# *Nehushtan*

## *The Search for Healing*

---

**Andrew DeWitt**

Book jacket design by Ryan Winkelman

ISBN 978-1-7326494-3-9

Andrew DeWitt Publishers
15368 Stacie Court
Dubuque, IA, 52001

# Dedication

I dedicate this book to my three children Alex, Aiden, and Abby are the inspiration for the teaching in this book.

> God is able to bless you abundantly, so that in all things at all times, having all that you need, you will abound in every good work.
>
> II Corinthians 9:8

# Forward

I spent the first few years of my twenties serving as a youth minister. My days were comprised primarily with planning youth activities, visiting students at school, and attending their various events. However, I ended each day kneeling at my bed, talking with Jesus. That was my favorite part of each day. In fact, I'd often find myself in my office at the church saying, "I can't wait to get home so I can pray." Then I'd chuckle a bit and tell myself, "I can pray right here, right now." That was true, but the time each night alone in my room on my knees was where it all happened.

My routine was simple. I'd turn on some soft, instrumental music in the background and just spend a couple of hours in prayer, talking with our wonderful, living God. He was so real and tangible to me during those times, and I enjoyed speaking with Him.

Yes, He spoke back.

Many nights I fell asleep still kneeling at my bed. It was the sweetest time, and I looked forward to it every day.

Now it's over twenty years later and I serve as the Healing Rooms Director at the International House of Prayer of Kansas City (IHOPKC). Andy DeWitt and I have been good friends for more than a decade and a half, and when he speaks of me, he says that I pray for a living. That is true. It is a great honor for me to serve in a ministry that prays and seeks the face of God 24/7. It's also my pleasure to lead a team who prays for the sick seven days a week. As part of a healing team, I've witnessed God heal in answer to my prayers over and over again, but it's definitely not because of me. I've seen Him heal when I've prayed for people in all kinds of circumstances. I've seen Him heal when I've felt strong and confident in my prayers. I've seen Him heal when I've felt weak and disqualified from being a minister of any sort. The simple fact of the matter is that it's not about me, it's God who heals. He is a healer, and it's His desire for all of us to be well.

As much as I enjoy ministering to the sick, the part of my job that I truly love is when I'm involved in training and encouraging others to pray for the sick. I love seeing God answer someone who reaches out their hand in faith for the first time, asking Him to heal the person in front of them. There is no special prayer to pray, or technique to use. This is an important point. God never prescribed any special prayer or ceremony guaranteeing someone's healing. It's simply us asking Him to heal. He responds to our prayers as they're offered in faith.

Every believer in Jesus can see the sick healed. You don't have to be at a place like IHOPKC to see it happen. You don't have to have a special gifting or calling. It's not only for those with special training. It is for everyone who believes in Jesus. Just reach out to Him with the faith you have and ask Him to heal. In the end, it's not about us and what we bring to the table it's about who He is and how much He loves us.

In *Nehushtan: The Search for Healing*, Andy tells a fun and engaging story with scriptural truths about healing brilliantly woven throughout the pages. I especially appreciate how he discusses the need for faith and the wrestle with our human nature that wants a concrete, tangible guarantee of healing. I enjoyed this novel very much, and I hope you do as well. May you grow in your understanding of Jesus as our healer.

Brian Pendleton
IHOPKC Healing Rooms
*Exalting Jesus by healing the sick*

# *Disclaimer*

This is a work of fiction. Names, characters, corporations, and government entities are either entirely imaginary or are used fictitiously. Any resemblance to actual persons, corporations, or government entities is noting more than a coincidence and doesn't mean a thing.

# Chapter 1

## *Ein Gedi, Israel*

Dolly Jane DeWitt plunged her four-inch spade into the warm dry earth. She had been digging and scraping, clearing rocks, soil and debris through the past two weeks. It was an ideal way to spend her Christmas vacation. She enjoyed being at the lowest point on earth where the sunny winter months reach 65-70 degrees, making work outdoors especially attractive when looking to escape snowy conditions of the American Midwest. Shovels, buckets and wheelbarrows were in her hands constantly as she labored with the archeological team.

Dolly Jane stood up and leaned back, easing the strain on her lumbar spine. Then she relaxed in a practiced pose. She wore capris and a deep red tee shirt emblazoned with the Iowa State logo. Free from any type of make-up, her facial features were strikingly beautiful. Her sunrise golden hair was tied up in a ponytail that danced across her shoulders and allowed the breeze to cool her neck. She often broke into a disarming and inviting smile, lighting up any room with her dazzling angel-white teeth. A sculptor could not have crafted a more perfect person.

In contrast, the rocks and cacophony of briars and thistles surrounded her in the desert. Again and again she sunk her spade into the soil, retrieving samples to be sifted and sorted through. She brushed her hair aside in a move like that of a practiced model.

She had volunteered for an archeological dig as part of her anthropology and archaeology degree. Under the authority of professor Janet Zimmerman, she signed up. Janet handed her a handful of digging implements and said, "Every society from the beginning of time has had to deal with their dead. While a few burned them in religious ceremony, or mummified their leaders, most buried them in graves of reasonable depth. But here, in the desert, no team had ever found a human bone. If we can find even one bone, this will be enormously helpful in understanding this ancient culture."

Dolly Jane worked her small section of the harsh mountainside on the map. The Ein Gedi archaeological site is literally an oasis in the desert and a nature reserve in Israel just west of the Dead Sea. Dolly Jane had fallen in love with the region during her first few days there. She enjoyed the history of nearby Masada, and more than once took the gondola or made the strenuous hike to tour the ruins on the mountaintop. She frequently stole away at lunchtime or at the end of a long day of digging to the base of David falls and kicked off her shoes and let the cool water bring refreshment. On her first visit to the falls, she dove into a worship experience and felt God asking her to place her hands into the water. At first she hesitated because she didn't want her iWatch to get wet. Then she removed it and plunged her hands down by her feet in the cool aqueous bath. Immediately, she felt a symbolic separation from social media as a part of her closeness with God. This place was special to her.

The site has been excavated many times over the years, and currently the group was a mixed bag of students from various parts of the world. French, Bolivian, German and Israeli students were hunkered down in various stages of exploration. A variable cornucopia of linguistics within the ditches of the dig site yet, and Dolly Jane did her best to learn the basics of their native tongue and communicate with each of them in their own language as much as she was able. Time was plentiful as they dug slowly and carefully and carting the treasured earth one wheelbarrow load at a time to the makeshift shelter where the soil and anything that came along with it was sifted, strained, and sorted. She had been working long days for two weeks and her time in the country was coming to an end.

She loved the camaraderie but today she worked alone. Dolly Jane stood up straight. From her assigned quarter she could see a wide array of desert wasteland on one side and rich green foliage on the other. Her assigned digging site was several hundred yards from the visitor's center and within view of several caves and the beautiful stream. Ibexes sauntered along unafraid of the human encounters, kicking up rocks as they traversed the hillside above her. Thankfully, their camp was on the other side of the embankment from the paths normally traversed by tourists.

Almost a year previously, a series of earthquakes ranging from 5.2 to 6.3 caused the Israeli government to shut down the site for safety reasons. When they re-opened, a team of geologists was first to assess the region and concluded that, while there was no current seismic activity, deeper changes within the subterranean regions were afoot and danger was still present. Without hard evidence to prove their case, they acquiesced to pressure from the tourism industry and re-opened to the public. The twenty-two seconds of undulating earth movement created several precious new openings into the mountain. This unearthed a treasure trove of never before seen archeological ruins. When the site was re-opened, scientists from all over the world descended on the area and a flurry of archeological activity ensued. Digging in their small confines of the site, Dolly Jane's group had come across a few fragments of late first-century Roman pots and bowls. But certainly they had found no evidence of bones in the settlement. Without bones, the dig would have to find a creative way to call the exploration a success.

Through the course of the day, Dolly Jane had slowly migrated away from her team. She could see the vast site, but the only active digging was around the hill behind her. Away from the constant chatter of the other students, she was peacefully alone with her thoughts and her spade. The mountain was significantly steeper in this section; she had to constantly work to keep her feet from slipping down into the underbrush beneath her. She passed through a collection of native jujube and acacia trees when she noticed something glinting beneath a large light brown boulder against the hillside. She ignored the boulder, which had an unnatural smooth surface. Instead, like a distractible teenager, she focused on the shiny object. It was neat and tidy, almost as if a giant hand had placed it there. Although she couldn't make out what the object was, or it's size, she expected that she could get around it with a few minutes of careful exploration.

She knew she was obligated to fetch someone, at least tell professor Janet about what she saw. Dolly Jane was not a trained archeologist, just a student with high aspirations and some anthropology and archeology classes on her resume. This was scheduled as her last full day on site and she wanted to prove herself. If she went back down to the main camp and admitted that she was onto something, everybody would be involved, and it will no longer be her discovery. But if she came back with something shiny, it would be catalogued as Dolly Jane's discovery, her name forever embossed in the annals of historical record.

She knelt down on the ground and leaned her hip and shoulder against the rock for support. Then, with a flutter of excitement, she pushed her fingers deep into the dark, blind earth. Straight away, she knew her instincts were correct and that she had been onto something worth finding. It was smooth and shiny to the touch, metal not stone. Grasping it firmly and telling herself not to expect too much, slowly, slowly she eased the object from the mooring of the earth and out into the light. The dry earth seemed to shudder as it reluctantly gave up its treasure.

She was lost in the past, captivated by the piece of history she cradled in the palms of her hands. A heavy round buckle.

It was deep yellow with hints of green around the edges, possibly corrosion from a lengthy burial. At first glance, it looked to be Roman. Could it be the sort of buckle used to fasten a cloak or robe?

She rubbed it with the corner of her shirt.

Was it bronze?

She looked closely, it was inscribed with a lettering she had never seen before:

üfürükçü

She knew the dangers of jumping to conclusions or to being seduced by first impressions, yet she could not resist imagining its owner, long dead and gone, who must have walked the paths on this very mountain, wearing a robe, a stranger whose story she had yet to learn. Lost in the past, she connected with the timeframe thousands of years before. The world seemed to be suspended, out of space and out of time. The object in her hand mesmerized her. She didn't notice the boulder shift at its base.

Then something, possibly a sixth sense made her look up from her treasure as the ancient slab of stone swayed and tilted then gracefully it began to fall directly towards her. As the wall of rock came crashing down towards her the spell was broken and she returned to the present. She leapt out of the way throwing herself from the deadfall trap that she had created with her digging. The boulder hit the ground with a dull thud, sending up a cloud of dark brown dust.

She tumbled down the hillside and landed in the underbrush. She lay sprawled in the dirt, dizzy, disoriented, and disheveled. She lay still, waiting for the world to stop spinning. It began to sink in how very close she had come to being crushed.

Gradually the pounding in her head settled down. Then she could feel the rapid pulse in her chest and realized that she hadn't taken a breath in a long time. She exhaled and panted, respiratory rate matching her anxiety. Her knees had the epidermal layer removed and lines of red began to seep forth onto the surface. Her left hand was grasping a poplar tree. When she found that she was stable and no longer disoriented, she let go of the tree. She felt her right wrist and realized that she was still clutching the buckle in her hand to protect it.

"I'm not hurt," she managed to stammer.

She ambled to her feet and dusted herself off. She realized that in her myopic digging, she failed to look around her and had completely caused the catastrophic failure with her ignorance. She climbed back up the hillside and looked down at the boulder, smiling at her nemesis. Then she peeked around the corner and realized that the fall had been on the opposite side of the hill from the camp and nobody had heard the crash.

She raised her hand with the buckle in it and was about to call to attract the attention of one of her fellow students when she noticed a rectangular opening in the side of the mountain where the boulder had been standing. Like a doorway cut into the rock.

The mountain was riddled with caves. Some shallow and some went deep with hidden passageways, so she wasn't surprised. *Why was that boulder covering this very opening?*

She knew she should call for help. Nobody knew that she was over this far. It was stupid and possibly even dangerous to go any farther without backup. She knew what sort of things could go wrong, but something was drawing her in.

It was personal.

It was her discovery. She told herself that there was no sense in disturbing the whole camp. They were busy working on their own projects. Who knows? It might not be anything worth discovering and she didn't want to waste their time. She wasn't going to dig much. She wouldn't disturb anything. She just wanted to look.

She whispered to herself, *I'll only be a moment.*

There was a deep depression in the ground where the stone had stood guard over the mouth of the cave. The cool dry earth was suddenly exposed to the infrared rays of the sun after so long. Her hat and trowel lay on the ground where they had fallen. She slid the precious buckle into her front pocket and looked into the darkness of the cave. The rectangular opening was no more than four feet high and a foot and a half wide. The edges were irregular and rough. She ran her fingers up and down the rock surface and found the edges were curiously smooth where the boulder had rested. She ducked down and stepped inside.

As the rods of her retina slowly adjusted to the minimal illumination, the deep blackness gave way to charcoal gray and she saw a long narrow tunnel. The hair on the back of her neck rose as if to warn her that something lurked in the darkness, something better off left undisturbed. She smirked at the thought and realized that this cave, while ripe for childish superstitions and ghost stories, hadn't seen the light of day for hundreds of years and certainly nothing alive could be there.

Nothing dead could bother her.

The smell of long-hidden subterranean air enveloped her as she bent down and stepped into the cave. The cool, damp surroundings were a striking contrast and a welcomed reprieve from the oppressive heat that she had dealt with since landing in Tel Aviv airport three weeks earlier. Step by step, she made her way through the tunnel. The coolness of the cave chilled her. She couldn't tell if the tunnel was getting narrower, or if it was an optical illusion from the progressive darkening due to the distance from the only illumination at the mouth of the cave. She felt in her pocket and felt her cell phone. She used it as a flashlight in front of her and could tell that indeed, the tunnel was narrowing.

She proceeded onward.

A few feet farther, the tunnel opened into a large chamber. She stepped into the middle of it. An irregular oval shaped room that she could easily stand up in. She scanned the room with her light and could see the ceiling far above her, and the walls were replete with carvings and imagery that she didn't recognize.

Then she looked at the floor. Perpendicular to the wall was an amorphous mound lying just above its surroundings. She walked over to it and bent over. With her light pointing at the ground she hoped to find some pottery or maybe even ancient coins. Instead, she saw a human skull.

She recoiled and stumbled to her left. She tripped over a skeleton and fell. She landed on her hands and knees, directly over a third pile of bones. Without intent or conscious thought, she let out a high pitch shrill that embodied the emotions that ran through her. She looked down.

The blind sockets of a skull stared back at her.

She could feel malevolence crawling over her skin, her scalp, and even the soles of her feet. She scooted backwards and looked around. She saw a row of skeletons lined up against the cave wall. A shiny metal object lay between two of the bodies. She looked closer and though aged, it was clearly a dagger.

She should not be in this place.

Dolly Jane heard footsteps. They were not in the direction that she came from. Clearly someone was coming towards her from the opposite end of the cave. She turned and tried to run towards the tunnel she came from. Her hand struck the cave wall and she dropped her phone. It landed with the light facing the dirt and darkness instantly engulfed in the abyss that she shared with a series of dead bodies.

Her foot tripped over a skeleton and she fell downwards. She felt her body tumble to the ground and her head struck something solid.

She tasted metal.

Though her eyes were closed, she saw a bright light.

# Chapter 2

---

## *Chicago*
## *Congress Plaza Hotel Ballroom*

Standing in front of his display, Billy DeWitt shifted his shoulders and adjusted his tie and heavily starched shirt. He was sharply dressed in a new shirt, shoes, and sport coat - all purchased specifically for this trip. After he won first prize at the State Science Fair in Des Moines, Iowa he had been invited to the prestigious Intel International Science and Engineering Fair (ISEF).

He wasn't a model, but he should have been. His eyes had the startling clarity of a mountain stream. His aquiline nose complemented his prominent cheekbones and masculine jaw line. He seemed molded from a different cast as his Spartan shoulders and athletic build resembled Dwayne Johnson yet in his suit and tie, it spoke of quiet strength. He walked with confidence, purpose, and authority revealing his Ivy League status.

Flamboyant of character, he would fill every room with his joy as he greeted those around him with his story telling. He often dropped into a variety of hip-hop dance moves, which drew crowds wherever he went.

However, standing at the ISEF, after checking his poster, video and the robot, he stood stationary, steadfast and stagnant as he waited for judges to evaluate his invention. He had made the trip to Chicago to present his invention, and he was ready. He loved the antique feel of the Congress Plaza Hotel. What it lacked in modern amenities, it made up for in character – plaster crown molding, heating registers, and original rickety door handles graced each private room.

Billy watched the judges observing the presentations to his right and left. They observed, read, and asked questions. He waited for his turn.

He relaxed by pulling his iPhone from his pocket. He pulled up the web site for the science fair and read again:

> The Intel International Science and Engineering Fair (ISEF) is the world's largest pre-college science competition. Each year, approximately 1,800 high school and college students from more than 75 countries are awarded the opportunity to showcase their independent research and compete for over $4 million in prizes.

His presentation was classified as a "poster". But like the long line of entries on either side of him, there was much more than a simple description in a vertical written format. A white and black cylinder about the size of a basketball sat on the table, a few curved tiles lay behind it. He also had a computer screen that showed a looping video of his presentation. Any minute, doctoral level scientists would soon be standing in front of him to review and judge his work. He spoke calmly to himself, "It's a privilege just to be here. Relax and tell them what you know."

Billy had checked and rechecked the presentation countless times and was confident that what he had on the table represented his best possible work.

A grey haired gentleman in a rumpled sport coat and disheveled tie sauntered into Billy's view and without a word, stopped in front of him. Billy had no idea who he was. His nametag simply read "ISEF Judge". The judge didn't look at the poster at all, rather, he stared at Billy motionless.

Billy pressed the button on the video. Gentle music provided background to a recording of Billy's voice that said, "Tunneling is one of the most complex engineering issues that we face."

The judge gave him a blank stare, "Shut the video off."

"Certainly, sir."

"If you want to compete, you have to tell me about it in person."

Billy didn't miss a beat. "Absolutely. My name is Billy, and I want to introduce you to my robotic tunneling robot. Tunneling projects are plagued with several issues. First, the ceiling is unpredictable; subject to collapse. Second, subterranean navigation is a huge challenge. To find the target on the other side of the dirt is always difficult. Finally, they have to do something with the dirt. You can never tunnel in secret. Tunneling prisoners take pockets full of dirt to clandestinely scatter them in the exercise yard every day, removing the dirt from their secret tunnels a handful per day."

While Billy spoke, the judge was looking down at his phone. Billy couldn't tell if he was interested and making notes, or checking Instagram. His facial expression revealed nothing.

Billy motioned to the table. A three-foot long cylinder about the width of a basketball sat next to a spiral shaped tile. "With my robot, each of these problems is solved."

The judge put his phone in his front pocket then looked away. He scanned the ballroom floor and assessed the other candidates.

Billy attempted to regain his attention, "Sir, if you look at the digging surface, you can see that the circular bit is far more complex than a traditional tunneling head. Hundreds of diamond burs dig tenaciously. The earth is guided into one of four pint-sized vaporizer chambers. The particles are heated and completely desiccated. When the chamber is 64% full of dirt powder, these two ports inject 0.1 gram of granulized calcium hypochlorite and aerosolized polyethylene glycol."

The judge's eyebrows raised, "You're going to blow it up?"

"You know your chemistry!" Billy said. "Great! Let me tell you a quick joke. What do you do with a sick chemist?"

The judge rolled his eyes.

"If you can't helium, or curium, then you barium," Billy chuckled.

The judge stared at him motionless.

Billy cleared his throat and continued, "No sir. No explosion. Quite the opposite, actually," Billy said. "As the injection is complete, the dormancy period of the reaction is utilized for the piston to compress the chemical mixture along with the dirt particles into a custom made molding. The heat from the reaction transforms the dirt from the tunnel into a rock hard porcelain tile. As the piston returns to its original position, the tile gets positioned into place, more dirt is injected and the process repeats."

Billy grabbed a few small curved tiles from the tabletop and snapped them together as he spoke. "The tile is set into place at the back end of the robot where it cures to completion as it cools. As soon as the first tile is placed on the tunnel floor, a second tile is sent against it on the left wall of the tunnel in a spiral-interlocking pattern. Each tile is secured with a robotic arm until the next tile is set into place."

Billy snapped two more tiles in place, demonstrating the formation of the tunnel formation. "Like a jigsaw piece interlocking with the first piece and setting up the spiral. As soon as it clicks into place, the robotic arms are released and the machine ambles forward placing another tile every other second. The process is dizzying in its quickness. Checkers can tunnel ten meters a minute."

The judge inquired, "Checkers?"

Billy smiled, "Based on her alternating white and black, pattern, that's my nickname for her."

Billy took a breath. He stepped back and waited for the judge to digest his statements.

The judge said, "New robots are a dime a dozen. What makes yours special?"

Billy said, "The dirt never has to be removed. It's used to create the walls of the tunnel that it digs."

The judge said, "To what end? Who tunnels in secret?"

Billy had a blank stare. He had poured his life into this project. He had always been told that he was smarter, more creative, and more driven than everyone around him. This may have been the first time in his life when his work had actually bored a person in a position of authority. He was speechless.

"Do you plan on doing something illegal with this robot?"

Billy stammered, "No sir."

"I would hope not." The judge took a step back, making it clear that he did not want to associate with him. "Tunneling in secret indicates deception, and secrecy. These are not attributes to inventions with commercial application. He walked away and began analyzing the next project.

*Oof*, Billy thought.

The trip from Iowa to Chicago had been full of anticipation and great expectations. Now, when he had the opportunity to present his genius to someone of stature, he had completely been brushed off. He wondered who the judge was.

Billy retreated to the comfort of his iPhone. He pulled it out and reviewed the protocol for the day. He saw that through the remainder of the morning nine judges would evaluate him. He slumped over and sighed. Did he have the stamina to take that amount of criticism?

He looked up from his phone and saw another competitor at the table across the aisle from him who was also in between judging sessions. They made eye contact. In his mid-twenties, the young man extended his right hand for an expectant handshake.

"My name's Chase Johnson." Chase's firm grip was like a warm embrace to Billy's clammy hand. His sandy blonde hair waved aimlessly above his piercing blue eyes. He was ruggedly handsome. His well-manicured beard surrounded an inviting smile. He wore a black suit, plain dress shoes, and a confident demeanor.

Billy motioned to the judge and asked, "Who is that guy?"

Chase grinned, "That judge was Doctor August Remkin. He's a chemistry professor at Harvard."

Billy's shoulders slumped. His previous competitions were all at the local or state level. He had never expected to be surrounded with expertise at this level. "I picked the wrong guy to tell a stupid chemistry joke."

Chase laughed, "Relax. Remember, they aren't judging you, they are just looking at the marketplace in which your design might be used."

Billy had no idea what he was talking about.

Chase continued, "I heard your presentation. It sounds intriguing."

Just then a pair of judges approached. A lady in her sixties locked eyes with Chase then looked at his poster. A black haired man with a grey sweater took his position at Billy's table and stood squarely, perusing his poster. Billy assumed he was a professor in some field of science with sky-high credentials who had forgotten far more than Billy ever would know.

Billy dove into tunneling technology as before but with a more abbreviated speech. "The robot digs forward upward, downward right or left, guided by its own sensors, looking through the dirt like a GPS guidance, to find the best path to eventually arrive at its target. Whenever possible, it avoids rocks, water, oil, or man made structures. None of these represents a true obstruction, since the robot has a means to grind and process almost every type of geological structure, including petroleum."

The judge asked, "You can tunnel through an oil deposit underground?"

"Absolutely! However, any liquid under pressure inevitably will be expelled through the tunnel it creates. Therefore if it must travel through such a pressurized well, it seals off the tunnel with a circular wall at the posterior, in the shape of a man hole cover prior to entering the formidable environment."

The judge remained silent.

Billy continued, "When Checkers goes through an oil deposit, it seals off the tunnel behind it with a circular tile, like a manhole cover. Then begins making tiles from the oil-compound. These tiles are technically classified as a type of plastic! They harden immediately and she continues building the tunnel."

The judge shifted his weight, hoping for him to conclude.

Billy said, "Don't worry, I got this. The robot continues to its destination, takes a short detour to an air pocket and creates a vent into the tunnel..."

The judge interrupted, "What is the commercial use of this product?"

Billy was stunned. Once again he had been stopped from completing his presentation with a question that he had no answer to.

The judge was tapping on his phone as he spoke, "We don't tunnel through oil, son. We pump it out. It pays the bills. Thank you for your efforts." Without making eye contact, he walked away.

From then on, Billy wanted to say, *Hold my beer and watch this. The robot can do so much more!*

Billy was given no rest. The judges came quickly, one after another.

The next judge actually introduced himself, "I'm professor Clyde Wilkins from MIT, department of Geology."

He watched Billy's presentation closely, then interrupted, "How does the robot know where to go?"

Billy was quick to answer, "The route is programmed in ahead of time."

"So it has no autonomy?"

Billy thought for a moment. Then said, "No."

"So if the underground terrain is different from what you expect – which is always the case – then the robot will be nonfunctional."

The boy genius' frustration was palpable. Why couldn't they see it? Nobody else had ever done what he had done. Why was it his responsibility to produce commercial applications for the robot?

By the end of the morning, all nine judges had evaluated his project and had asked questions that left him demoralized and exhausted.

He wanted to get into the details of the programming, the chemical injectors, or the creative movements the robot was capable of yet it seemed that all the judges cared about was making conclusive statements about the robot's commercial use.

Billy stood in the position of a judge, folded his arms across his chest and thought about leaving the entire project there and just walking away. He had no chance of winning. No chance of getting his technology out into the world. He took a few steps forward and put a hand on his precious Checkers and sighed. In a quick motion he placed the robot in his suitcase and shoved the poster in. Though he had a few hours before his flight Billy prepared to take a taxi back to the airport. He found himself staring out into the distance. Never before had he been so frustrated.

"Quite a robot you've got there!" A voice from behind him blurted out.

Billy didn't move.

"Tunneling is a huge challenge, but all they care about is using it for oil and gas discovery."

Billy turned and looked at who was speaking.

Billy didn't move.

Chase Johnson strode into his view and said, "Your robot might not be what they are looking for, but I think you might be interested in my project."

Billy tilted his head to the side, his interest awakened.

Chase squinted. "This morning didn't go the way you wanted. But did you at least get a chance to see any of the other entries?" Chase asked.

He shook his head and looked at the pattern on the carpet, "Why bother?"

"Let me buy you lunch."

"I've got a flight later in the afternoon."

"I've got a hunch you'll like what I have to say. If I'm right, you won't want to get on the plane at all."

# Chapter 3

## *Ein Gedi, Israel*

Pain pierced Dolly Jane's head. Though her eyes were still closed, she could hear footsteps around her. At least four people were talking, some close, others farther away and barely perceptible. She noticed an unfamiliar echo.

Where was she?

She couldn't tell if she was dreaming, or if she was awakening from an awful nap. Reality came slowly as she realized where she was. She forced her eyes to open.

The cool dark walls of the cave were illuminated with battery-powered lanterns. Janet offered a warm smile as she offered Dolly Jane a water bottle. Dolly Jane obliged and took a sip. She tried to sit up but Janet placed a motherly hand on her shoulder and said, "Relax, we're not in a hurry. You took a nasty spill and need to go slowly."

Dolly Jane looked around her. Khaki clad professors surrounded her. They had placed stakes throughout the cave and had sectioned it off, protecting each of the skeletal remains. The curiosity that Dolly Jane had stumbled into had become a major archeological find. The team was preparing to spend an inordinate amount of time inside the cave. They planned to photograph every inch of it, then every artifact within the confines would be unearthed, scanned, and analyzed according to precise archeological protocol.

Dolly Jane looked at the skeleton next to her, then back at Janet. Those motherly eyes gave her a sense of calm and security, in spite of the setting. However, lying in the cave filled with remains of the dead, she was no longer in her comfort zone.

Dolly Jane began to regain consciousness and asked, "¿Qué pasó?" She squinted, realizing that what she said didn't sound right. Then she said, "מה קרה?" Somehow, that didn't sound correct either. She looked at Janet and uttered, "What happened?"

Janet laughed, "You might have a concussion, but it's clear that you've made a major discovery!"

Dolly Jane said, "I thought I was going to die!" Then knowing that she had made an overstatement she corrected, "Just kidding." She looked around at the team within the cave and asked, "How did you find me?"

"Our team was on the opposite side of the cave, working on a tunnel into the mountain. We thought it was a grave site, and were proceeding slowly when we heard you scream."

Dolly Jane closed her eyes and shook her head.

Janet continued, "The tunnel we were in wasn't a grave, at all. It was a doorway to this!" She waved her hand around the cave.

Dolly Jane said, "I shouldn't have gone in by myself."

Janet nodded, "That's true. But you did and you sped up the process of finding all of this." She waved her hand as she spoke.

"What is it?"

"We've only been at it for less than an hour. We haven't had time to process what this cave is, or was. What we do know is that there are at least five corpses lined up, and not intentionally buried. There is also a collection of pottery at the end of the cave. We will certainly spend some time looking at the markings on it to date it and process the details." Janet shook her head and said under her breath, "Honestly, this looks more like a tragic hospital ward that ended poorly than a burial site."

As she said it, she looked up in excitement. "What if this was the last of the ancient society?"

Dolly Jane squinted. She didn't understand.

Janet continued speaking, but mostly to herself. "The society vanished and we don't know why, but now, we find the first bones! Skeletons are intact! Lined up in a row, here in this cave."

Janet spoke quickly and quietly, "Were they sick? Was there a plague? Were they trying to hide? Were they royal?"

She looked at the other workers and ordered, "Make sure we follow protocol and get every aspect of this dig catalogued as meticulously as possible." She motioned around the cave with her hands. "It looks like this will be our new home for a while. We'll be in the cave for months. Let's get it right."

Dolly Jane was still lying on the ground. She felt her head and noticed a lump next to her ponytail. Then she felt the ground. It was cold, hard and smooth. She sat up and felt where her head had struck the ground. She brushed the dirt to the side and saw a glimmer. She began digging and unearthed two sides of a metal entity.

Janet saw what she was doing and grasped Dolly Jane by her hand. "Wait a moment." Her face was serious. She took out a paintbrush and began dusting around the edges. With the skill of a sculptor, she removed the surrounding dust from the metallic structure. Dolly Jane looked up from where she was sitting, she gave the professor room to work.

Janet remained focused on her task. She worked the ground for about half an hour. She painted, sculpted, and painstakingly unearthed the relic while Dolly Jane found a comfortable place with her back against the cave wall, sipping water, waiting for her double vision to fade.

Janet looked up. Her eyes widened. She remained silent. Her work had almost completely relieved the metallic structure from the ground.

It was a bronze snake.

A skeletal hand was grasping a triangular head indicative of a venomous snake. But the bronze had clearly been broken. The head was a roughly hewn image, but it was smooth and ancient in appearance. However, the body of the snake was several inches in diameter and the snake should have been at least 3 feet long to be an adequate representation of the animal. It was too short. It measured only ten inches from the nose to the severed edge. The skeletal hand that grasped the snake still remained partially buried.

Janet paused. Instead of starting the process, she sat back and put her hand over her mouth. She gasped. She stepped back and looked up and to the left, mentally processing what she had just seen.

Dolly Jane had never seen her so surprised. "What is it?"

Janet's face revealed wonder and joy. She brought her hand to her forehead and smiled from ear to ear. Then suddenly, her mouth dropped open and her body became rigid. Fear crept over her face and stayed like an unwelcome visitor.

Dolly Jane watched as Janet suffered through her emotional rollercoaster. She calmly asked, "What is it?"

Janet quickly stuffed the relic up the sleeve of her shirt and hid it the best she could. She looked around to see if anyone had witnessed her actions. They were all occupied with the array of human remains and were paying no attention to Janet.

Dolly Jane was shocked, "Janet!"

Janet said, "The two of us need to get out of here. Now! Let's use the excuse of getting you to a medic."

Dolly Jane rubbed her forehead, "What are you talking about?"

Janet whispered, "Nehushtan!"

# Chapter 4

## *Chicago*
## *Congress Plaza Hotel Ballroom*

Billy left his belongings with the bellhop and set out across into the vast expanse of human activity on Michigan Avenue. He followed Chase's brisk pace down the sidewalk. He saw the Osaka Sushi bar and restaurant and Billy feared that he might have to feign interest in raw fish. The smell, though faint was repulsive to him as they passed by. A few paces later, they entered the Downtown Hilton. Billy was puzzled, *Why had they gone from one hotel to another?*

They passed through the luxurious lobby and entered the 720 Bar and Grill. Chase greeted the host who walked them through the busy tables and showed them to a booth along the back wall. They made themselves comfortable at a table and he handed them menus.

Chase already knew the menu and he waited for Billy to acclimate and view the choices before him. He reminisced about his younger years. Having graduated high school as a valedictorian he had always been told he had great potential. He attended the University of Iowa's engineering program while working at Rockwell-Collins. While at the company, his outstanding work received instant notoriety and his project manager advanced him to be the team leader. His supreme intellect drew the other engineers to him like flies to a streetlight, regardless of their age difference.

Chase's domineering leadership style worked well for a certain subset of introverted engineers. After a year on the job, he was a section chairman. He recruited a team of twenty quiet unassuming intellectuals who enjoyed having a cubicle at a large company in which to work every day and didn't oppose the authority structure. Chase worked the team to the bone. He held large group meetings, smaller meetings, and also met with each member one on one. He tasked each of them with two or three projects at a time and demanded regular updates. In the midst of the confusion, he wove into their assignments a number of side projects, which he quickly updated as soon as they were completed. These side projects were the technical aspects of his personal research project for his master's degree. Broken down into many parts with so much going on, none of the team members ever knew that the others were working on similar projects. His minions completed his research. Chase also tasked an engineer who had a talent for writing with a number of very specific writing projects and an extensive bibliography. Chase compiled them into his master's thesis and was able to finish both a bachelors and master's degree in four years while working full time.

After graduation, he moved to Chicago and opened his own business specializing in scanning technology. He longed to make his mark on the engineering world. He endeavored to build an empire in the arenas of global security and make his fortune. Though he had only been in the competitive city for a few weeks he already had a few customers and was looking for talent. He entered one of his previous projects into the Intel International Science and engineering Fair (ISEF) as a way to analyze the talent field. When he saw Billy, and his ingenious digging machine, he knew that he was among an intellectual peer.

They sat at the table together in the dimly lit restaurant. Chase scanned the menu quickly, decided on his lunch order within a few seconds and put the menu down. "I was presenting just a few yards from you. I heard variations of your presentation a couple of times while I was waiting. The judges didn't give me the time of day, either."

"So we're just a couple of losers sitting here."

"Not at all! Your tunneling tech is fantastic."

"I thought nobody cared," Billy lamented. "Since I've been here, I haven't had any significance at all. I've been just another number."

The waiter visited and Chase ordered a Diet Coke, Billy asked for ice water.

"Tunneling is a huge industry with big dollars."

Billy said, "I guess so. Oil pays big."

Chase added, "Not just the oil companies. Governments and private companies alike have been digging tunnels for thousands of years for irrigation, city defense, and mining. Entire civilizations have been saved simply because they've had good tunnels."

"Why did you want to talk with me?"

"Your little robot is on the verge of something huge. It's just missing a single piece of technology."

"The judges said they wanted something more. But what?"

"I don't care about the judges. I care about what will work. Have you seen my presentation?"

"No."

"Ground penetrating radar."

"I don't know much about that."

"Engineers use GPR for nondestructive testing of buildings and pavements, locating buried utility lines and studying bedrock and soil."

"Sounds fascinating, I don't –"

"Let me finish. Ground penetrating radar is a geophysical method of using radar pulses to image below the ground's surface. It's uses electromagnetic radiation in the microwave band of the radio spectrum to detect subsurface structures. GPR is used in rock, soil, ice, fresh water, pavements and other structures."

Billy asked, "So if it's so good, what needs to be improved?"

Chase answered, "It sucks!"

Billy raised his eyebrows.

"In the right conditions, GPR can detect subsurface objects, changes in material properties as well as voids and cracks. A GPR unit sends high-frequency radio waves from 10 MHz to 2.6 GHz into the ground. A receiving antenna records the variations in the signal return and interprets the signals. The electrical conductivity of the ground, the transmitted center frequency, and the radiated power all limit the depth range at which GPR is effective."

Billy said, "Sounds okay so far."

Chase continued, "The way it works is the operator drags or rolls a scanner over the surface with a GPR antenna that must be in contact with the ground for the strongest signal strength. Higher electrical conductivity attenuates the electromagnetic wave and decreases the penetration depth. GPR is frequency dependent attenuation, the higher frequencies don't penetrate as far as the lower frequencies, but they provide better resolution. So you have a tradeoff between penetration and resolution."

Billy said, "Doesn't sound like it sucks."

"It's fine in the bedrock on, say, Greenland. Studies there show penetration up to several thousand meters at low GPR frequencies. However, fine-grained sediments, like clay and silt, cause a loss of signal strength. Rocky or mixed sediments scatter the signal and cause extraneous noise. Dense dry materials like limestone or granite only allow a penetration of 1.5 meters. The worst resolution is when we are looking at moist or clay soil. There, penetration is negligible, only a few centimeters."

"That's pretty useless."

"The principle disadvantage of GPR is that it is severely limited when environmental conditions aren't ideal. Guess what type of soil is on most of the planet."

"Not good."

"Exactly."

"So it sucks. Why did you present on sucky tech?"

Chase asked, "What have you heard about Archaeological Geophysics?"

"Aren't you gonna tell me that you've made something better than traditional GPR?"

"Archaeological Geophysics is a new field that looks for artifacts, features and patterning deep within the earth."

"That's another field of study that I've never heard of but would probably love."

Chase said, "And that brings me to my project."

"You developed a better GPR?"

"With one point on the surface, and the other in the drill bit. Sonographic and laser data are sent and received from both points simultaneously. This allows a three-dimensional image to be calculated. The computer generates a tomographic image that is accurate beyond anything we've seen before."

Billy was thinking faster than Chase could talk. He interrupted, "This won't work. It takes three points to calculate position."

Chase smiled, "You sound like the judges at the symposium."

Billy smirked. He had been enjoying the distraction from his painful morning.

Chase continued, "We have way more than three! The sensor makes the reading and as soon as the drill bit moves, we have the third point for our calculations. In fact as it continues to move, we have an infinite number of points!"

Billy looked stunned. "If the numbers are good, then you could map out the area underground with amazing accuracy."

Chase smiled.

"Do you have any examples of this working?"

"Not yet, judge." Chase smirked. "That's what they kept asking me. What if we put my ground penetrating radar on your robot! Well, we'd really be onto something."

Billy sat back in his chair. He didn't know what to think. The waiter brought the Diet Coke and water. Chase ordered a burger. Billy realized that he wouldn't be picking up the tab and ordered a root beer and a New York Strip.

Billy thought about the issues he had encountered with tunneling and asked, "What about issues like dry sandy soil?"

"Most lasers are single wavelength, and limited in use to their specific function. My laser is a modulating frequency, changing in wavelength and power hundreds of times every second. It's the same with the sonograph. The data gained from different points as they process through multiple lines of data is dizzying.

"What did the judges think?"

"Short sighted."

"Absolutely. Their myopic viewpoint shouldn't halt progress."

The two overachievers continued their conversation wading far into the weeds where tech lovers live. They discussed sensors, computer models and geological challenges. The waiter brought two plates and they continued their conversation over the burger and steak.

Equally satiated by the meal and conversation, Chase said, “I’m confident that this thing will work. The computer simulations show it.”

Billy sat back in his chair and pondered, “You want to steal my idea.”

“Not at all. I want to partner with you.”

As the last piece of steak was loaded onto his fork, Billy said, “I’m supposed to head back home later today.”

“Change your plans so you can stay an extra day or two. You’ll enjoy my lab in my apartment. I live just a few blocks from here.”

Chase paid the bill and they exited the hotel back to Michigan Avenue and leisurely walked back to the Congress Plaza Hotel. As he saw the pattern of the carpet, the scent of the building hit him. His feet were glued to the floor as frustration filled him. Billy was taken back to the emotions of the morning. He grieved in failure as his efforts had been blocked, defeated, and obstructed.

Chase, in his optimism had soared five paces ahead of him before he noticed that Billy had stopped. “Did you forget something?”

Billy looked up. He was speechless. He didn’t know what to say. He pressed through the frustration of the morning and said to Chase, “Let me grab the bag from my room and we’ll blow this joint. They walked through the lobby past the concierge and the bank of elevators. Around the corner, the ISEF award ceremony was taking place. Billy and Chase poked their heads into the conference room.

From the podium, Dr. Remkin announced, “The winner of the Gordon E. Moore Award. The Moore Award recognizes the Best of the Best among the outstanding students from around the world who participate in the Intel ISEF.” Billy recognized the man speaking as the Harvard chemistry professor. He continued, “$75,000 is awarded to the student with the most outstanding and innovative research, as well as on the potential impact of the work.”

"And the winner is," he paused and a hush came over the crowd. "Alistair Nichols, with his window washing robot."

Applause came from the crowd and Billy stepped back into the hallway and saw the elevator door spring open.

"Window washing robot? That's so dumb."

Chase whispered, "I saw his presentation. It's a pretty simple robot, but has immediate commercial application. It's perfectly suited for skyscrapers! Spritz, scrub, squeegee, repeat. Washing windows on skyscrapers is a dangerous job. If this is used by companies, this robot might be able to pay for itself after cleaning just one 7-story building."

Billy shook his head.

They waited for the elevator in silence. Together they boarded and rose to the seventh floor and exited. Chase said, "Your robot is far more complex than Alistair Nichols'. The operations it perform are far more complex than what the simple window washer does."

Standing in front of his hotel room, Billy aligned his keycard with the pad on the lock. He paused and thought about the locking mechanism. Billy looked at Chase and said, "This little lock is so much better than the window washer."

Chase raised his eyebrows.

Billy held the key in from of the door, "The radio-frequency identification induction loop transmitter sends a signal that is read by the sensor within the lock. The key's RFID chip could normally be read at up to eighteen inches, but the antennae within the lock limits the distance to an inch or two." As he tapped the pad, he said, "The latch bolt retracts with an emergent thumb turn while the inside lever remains free for immediate egress." Billy turned the handle and the door opened. "Seriously?" He said, "This doorknob, and my robot are more complex than a ridiculous window washing robot!"

Chase agreed, "Commercial application."

Billy nodded.

Chase said, "Together we'll dominate."

# Chapter 5

## Michigan Avenue
## Chicago

The street view of Michigan Avenue was thrilling to Billy. Though he had grown up in a small Midwestern town, he always felt more alive when in the middle of the city. Billy loved the city. He was pleased when Chase led the way across the street to the expansive Buckingham Fountain and Gardens. They enjoyed the beautiful 70-degree sunny day as they strolled along in the park. Between Columbus Drive and Lake Shore Drive the expansive park gave views of glass skyscrapers to the north and west. Billy looked South. Though Soldier Field was blocked from his view, the cityscape beyond the stadium was breathtaking. Lake Michigan on the east was a beautiful and striking contrast.

He rolled the metallic suitcase that contained Checkers while Chase graciously took his other bag. The wheels rolled smoothly along the modern red brick path. They made a straight path and enjoyed the manicured flowers and the occasional licensed street vendor. The walk through the park was exactly a mile, yet the refreshing city park worked like an infusion of life for Billy.

When they approached Aqua Lakeshore Apartments on Columbus Drive, Chase said, “Home sweet home.”

Billy looked up. Above him, the glass and concrete structure extended high into the clouds. Surrounded by extended balconies in every direction, they were smoothly irregular, an architectural work of art. It made the image of undulating concrete waves as it rose upwards. Around the building was perfectly kept rare inner city green space.

Chase pressed a button on the array of choices on the elevator wall and the number eighteen became luminescent in the dirty elevator. They exited and walked down the hallway and he inserted his mechanical key to open the door. Billy could see the entirety of the 800 square foot apartment from the hallway. He was instantly drawn to the far wall, floor to ceiling window. Billy opened the sliding door and sprang out to the balcony. He was taken back by the view of Lake Michigan. He leaned over the railing and saw the pool far below.

"Chicago is a beautiful city." Chase said.

Billy said, "From this elevation you can see Muskegon on a clear day."

Chase declared, "You know Lake Michigan!" We are two floors shy of the penthouse. When we get rolling in the business, I'm moving up."

Billy turned around and viewed the inside of the apartment. Against the wall was a desk piled high with electronic devices, wires, and laptop computers. A bed in the corner, restless sheets in a flurry hung down to the floor. On the wall was a forty-inch flat screen television, the remote control on a brown padded office chair. The only other chair in the space was a folding chair lying against the counter, which held the sink. Between the sink and a tiny refrigerator was a counter space with a bowl with a few pebbles of captain crunch marinating in warm milk. The space could possibly have been called a kitchenette in a hotel setting, but here the hotel web site called it a gourmet kitchen.

Chase sat down in his seat at the desk. He spread his arms and said, "This is where the magic happens!"

Billy was speechless. He had never seen an apartment so diminutive, or free from the confines of cleanliness. He finally said, "I can't believe you live here."

"Sure! It's home sweet home. My roommates and I live and work from here."

"How do you have space for roommates?" Billy asked.

"It's the only way to pay the rent, for now. We make it work."

"Where do they sleep?"

"There's a little bedroom across from the bathroom."

Billy took a few steps in the direction Chase indicated and peeked inside. A cot about half the size of a twin mattress lay on the floor with sheets strewn about. Billy said, "That's a closet."

Chase laughed, "It's small, but with the extra bed, I can share rent. We sleep in shifts, which is fine because we each work a different shift. Fuzzy just finished grad school and works two jobs to pay off loans. Whenever he comes in, he sleeps. My friend Maddy is a computer engineer who works second shift during the day and is also getting her master's degree. She lives across the hall but is rarely around."

Billy looked around the room, "What do you do for a living? I mean, how do you pay the bills?"

"Right now, I'm a freelance security contractor. I work for a variety of companies developing security plans. I'll analyze blueprints, and look at their geography, traffic patterns, and daily workflow of businesses to develop a security system for them that will achieve security with maximum efficiency. I send a schematic to their engineer that shows which security elements to put where. A lot of science goes into knowing which sensors are best in various situations."

Billy said, "Sensors. I think I see a theme developing here."

Chase opened a desk drawer and pulled out a handful of various sized black plastic components. "These little guys came out two years ago. They are marketed as thermal imaging cameras, but with a little modification, they can transmit data on motion and temperature to a security center."

He opened another drawer and pulled out a pillbox with two-centimeter boxes labeled Monday-Sunday. He opened the box labeled Tuesday and using tweezers, lifted a black pellet about the size of a grain of rice and set it on a white velvet surface. "This is what I wanted to show you."

Billy leaned closer, but couldn't see enough to be impressed. Chase brought over a desk-mounted arm with illuminated magnification and Billy stood at the desk while he held the sensor with tweezers and examined it closely. He was able to view the lettering and a few indentations on the side of the pellet.

Chase spoke while Billy investigated. "This little guy is a beast! It is the most powerful modulated laser and sonar sensor ever developed."

Billy shoved his hands into his pockets as he watched. He realized that though he had checked out of the hotel, he still had his hotel keycard in his pocket. He withdrew it and tossed it on the desk with an embarrassed grin.

Chase tapped his finger on the Congress Hotel keycard and said, "This is a whole different ball game from an RFID chip. The hotel key is based on the ISA 14443 air-interface protocol designed for short-range transmission."

He tapped his laptop screen and an excel spreadsheet appeared. After a few keystrokes, numbers filled the screen. "The calculations are convincing."

Billy took a few moments and digested the information. He loved spreadsheets. The numbers told the story of everything the sensors did. They emitted signals of various wavelengths, and constantly made readings. To most people, the screen full of numbers would be fodder for somnolence but Billy read it like a mystery novel.

He asked, "How strong is it?"

"They send signals a thousand meters, and receive the information back again — to this." He pointed to a black box on the first shelf. "This is the ultrahigh frequency reader. It houses a coiled beam-steerable phased-array antenna that can interrogate passive tags at long distances without obstructions. They are incredibly sensitive."

Billy shook his head, "That's not what I mean." He picked up the sensor and tried to crush it with his fingers. Then he flexed his muscles like a weight lifter and repeated, "How strong is it?"

Chase smiled.

He reached for another drawer and grabbed a hammer. In one fluid motion he slammed the hammer down hard on the table. A sound reverberated within the walls of the apartment like a gunshot and the tiny sensor took the brunt of the punishment. Billy jumped back at the sudden outburst of violence. In shock, he looked at Chase with the hammer in his hand. Billy stepped up to the desk and gently picked up the sensor with tweezers once again and examined it with magnification. It was completely unharmed.

Chase smiled, "The outer casing is a high molecular weight duo ethylene polymer. The shell provides rigidity and contains the chemical content that also serves as the battery, which helps decrease size."

Billy's eyes brightened, "Is it strong enough to withstand the constant punishment of a drilling machine?"

Chase smiled confidently, "Absolutely."

Billy asked, "What's their range underground?"

Chase grinned from ear to ear. "We don't know how much the ground will attenuate the signal, or how having the sensor working in motion will change it's readings. These are the first of about a hundred questions we need to look at."

Billy raised his eyebrows. "We?"

Chase nodded. "Your little robot is just the tip of the iceberg. Once we modify that little guy with these sensors and some eyes underground, there's no end to what he can do."

Billy said, "I'm honored."

Chase replied, "Stick with me kid. We've got all kinds of potential right here in this room."

# Chapter 6

## *Ein Gedi, Israel*

"What is Nehushtan?" Dolly Jane asked, her head still pounding.

Janet said, "That question will have to wait until we are alone." She stepped back from the snake in the skeletal hand. Her mind was swimming with the revelation of the bronze snake surrounded by dead bodies in the middle of an ancient site. She looked at Dolly Jane and quickly shifted gears to a motherly role. She spoke loudly so that everyone in the cave could hear, "That's a nasty bump on your head. We need a medic to take a look at you. Let's get you back to the camp."

They exited the cave and headed back toward their base camp. On the path with the bright sun shining overhead Dolly Jane appreciated the warmth of the infrared sunrays on her skin. Still surrounded by team members, their conversation would have to wait. Dolly Jane thought back on how they had met.

. . . . .

Janet Zimmerman held the title, "Professor of Anthropology" at Iowa State University and specialized in

Archeology, a subunit of the larger field of Anthropology. Like most tenured professors she specialized in one of the various fields within Archaeology. Her studies emphasized research in and around the Dead Sea. For the past thirty years, she had led teams of eager college students to unearth and study dry sandy dig sites. Her most favorite sites were in Israel, especially the calming desert regions of Ein Gedi.

Dolly Jane first met her when she took an elective course "ANTHR 128: Archaeological Methods and Techniques". She had no interest in anthropology or archeology, but was taking the elective to fulfill a liberal arts requirement. She expected the class to be little more than a boring rendition of ancient stories with names and dates to memorize. With the bar set low, she threw her bag over her shoulder and rode her bike to Pearson Hall.

The brick edifice housed the anthropology and world languages department. Other than her Spanish classes she hadn't paid attention to the building at all. Dolly Jane pressed the aluminum handle that covered Pearson Hall's glass door. She followed the human flow of backpack wearing energetic students up the stairs to room 323 where she settled into a seat in the small lecture hall.

Dolly Jane was pleasantly surprised when Janet addressed the class on the first day. She took center stage in the classroom and had a commanding presence. Her dark brown shoulder length salt and pepper hair was left unbound to tumble. Never one to wear make-up, she exuded confidence in who she was. Her eyes sparkled as she spoke, "Archeology is placing yourself in another person's shoes. Imagine living life in another time, a different culture. Imagine what their daily routine would be like. What did they do when they woke up in the morning? What was for breakfast? How did they make their living? What did they do for fun? What were the major issues of the day? What were people gossiping about on Instagram and at the local Starbucks?"

A few students chuckled at the insertion of a modern coffee shop and social networking into the doldrums of antiquity. She continued, "Using the clues that we have to look at from other cultures and times, we can learn a lot about their life. It is as though we are viewing a home through the keyhole of the front door. The more information we have about a culture, the better the view of their lives we can discern."

Dolly Jane was pleasantly surprised. She sat up in her chair and began to take notes. This was nothing like any previous classes that she had experienced. The lecture continued with a description of how coins, pottery and parchment are used to piece together images of life in other times.

Dolly Jane went back to her dorm room with a wide smile and read the syllabus cover to cover. The course intrigued her in a manner unlike her previous course of study. In every previous field of study that she undertook, she would enjoy the subject, and effortlessly memorize the material and master it quickly. But nothing had gripped her like this new world.

When Dolly Jane arrived at the classroom for their second lecture, she was surprised to see the class broken up into sections. Janet instructed the class to arrange themselves in groups of four, then she gave each of them a sealed plastic bag. Then she said, "The bags contain replicas of ancient coins, maps, and reproductions of an original ancient manuscript. All electronic devices must remain off. Using only the information in your bag, find the topic, and write an analysis of the subject. This will be your first graded assignment for the semester. You have 15 minutes."

Dolly Jane dumped the contents out onto her desktop and dove in. The two bronze coins were accompanied by a detailed description:

> **501404**
> **CONSTANTINE I.** 307-337 AD. Æ Follis (19mm, 2.70g). Struck 328 AD. (anepigraphic,) Rosette-diademed head right, looking upwards, (eyes raised to God). / **CONSTANTINI-ANA DAFNE**, Victory seated left on cippus, head right, holding palm branch in each hand, trophy and captive before; **Γ** / **CONS**. (mint of Constantinople). RIC VII - ; Hunter -; Cohen -; LRBC -. VF, earthen black patina. Rare. **VERY RARE anepigraphic type.**

She set the coins aside and quickly studied the map. It showed the Middle East and was definitely a map of Turkey, but no cities were labeled. The city in the northeast portion of turkey was highlighted along with the roads to and from the area. They came from every direction: Asia Minor, Egypt, Greece.

She picked up the two pieces of parchment. She felt the texture and smelled them. Nothing. They were obviously cheap replicas, appropriate for this exercise but providing nothing in terms of tactical information. She smirked and looked over the writing. She attempted to read the first line:

> Πιστεύω εἰς ἕνα Θεόν, Πατέρα, Παντοκράτορα, ποιητὴν οὐρανοῦ καὶ γῆς, ὁρατῶν τε πάντων καὶ ἀοράτων.

Dolly Jane recognized it was written in ancient Greek, but her limited literary skills were unable to penetrate beyond that.

She held up the second parchment. It was of equal quality:

> Credo in unum Deum,
> Patrem omnipoténtem,
> Factórem cæli et terræ,
> Visibílium ómnium et invisibílium.
> Et in unum Dóminum Iesum Christum,

"Latin," she pondered. Her knowledge of Spanish gave her a window into some of the words. "Obviously an important enough document to be translated very early on."

A white 3 x 5 card revealed the translation:

> We believe in one God, the Father Almighty,
> maker of all things visible and invisible.
> And in one Lord Jesus Christ,
> the Son of God, begotten of the Father.

The document continued, but she didn't need to read any further. She closed her eyes and replayed the first line:

> We believe in God the Father

She imagined that same line with music. Her mind drifted to the song by the Newsboys and replayed the second line as well:

We believe in Jesus Christ

While it is certainly not a word for word rendition, nor was it a comprehensive theological statement, the Newsboys did shed a little light on basic Christian tenants of faith. They also used some of the words from the ancient document in their lyrics. A moment later, she thought of the origin of the song and recognized it as the Nicene Creed. She instantly referred back to the English translation on the parchment.

God of God, Light of light, true God of true God,
Begotten and not made;
Of the very same nature of the Father,
By Whom all things made into being,
In heaven and on earth, visible and invisible.

She placed the parchment back on the table and whispered, "The Nicene Creed".

The other students at the table held blank stares. She closed her eyes and thought for a moment. While she didn't remember all the details of the theology that was laid out in the creed, she did remember that is was a monumental landmark in the history of the Christian church.

She returned to the map and pointed to the highlighted region. She said, "This city in Turkey must have been the ancient city of Nicaea." She picked up a coin and said, "The coins showing Constantine the Great show him in a pious heavenward gaze. This means that we must be talking about the cultural shift that happened when Constantine adopted Christianity as the religion of the Roman Empire."

While her knowledge base was lacking on the history of the 1200 leaders who attended the meeting. She knew enough to recognize that all the clues on the table pointed to the Nicene Creed. Dolly Jane returned to her desk. She inhaled deeply and pursed her lips as she exhaled. She put herself there in the region surrounding Nicaea in 325 AD. She saw the streets bustling with people who had traveled to the conference from all over the world. She understood their excitement. She imagined going in and out of her favorite bathhouse and Ecclesia. She imagined the rifts that sprung up due to the vast differences that came from divisive teaching. For Dolly Jane, she pictured the Council of Nicaea as a turning point for the church, and for world history.

She took a quick glance at her watch and realized that she still had nine minutes to write something on paper. She thought from the point of view of a girl her age working at a coffee shop as the religious leaders from all over the world descended into her town. Her thoughts poured onto the page as effortlessly as water flowing down a stream. Putting her pen on the paper, she described her day not only serving coffee in fine porcelain cups, but the various leaders that she waited on, about the importance of the council meeting, and how it would impact the world. Her hand moved swiftly over the page as she wrote.

> The world's religious leaders sifted in and out of her tables, and she could hear their conversations. The majority of religious and political thought in the history of the world was conceived with caffeine in hand.

She smiled as her imagination combined with the facts in her story. She wrote swiftly and told a fictitious account of a young coffeehouse waitress serving the religious leaders.

Janet interrupted her thought process. "Go ahead and hand in what you have so far,"

She looked up from her desk and noticed that she had several pages written. In contrast, the other students around her had barely scrawled out a few lines. Shocked and slightly embarrassed, she passed her work forward and sat slumped down in her chair.

Dolly Jane thought for a moment. She realized that she hadn't touched any of the theological concepts that were dealt with. She hadn't commented on Constantine, or even mentioned that the subject matter was the Council of Nicaea. She had completely ignored all of the historical facts. She was certain that she was off track and was bound to fail the assignment.

Janet collected the papers and scanned them. Most had written “Council of Nicaea”, “Religious liturgy,” one had erroneously written, “The city was named Constantinople,”

When she flipped to Dolly Jane’s paper she read for a few moments then looked up at the class. She tried to read the faces to discern who had written it. Dolly Jane shrunk down in her chair trying not to be noticed. Janet read aloud from Dolly Jane’s paper. She put emotion into what she was reading and the words came to life. She read the entire 748 words that Dolly Jane had hastily scrawled out by hand. When she finally set it down, the entire class was confused, including Dolly Jane.

Then she said, “Archeology is not about finding relics. It’s not about knowing the names and dates of the kings or knowing the results of the wars. It’s about putting yourself into another time and culture and experiencing what they did in their context.” She held up Dolly Jane’s paper and continued, “This journal entry is an excellent piece of work. While it didn’t recite any historical facts, about the Council of Nicaea it showed them through the eyes of a teenage waitress. Show, don’t tell.”

Dolly Jane beamed.

Janet quickly recognized the author of the paper and made eye contact with Dolly Jane. Making no attempt to give Dolly Jane anonymity she gave her an affirming nod.

During the course of her first two years at Iowa State University, Dolly Jane switched her major and took every class that Janet offered. With every one, Dolly Jane looked forward to class time like never before. She found herself reading not only the syllabus and required reading well ahead of time, but further reading came naturally. She enjoyed the stories of archeological relics more than a good novel. She also added a few Hebrew classes and eventually completed a minor in Hebrew.

Ironically, once Dolly Jane knew who Janet was, she seemed to spot her at other venues around campus. Janet was a volunteer at SALT, the Christian outreach through Cornerstone Church, where Dolly Jane attended. She emulated the life and generosity of Jesus, she lived in a villa just around the corner from Dolly Jane's sorority house and worked out at the same facility that Dolly Jane did.

Dolly Jane began attending the small group Bible study sessions that Janet led. Janet quickly saw leadership potential in Dolly Jane and had her facilitate several discussions in the group. She seemed to lead with effortless skill and was a natural choice to take over when Janet was unable to attend. Soon, Dolly Jane assumed leadership of the group and Janet started a new group with other students while she continued to meet with Dolly Jane once a week for coffee.

For Dolly Jane to attend an archaeological dig was no stretch of the imagination, or a lofty goal, rather it was the logical next step in her education. Killing two birds with one stone, she received credit for her Hebrew minor by staying with local Jewish families and exercising her language skills, she attended Hebrew classes in the morning, and archaeological digs in the afternoons.

. . . . .

Once they had progressed down the hillside and were out of sight of any of the teammates on the dig, Janet slipped the bronze snake out of her sleeve and into her bag.

Janet said, "I know this looks bad."

Dolly Jane was shocked, "Looks bad? Are you kidding? Theft of a archeological site!"

Janet said, "It goes much deeper than you imagine."

Dolly Jane stammered, "I can't even count how many laws you've just broken!"

They continued walking and Janet said, "What I've done is much more than simply taking a historical artifact. This little piece of metal is easily the most important find since the Dead Sea scrolls. We have to protect it."

Dolly Jane shook her head, but decided to trust the wisdom of her mentor. They proceeded down the desolate, brown, rocky hillside and followed a well-worn path into a wadi, a natural dry riverbed in the desert. Their route appeared no different than the trails to the famous David's Falls, or the more difficult terrain to Shulamit's Spring with the single exception of the water pools along the way. Janet found a shade tree along the creek and sat on a smooth boulder. Dolly Jane was uneasy, but sat in spite of her confusion and frustration.

Janet asked her, “What’s the most famous verse in the Bible?”

“John 3:16.”

“Correct. Can you quote it?”

“For God so loved the world that He gave his one and only Son, that whoever believes in Him shall not perish but have eternal life.”

“Why is that verse so famous?”

“It’s the basis for all of Christianity!”

“Correct. So what is the lead up to that amazing statement? What verses precedes that one?”

Dolly Jane had never thought of that. She didn’t have much of an answer and said slowly, “John 3:14 and 3:15?”

Janet laughed, “Creative answer. Can you quote those?”

“No.”

“Okay, most people can’t. In the verse, do you know who is talking?”

“No.”

“Do you know who they are talking to?

“No.”

“Ah, the quest for learning has begun.” Janet laughed. “John 3:14 says ‘Just as Moses lifted up the snake in the wilderness, so the Son of Man must be lifted up.” She looked over the desolate dry region and said, “The story Jesus is referring to is in Numbers chapter twenty-one. The Israelites traveled from Mount Hor to go around Edom. The people were grumpy and complained that they didn’t have any bread or water.”

Dolly Jane nodded, “I remember that story.”

“They complained about the manna God was giving them and said, ‘We detest this miserable food.’”

Dolly Jane chimed in, “Right. Then the Lord sent venomous snakes among them; they bit the people and many Israelites died.”

“Exactly. Then the people came to Moses and said, ‘We sinned when we spoke against the Lord and against you. Pray that the Lord will take the snakes away from us.' So Moses prayed for the people."

Dolly Jane furrowed her brow, "What does any of this have to do with John 3:16?"

"Hang on there kiddo. Listen to what the Lord said to Moses, "Make a snake and put it up on a pole. Anyone who is bitten can look at it and live."

Dolly Jane said, "Oh. I get it. Moses' snake was a metaphor."

"Certainly, it was a teaching point for Nicodemus. But there is much more to it.

Dolly Jane raised her eyebrows.

Janet continued, "God anointed the snake with the power to heal. When the Israelites were bitten by a real poisonous snake, they simply had to look at Moses' snake and they received real physical healing."

"You're talking historically, now, not metaphorically. This is something that really happened. Not a story to teach about repentance."

"Absolutely."

Janet stopped walking and held Dolly Jane by both shoulders. "What happened to the snake after that episode in scripture?"

"I dunno," Dolly Jane said.

"Most people don't. But this is where archeology come in. What were their options?" Janet asked.

"They could have melted down the metal and used it for other things," Dolly Jane said.

"What would most religious people do?" Janet pondered.

"It became an icon. An idol for them to worship," Dolly Jane lamented.

"They kept it," Janet concluded.

"Yes! Where?" Dolly Jane inquired.

"It was a relic like the tablets that had the Ten Commandments and Aaron's staff that budded. So they kept it, and worshipped it," Janet said.

Dolly Jane was shocked. "What?"

They continued walking back to the camp, and Dolly Jane felt like she was regaining her strength. Janet said, "The bronze serpent of Moses accompanied the Israelites from the desert to the Promised Land, where it ultimately became of symbol of worship in its own right and became known as Nehushtan. Eventually, it was placed in the Temple of Jerusalem in the holy place. The Israelites worshiped it as an idol. They burned incense to it, and it continued to bring healing."

Dolly Jane was speechless.

"Yep, every leader after Moses: Joshua, the other judges. Then the kings: David, Solomon, all the kings worshipped Nehushtan for it's healing powers all the way up to King Hezekiah."

Dolly Jane shook her head. Then she said, "What did Hezekiah do with it?"

"When Hezekiah became king, he moved against the local shrines and closed them down. In effect, this act was the first time that the offering of sacrifices was centralized to the altar in the Temple of Jerusalem. He got rid of idol worship all across the country and Jerusalem became the sole remaining site."

"What happened to Nehushtan?"

"Hezekiah used it."

"How?"

"The story is recorded in 2 Kings 18-20, and again 2 Chronicles 32. He became sick to the point of death. He entered the temple and prayed to God for his life. God granted him an additional fifteen years."

"I think I remember that story. Didn't he ask for a sign, and God allowed the sundial to go back fifteen steps or something?"

"Yes, he received his sign and his healing. Then Hezekiah broke Nehushtan to pieces and hid them."

Dolly Jane felt the bump on the back of her head. She was confused, "That's not how I remember the story."

Janet offered her a drink of water and said, "There is no date given for Hezekiah's reforms. No explanation concerning Hezekiah's motivation and goals."

Dolly Jane said, "The first reform that Hezekiah did was to destroy the high places. I had forgotten about the snake, but I'm sure that was right there among his first reforms."

"Very good. You remember the story correctly, but the Biblical record is written for a number of reasons. To set down the history as they perceived it, sometimes things aren't written in chronological order."

Dolly Jane smirked.

"For example, Hezekiah's 29-year reign was from 727-698 BCE. Right?"

"If you say so."

"And in that time, he defended Jerusalem from invasion by fortifying it with a new wall, bringing water into the city with a tunnel, and building up supplies of food and weapons."

"Sounds like a good king!"

"Absolutely! Teacher Ben Sirah included Hezekiah among the praiseworthy ancestors of Israel, right along David and Josiah. He's even listed in the lineage of Jesus."

Dolly Jane laughed, "Ya, but so are Rahab and Tamar and they were prostitutes."

Janet burst out laughing. She saw that they were almost back to the camp. They had just two hundred yards of easy hiking left. She continued, "When we look at non-Biblical sources we see an Assyrian inscription of King Sennacherib that describes his campaign to the West in 701 BCE. He speaks about 'Hezekiah the Judean' and calls him a stubborn and mighty enemy. Sennacherib claims that Hezekiah was forced to surrender to Assyria's superior might."

"What?"

Janet continued, "The Assyrian victories in Judah were memorialized in a relief engraved on a wall in Sennacherib's 'Palace without Rival' in Nineveh that depicts the battle and capture of the city."

Dolly Jane said, "You're kidding!"

"We would expect a multiplicity of views as we encounter various points of view in what is a truly variegated past."

"I suppose."

"The trove of written and visual documentation is augmented by the findings from archaeological excavations at major cities attacked by Assyria, Lachish and Jerusalem. Taken together, these rich materials make it possible to reconstruct a vivid picture of the last quarter of the eighth century BCE."

Dolly Jane pondered, "If Hezekiah had used the bronze snake to heal himself, then why did he break it up."

"His revelation that Nehushtan was a stumbling block to worshiping God came later."

Dolly Jane said, "I understand. But what did he do with the pieces? Have they ever been found?"

"Nehushtan has been sought after by kings and generals alike for centuries. Imagine the influence you would have if you had the power to heal. With the snake in your possession, your soldiers wouldn't have to worry about death. Your people wouldn't fear disease or pestilence."

Dolly Jane was speechless.

"Imagine having the power to heal in your hands. What would you do with it?"

"I'd make it available to everyone!"

Janet appreciated her altruistic approach. She asked, "What would most people do with it?"

"I can't imagine."

"They would build a temple to house the relic. They would charge a very steep admission! If it heals, people would pay anything! Healing never comes free. They would rather be slaves than die."

Dolly Jane shook her head.

Janet said, "The power within Nehushtan could change the world, possibly rule the world!"

They entered the camp and headed past the collection and sorting tent toward the far side of the settlement. "Societies all around the world have embraced the image of the bronze snake. Many have used replicas of it as symbols of the healer." Janet continued, "Bronze snakes have taken a mystical role in symbolism over the course of history. What is the symbol for medical care?"

"I have no idea."

She Janet pointed across the camp, "The medical tent is right over there. What's the symbol on the front door?"

Dolly Jane squinted. She realized that she had seen the image thousands of times, but never really thought about it. She said, "I see wings on either side of a squiggly line and a straight line."

"Look closer. What is the squiggly line?"

Dolly Jane walked over to the tent and looked closer. She could see the image was clearly a snake wrapped around a pole. Her mouth dropped, "That's a snake."

"Nehushtan is the universal image of healing. That's because it heals!"

"I thought it was something from Greek mythology."

"Some day we can dive into a deeper discussion and explore the conundrum of Mercury and Hermes, the Rod of Asclepius and the Caduceus."

"What?"

"Many people conflate the Biblical account with the Greek stories. The archeological dating actually puts the Greek stories after the Mosaic account. The Greek mythology was partially based on established Biblical record."

Dolly Jane said, "That's not what the world history class teaches."

Janet said, "The truth isn't always popular. The Greeks used the understanding of the healing power of Nehushtan as the basis of their stories that include the Caduceus and the Rod of Asclepius."

"My head is throbbing."

"From which part? The physical trauma you endured? The historical lessons I just put you through? Or from the emotional aspect of what is in my bag?"

She wanted to scream at the top of her lungs, "All OF IT!!!" She knew raising her voice would make her headache worse. She didn't know how to process what she had just seen or heard.

They walked the final hundred yards to camp and entered the medical tent. It was vacant. Janet helped Dolly Jane onto the exam table and went to the cooler, bagged up some ice, and gently placed the ice on the back of Dolly Jane's head.

Janet said, "I'll go find someone to help."

Dolly Jane grabbed her by the hand just before she left and said, "Why did you take it?"

Janet tapped her bag. "If this relic were to be catalogued and registered, we would list it on an online database. You know what I'm talking about, you've done it with the pottery pieces that we've found in the past few weeks."

Dolly Jane nodded.

Janet continued. "As soon as it is catalogued, the whole world will know that Nehushtan is here. Listen, this is no piece of pottery. This relic is explosive! It's dangerous."

Dolly Jane said nothing.

Janet continued, "Dozens of treasure hunters all around the world have programmed automatic searches on their browsers looking for anything having to do with the words, 'Snake, Bronze, Healing or Nehushtan.' If they notice that someone is searching for the source of healing, they instantly hack into their computer and look into the rest of their search history. You can tell archeologists pretty easily from their search history. They would know if someone has found it and was looking for the next piece."

Dolly Jane shook her head. "You mean there is something like a secret society after this thing?"

"Not really, just individuals around the world who are passionate about finding Nehushtan. They're called Seekers, for lack of a better term. They would be here within a few hours with an armed team to steal it."

Dolly Jane was shocked. "Steal it?"

"Look around! Right now, we have no real security here. It's just a few folks like you and me saying 'Don't take our relics.' Granted, that has always been plenty, who would want to steal our piles of dirt? But now that's all changed."

Dolly Jane asked, "Are we in danger?"

"Not as long as we keep this quiet."

"Does it still have power?"

"You saw that it was surrounded by dead bodies, right?"

Dolly Jane frowned.

"The legend is that all three pieces must be recovered in order for Nehushtan to regain its healing power."

Dolly Jane said, "Do you believe in relics?"

Janet paused, "What is a relic? Who attributes the powers to relics?"

Dolly Jane said, "Legend, I suppose."

Janet said, "Folklore said that if you drink from the cup that Jesus used at the last supper, then you'd be immortal."

"The Holy Grail!"

"Show me that in the Bible."

Dolly Jane said, "What do you mean?"

Janet said, "The Holy Grail isn't in the Bible, except a brief reference to the cup being there. There was nothing about any powers attributed to the cup."

Dolly Jane was silent.

Janet said, "Show me the powers attributed to the true cross of Christ in the Bible."

Dolly Jane said, "There is plenty of power in the cross, but not the physical wood of the cross."

Janet said, "People love relics. When they go on vacation, they buy trinkets, memories of their trip. The Yad Kashish Souvenir Company sells millions of items every year. People value the trinkets and put them in their living room as a memory of the trip. But there is no power in the trinkets. They tell a story, but they are not powerful in and of themselves."

"So what are you saying?"

Janet tapped her bag, "Only when the relic has a supernatural aspect in the history of the Bible, then I believe.

Dolly Jane shook her head, "What makes it different from other relics?"

Janet said, "The Bible is clear. Nehushtan was the source of healing power in Moses' time. This is not a memory, it conveys power, and is documented specifically in the Bible."

Dolly Jane was silent.

They did not speak for a few minutes. The message of the importance of the relic sank in.

Finally, Dolly Jane asked quietly, "So where did Hezekiah hide the pieces?"

Janet smiled, "Now you're thinking like an archaeologist young lady!"

Dolly Jane grinned for the first time since before she entered the cave with the skeletons.

"We've got a lot of work to do. First, we need to date everything in here, and understand what happened. I expect that with the amount of pottery in the cave, we can date it pretty quickly. Then we will know the last time frame that had the snake. What we won't know is where they got it, or if they knew about the other two pieces."

Dolly Jane suddenly remembered the buckle in her pocket. She reached in and pulled out the relic and handed it to Janet. "I forgot all about this!"

Janet smirked, "So who's the relic thief now?"

Dolly Jane put her hands up defensively, "I was hit in the head. I didn't remember I had found it."

Janet said, "We both have our reasons."

Dolly Jane sighed, "Okay. What can you tell me about it?"

Janet looked at the buckle, "The inscription is Turkish. It says 'üfürükçü' which means 'Healer'. I suppose that would have been the designation for a doctor at the time."

Dolly Jane asked, "Why Turkish? That doesn't make sense here in Israel."

Janet said, "The Ottoman Empire ruled over this region from the thirteenth to eighteenth century. Turkish was the primary language of the government."

Dolly Jane thought for a moment, "The snake was not found in the original hiding place, it had been moved!"

"Possibly many times over the years. If it was used during the Ottoman Empire, who knows how many times it had been stolen or taken by acquisition over the years."

Dolly Jane inquired, "What are you going to do with the bronze snake?"

Janet was solemn, "We'll hide it in a secure place and put all of our efforts into finding the other two pieces."

Dolly Jane sighed, "How do we do that?"

Janet said, "The Book of the Kings tells the story of the details of the Kings of Israel and Judah. The location of the other two pieces will be there."

"What's the Book of the Kings?"

"First thing's first. Let me find you a medic."

# Chapter 7

## Lake Shore East Park
## Chicago

From the balcony of his apartment, Chase looked out over Lake Michigan then down to Lake Shore East Park. The six-acre botanical park within the heart of the city is surrounded by several of the tallest buildings in Chicago. The green space includes perfectly manicured trees and shrubbery. Though purely urban in every sense of the word, the greenery of the park is a pleasant addition to the surrounding concrete jungle. A community of urban canine owners frequents the south end, which is designated as a dog park.

Chase went inside and told Billy, "It's testing day!"

Billy and Chase walked in the greenery among dozens of joggers and picnic lovers. Billy rolled a black metal suitcase behind him on the cement sidewalk. Inside, the modified robot waited in expectation. After weeks of work, the pair had overhauled every cubic inch of the automated machine. They added the necessary sensory equipment along the front, stealthily hidden amongst the diamond burs. They created a new integration system between Checkers and the host computer to accommodate the vast increase in data. They revamped the steering mechanism to allow tighter turns in three dimensions. The only things they left untouched were the drilling mechanism, the tunnel creation tiles, and the nickname.

"Let's see what Checkers can do with her new brain," Billy said as he sat down on a bench.

He unzipped the suitcase and set Checkers on the grass. Chase was pulling behind him an empty rolling cooler. He removed the top and placed the entire cooler upside down, directly over the robot. He sat on the firm plastic cooler, shielding the robot from sight.

The pair spent a few minutes opening the two laptops and doing a few final checks on the software. Between the two of them, they had an array of windows open, monitoring dozens of parameters within the machine. Billy tapped a key and Checkers began a gentle hum, she was ready. At a glance, they could assess the details of the drill head, temperature inside and outside, ground composition, battery life, and distance of tunneling possible. On Chase's laptop screen were several windows but only the upper left was functioning. It showed a Google map of the surrounding area, they were in the center.

Within a few moments Checkers' sensors were fully functioning and data wirelessly poured into the computer like water over Niagara Falls. The computer silently converted the myriad of invisible ones and zeroes into three different images on the region. The upper right box showed an overhead view of the area, essentially a replica of Google maps with far more detail showing every tree, bench and bystander. Chase waved his hand back and watched himself on the screen in real time. The lower left showed the subterranean imagery. Data poured in and the screen came alive with details. He could see that there was nothing but healthy dirt for twelve feet before they found a pair of large concrete pipes. He tapped a few keys and the resolution changed, he could see within the pipes, one was a sewer line and the other contained a host of electrical and fiber optic lines. He tapped the screen again. He scanned forward and backward along the lines and could clearly see branching conduits going in various destinations.

The lower right window on the screen showed the underground thermal imaging. A mixture of reds, yellows, and blues revealed the temperatures. Chase let his fingers dance along the keys and the thermal image replicated the findings along the surface. His hands showed as though they burned red while his baseball cap illuminated a cool blue. Then he brought the image to the underground pipes and, while the detail wasn't as accurate as the lower left window on the screen, he had confidence in his sensors could tell the temperature of the sewer line and electrical lines to within a tenth of a degree.

On the far right of his screen, in a vertical column was a list of chemical elements with a series of numbers next to each: Calcium, Magnesium, Sodium, Iron, Water, etc.. Chase was able to mentally compute the soil composition from these chemical readings. He smiled proudly.

Billy was looking at his own screen. While it was naked from a photographic perspective, the data was impressive. Billy's windows revealed every aspect of the robot's internal performance: temperature and performance of the drilling mechanism, composition and moisture content of the dirt being recovered, performance of the calcium hypochlorite and aerosolized polyethylene glycol reaction, piston compression movement, tile formation, and of course, battery life. With a few taps on his keyboard, Billy could see every aspect of his beloved Checkers' upcoming subterranean dance. Like a proud father, Billy announced, "I'll watch her performance while you guide her through the terrain."

Chase said, "Let her go!"

Billy tapped a key and Chase felt a slight rumble under the cooler he was sitting on. After a moment, he felt nothing. He stood up and peaked under the cooler. Underneath there was nothing but a twelve-inch hole in the ground where Checkers was previously hidden. He felt the hole and was impressed with the clean tile lining that the little robot had built around the edges of the tunnel. It was warm to the touch.

"Excellent," he said.

The images on Chase's screen changed as Checkers moved deeper into the earth and turned east. He glanced at Billy's laptop and asked, "How's she doing?"

Billy was silently monitoring dozens of numbers, looking for anything abnormal. He smiled, "Fantastic."

Chase pointed to a boulder that appeared on his screen. “She’s doing great through normal soil. That rock over there looks like it’s granite. Let’s test her a bit.”

Billy was confident, “Sure.” He watched the numbers with an eye on Chase’s screen as Checkers approached the underground boulder. It stopped when it touched the surface. Billy watched as his screen showed that the gears shifted and drive mechanism moved into a low speed, high torque movement. The pressure against the boulder increased, and within a few seconds, it once again was moving forward.

Chase’s eyebrows rose, “She’s amazing!”

Billy bragged, “She works nonstop, independently, unnoticed, creating a sturdy 12-inch tunnel wherever she deems necessary. Checkers can dig through any type of soil, sand, clay, even marble. As you would expect, granite takes longer than sandstone, and requires replacement drill bits every 85 yards. The only limitation is subterranean water.”

Chase furrowed his brow.

Billy clarified, “You can’t make the tiles from water.”

Chase’s screen showed that they were approaching the opposite end of the boulder, having drilled directly through it. “How’s the drill head holding up?”

Billy had already analyzed the numbers, “Like a champ.”

Chase turned the robot south and was impressed at how quickly it changed back to swift motion once through the granite. He could clearly see the under surface of East Benton Place and the foundation of the building on the other side of the street. “Let’s take a closer look at this place.”

“Haven’t we had enough fun for an initial test?”

“Just a little more,” he said as he came underneath the building. The screen had shifted from a geological scan to an architectural analysis. 55-degree granite entities on the screen were steel pylons and reinforced concrete had been set in place in 1960. Chase stopped Checkers and scanned back and forth. Within moments, he mapped out the basement. He could see every plumbing and electrical entrance to the building. He scanned further and saw above the first floor and the thermal imaging brought up something red, walking down the hallway. A few seconds later, the image refined and a figure was kneeling at the base of a row of shelves. In the corner of the building, he could clearly see a toilet, shower and sink in a small room. Chase smiled, "Let's have some fun."

He directed the robot to the base of the foundation, directly underneath the bathroom and began drilling directly upward. Progress was slow. As Checkers inched forward, they were able to watch the worker continue to work in the next room.

Billy shifted nervously on his bench seat. "If we get caught..."

Chase aimed at the corner of the room, between the toilet and the wall. When they were an inch from penetration, he stopped Checkers. He progressed the robot into the concrete before the drilling mechanism dissipated into a thousand pieces. The resolution on Chase's screen changed. The windows that used ground-penetrating radar had negligible resolution. But the thermal imaging directly above him was incredibly clear. They could clearly see the bottom of the porcelain throne and the edges of the internal walls.

Billy was startled when a warm red head appeared. He said, "There he is!"

The man was looking around the bathroom. He poked his head into the shower and turned the water on and off. Chase and Billy watched as he looked over the sink, and then ducked his head under it. Eventually, he took a few steps back. Walking with a distinctive limp, he left the room.

Checkers backed up into the tunnel and sat still. Chase's screen resolution picked up once they were able to use GPR again. The man went into the next room, obviously looking for the source of the drilling sound.

With a hole left in the building, Checkers escaped backwards through the tunnel towards the privacy and comfort of the cooler Chase was still sitting on. He stopped just short of the tunnel entrance, remaining underground.

Chase was still looking at his screen. He panned around the region and could see the thermal imaging of the picnic table and surrounding area. He saw a lady with a stroller coming from the north, he zoomed in and could easily see the warmth of her skin by the red and orange coloring. He looked closer and saw her heart beating. He estimated 80 beats per minute.

Chase zoomed out and focused on the cooler he was sitting on. The blue and yellow hue revealed their comparative cooler temperatures. He zoomed in and saw his own heart, beating at about seventy beats per minute, then panned over to Billy, whose face was bright red, flush with increased blood flow on the skin surface. He focused eighteen inches down and to the left and saw Billy's heart racing.

"What did you think you were doing?"

Chase sat back and smiled.

"Hey Jack Wagon! That was completely un-called for!" Billy fumed.

"What do you mean? It seemed like an ideal test for the new sensors. Everything functioned perfectly!"

"You had no business drilling into the basement of a private building! We could have been caught! Everything we have built together would have been stripped from us and we'd be in jail."

"Jimmy is blind."

"What? What are you talking about?"

"I eat at III Forks Restaurant all the time. I know every inch of the building and pretty much everybody inside it. I knew it was Jimmy from his limp. He's a wonderful guy who works the storage room this time of day, but he can't see worth squat."

"That's why you chose this place? And why you were so quick to scan the restaurant?"

Chase interlaced his fingers behind his head and leaned back. "The machine performed great! That's an amazing robot you've created. If we add a few cameras at the front of it, we'll be able to see clearly after we've cleared the tunnel and gone above ground."

Billy was furious, "I can't believe you didn't tell me ahead of time! You knew what you were doing, and left me in the dark."

Chase ignored his rant and focused on the screen in his hands. He brought Checkers all the way back through the tunnel into the cooler. He stood up and gently kicked the cooler over, exposing the robust machinery whose black and white sides were speckled with brown dirt. It sat like a proud hunting dog who had successfully completed a training mission.

Chase squatted down next to it and said, "We need two other things. Once we've tunneled through, we will need to get the drill head out of the way and use a robotic arm to retrieve items on the other end. Then, we need to seal off the tunnel with some type of manhole cover. We need to produce a set of tiles that snap into place and cover our tracks. Otherwise, they can trace the tunnel all the way back to us."

Billy was stunned. His mind was swimming in a sea of bitterness and resentment. He had never envisioned what the end use would be for Checkers, he had simply followed his imagination and worked tirelessly until his amazing ideas had become reality. Yet it was his robot and he was shocked and alarmed that Chase forged ahead of him without considering Billy's thoughts or feelings. However, Chase's last two comments acted as an engineering challenge that swept over him like ocean waves preparing to crash on the beach. Billy recognized the feelings inside him. He could fight with Chase, and the wave would cause him to crash on the beach of unrealized engineering possibilities causing much of his work to halt because of a disagreement with how the test had gone. Alternatively, he could catch the wave and surf it, adding to his invention unprecedented robotic drilling performance.

After a few moments he took a deep breath and worked the problem. The robotic arms were easy, but it took him a few moments to come up with ideas for solutions to the other problems. When he had collected his thoughts, he looked at Chase. "We can add a secondary gearing system on the transmission to allow for the entire drill head to swivel like a butterfly valve. We already have four robotic arms for placing the tiles, they can be reconfigured to reach forward as well as backwards."

"Each of them?"

Billy said, "Sure. We can add a second mold that makes a man hole cover in three shapes like pieces of a pie. I have the mold back at my house. I've used it for other projects. The pieces snap together making a disc and it can cure in place, making a water-tight seal."

Chase was light hearted, "That was easy!"

Billy cautioned, "Well, it will take a while to do all of that. The easy part is coming up with ideas. Actually making the robot do everything, sometimes that feels like I'm trying to teach a monkey how to read."

# Chapter 8

---

### *Ein Gedi, Israel*

Dolly Jane sat on an exam table with a bag of ice on the back of her head for several minutes before the medic noticed that they had entered. When he responded, he apologized for not being more attentive. He took her vital signs and performed a cursory exam. "You've got a nasty bump on the back of your head. What did you hit it on?"

Janet spoke before Dolly Jane had a chance, "She tripped and fell and struck a rock on the floor of a cave."

The medic took his time and when he learned that she lost consciousness and carefully evaluated Dolly Jane. He simultaneously performed a mini-mental status exam while repetitively shining a pen light into her retinas. This was followed by gentle palpation of her head and neck. He inquired if she had any nausea, or other symptoms, all of which she denied. After a few minutes, he said, "I think you're going to be fine. Keep icing it and let me know if you become nauseated, have any visual changes, or if anything else changes."

Dolly Jane said, "Thanks for your help. I think I'll head back to my tent and get a little rest."

Janet led Dolly Jane to her tent. Dolly Jane asked, "What is the Book of the Kings?"

Janet said, "The Book of the Kings is written about several times in the Old Testament. At the end of any passage about a King's reign in the Bible, it says:

> As for the other events in his reign, aren't they written in the Book of the Kings?

Dolly Jane said, "I always thought that was metaphorical."

"Far from it. The Book of the Kings is a detailed daily account of every major action that the King did. It should be stored somewhere with the Kingly relics in Jerusalem."

"Or possibly with other long lost books."

Janet looked puzzled.

"Qumram was the site of the Dead Sea scrolls. Could it be there with them?

"Interesting thought. Hide the book with the other precious books."

Dolly Jane nodded.

"Qumram is one of the most important sites in the world. From the time of its discovery in 1947, it was investigated by thousands of archaeologists for over a decade. The site has been covered with a fine-toothed comb. The tens of thousands of documents they recovered have been catalogued and archived. They haven't found anything that could be the Book of the Kings."

Dolly Jane removed the ice bag and caressed her head. "So how do you go about finding an ancient book?"

Janet said, "I've got another idea about where the Book of the Kings is."

Dolly Jane gave her a blank stare.

Janet said, "What do you remember about Jeremiah being thrown into a cistern?"

Dolly Jane sighed, "Now you're reaching deep into the far reaches of Biblical minutia!"

"Jeremiah tells the story. Shephatiah, Gedaliah, Jehukal and Pashhur were officials of King Zedekiah at the time when Nebuchadnezzar captured Jerusalem. Those four men were not Jeremiah's biggest fans."

"I'm sorry, but this story is more confusing than normal."

"Before the city was captured, Jeremiah had been saying negative things over and over again. He was known as the prophet of doom. He continually warned Israel about the coming siege. The destruction of Jerusalem was foretold over and over again. Eventually the king's four officials had enough of him and threw Jeremiah into a cistern outside the courtyard of the guard."

"I'm not following."

"Jeremiah was then lifted from the cistern and kept imprisoned in the courtyard of the guard until the city was captured."

"Okay."

"They laid siege to the city for months. This gave them time to preserve things they wanted to preserve and we know that all the gold and silver in the temple were taken to Babylon."

"Do you think Jeremiah preserved something in the cistern?"

"What would Jeremiah have considered to be most important to preserve?"

"Most people would have wanted to preserve the national treasure, or the Ark of the Covenant. "

"He was a prophet. He didn't care about gold and silver. He cared about God. The most important things to him were God's name and His honor. While the city was under siege, he couldn't move the big visible things like the Ark of the Covenant but I'm convinced that he made a collection of ancient documents.

"You think he hid them?"

"He had first hand experience with the perfect hiding place. The conditions in a dry cistern are very similar to the Qumran caves – a perfect spot to preserve relics for millennia. Jeremiah preserved the documents there in front of the courtyard of the guard. We know exactly where it was. We know the palace, and the courtyard. These have been excavated very nicely. But the cistern was left alone."

Dolly Jane said, "If we can find the cistern outside the courtyard of the guard, we'll find plenty of well-preserved relics. Including the Book of the Kings. So we need to visit Jerusalem?"

Janet's mind was swimming in details of archaeology. "The process of getting a permit to dig and declaring a site to be of historical significance is a major political battle. One religious sect or another can consider any square foot of dirt between Egypt and Russia to be holy. The problem is that once a site is declared of archeological importance, the person who owns the property has it taken from them, and nobody can build there. Ever! It affects not only personal property, but plans for entire communities."

Dolly Jane asked, "How does any archaeology happen in Jerusalem?"

"It's almost impossible. During the 1967 six-day war, Jerusalem suffered damage from bombs and missile attacks upon the city. In the rubble that filled the Jerusalem streets afterwards, there was chaos. Once peace was restored, the city was disheveled and most of the peace loving citizens of the ancient city looked at the disaster zone and hurried to clean it up. They wanted to re-open their businesses and get back to a somewhat normal life. However, Nahman Mavigad PhD looked at the situation a bit differently. As an archaeologist at Hebrew University in Jerusalem he walked through the destruction like a kid in a candy store. He gathered a team and quickly sorted through as much of the rubble as possible before the bulldozers came through to smooth over the past once again. In the middle of the Jewish Quarter of the city, at the base of a missile crater he discovered, among other things, an ancient wall. With some effort, his team found that they were looking 2700 years into the past as they actually laid eyes on Hezekiah's Broad Wall. The unbroken length of wall they uncovered ran 210 feet and was preserved in places to a height of almost 11 feet. It certainly was not the whole wall, but it represented a great time in history."

Dolly Jane asked, "He was one of the great kings in Israel's history. Is there a museum in his honor?"

Janet answered, "No, there is not."

"There should be. They should build one right beside the Broad Wall. That would be the proper way to honor such a great king."

Janet said, "You've got a point. But the story of the Broad Wall is not a typical dig."

Dolly Jane smirked, "They didn't get a permit and parse through the dirt with a spade and sifter like you taught us to."

"Far from it. Bombs are not the preferred digging technique. But in order to preserve the structure, four families had their property confiscated by Israel's Ministry of the Interior. They had lived there for generations, and then with the stroke of a pen by the Anglo Israeli Archeological Society, they had nothing. Their homes had been destroyed in the war. The enemy's bombs had destroyed everything they owned. All they had left was their land. Then their own government took it from them."

"That's not fair."

"Not much in the world is. If we were to have evidence that the book of the Kings is located somewhere in a special site, it wouldn't matter how important the find, there would be a major fight to get a permit to dig. Nobody wants their property taken from them."

"Then how do you go about finding more of the history?"

"The city is almost impossible. It took a bomb in the middle of Jerusalem to unearth Hezekiah's Broad Wall, otherwise nobody would ever have dug there! In the desert, like Ein Gedi it's easier, but even here it's still a tourist destination and our university lawyers endured a three year battle to get access to this site."

Dolly Jane lay down on her bunk as Janet continued, "Paperwork, political battles, and money. That's what archeology boils down to when you aren't looking at the relics or lectures. It's all dirty and nasty battles, and it requires dollars. Before and after any dig there is nothing but fighting."

"It's a good thing you didn't start your first lecture with that angle."

Janet chuckled, "I wouldn't have a significant following if I told the nasty truth up front."

Dolly Jane smiled, "You never know. I might still be here."

Janet replaced the ice bag on Dolly Jane's head. "You very well might be, but you'd probably be the only one."

Dolly Jane said, "Okay, so where is Jeremiah's cistern?"

Janet looked up to the sky, "Hidden within the relics in unearthed dig sites somewhere in Israel. I've been to every dig site, active and inactive. I've read their reports and investigated them myself. Nobody knows where the cistern or the Book of the Kings is." Janet leaned back in her seat and said, "The main problem with dig sites is in the nature of archaeology itself."

"The paperwork?"

"The whole country is holy land. When a relic is found, the property owner is out of luck. The land is basically stolen from them by the government and forever turned into a dig site."

"That's terrible."

"And it's also why we have such difficulty getting any further in any site within Israel."

"But the book!" Dolly Jane said. "There have to be some leads on where it might be."

"Oh yes. I have a few thoughts. I would certainly apply for permits in two or three places. Even if we got them, we will still have trouble getting the grant money to perform the digs. Until we've made a discovery in a certain site, it's tough to get people to sign up."

"I'd sign up. "

"Slave labor, like yours, is all we can afford!" Janet laughed.

"If we could discover that book, then we could find the pieces of Nehushtan." She paused for effect, "And have healing power in our hands." Dolly Jane rearranged the ice on her head, "Until then, I would prefer to lie down."

Janet waited.

Dolly Jane's eyes brightened as she said, "You taught me that everything is 'PEOPLE PLUS!'"

Janet closed her eyes and shook her head. "You've always listened, haven't you?"

Dolly Jane said, "To every word. PEOPLE PLUS. That's what you called it. Every endeavor you are involved in is about people. It doesn't matter if you are a ditch digger, the president of a major company, or anything in between. Every job boils down to not only doing the task at hand but also being good with people. It's about dealing with people plus digging the ditch. People, plus running the company. In the end, all that really matters is how we deal with people. Honestly, with integrity, and love."

"I said all that?"

"Over and over again."

Janet embraced Dolly Jane with a reassuring hug. “Reading hundreds of books and knowing history from every angle, moving dirt to uncover a bronze snake…”

Dolly Jane finished her sentence, “It only matters if we deal with people with honesty, integrity, and love.” She removed the ice bag and caressed her head. “It looks like we’re gonna have to find a creative way to explore an ancient cistern.”

Janet said, “Did I tell you that one of my favorite people is Nahman Mavigad PhD?”

Dolly Jane was surprised, “You know him?”

Janet smiled, “Oh yes, we met years ago. In preparation for my dissertation on the Dead Sea Scrolls, I interviewed him numerous times. Our professional work turned into a friendship and as I spent more and more time in Jerusalem, he saw that even as a graduate student, then later as a young professor. (I was a committed archeologist like him). He saw me as his protégé. He knew I lived quite meagerly, with most of my salary going to airline tickets to do the work I loved, and he helped were he could. His family owns a small apartment in the Old City. It’s far too small for his family, so it’s vacant. Whenever I come to Jerusalem, he insists that I stay there.”

Dolly Jane was impressed, “That’s fantastic. Like you say, PEOPLE PLUS!”

Janet bowed her head, “He’s a wonderful man. Over the years we’ve collaborated on numerous projects within the city of Jerusalem, Masada, and Qumran. I think I’ll look into possible dig sites near the Temple Mount, then consult him about options on how to proceed.”

# Chapter 9

## Aqua Lakeshore Apartments
## Chicago

Chase and Billy returned to the apartment in silence. Billy was fuming over his new friend's reckless entrance into the restaurant. Chase didn't know what had bothered Billy but was thrilled with the test's outcome and was happy to wait to talk it through with him. When they entered the apartment, Chase' next door neighbor Maddy was sitting on one of the three small chairs eating a bag of Doritos, watching the Hawkeyes take on the Iowa state Cyclones at Kinnick stadium.

Chase was elated. "Fantastic! You're here!!"

Billy greeted her warmly. The two had met intermittently during his brief stay with Chase. Maddy had been a basketball star in college as a starting guard for DePaul. Her work ethic in the weight room was also evident in the classroom. After graduating Suma Cum Laude from DePaul, she pursued a master's degree at the same University, just a block away from her apartment.

"Grab a piece of pizza and a chair and enjoy the game," Maddy said.

"Thanks," Chase said. "Jimmy says hello."

“You saw him? Were you at the III Forks?”

Billy interjected, “Technically, he didn’t say ‘hello’ but he was waving.”

“What are you talking about?”

“You know our little project that we’ve been working on? Today was the inaugural test flight, so to speak.”

“You dug under the restaurant?”

Chase nodded.

Maddy pulled up a chair, “How did Checkers perform?”

“Beautifully.”

Billy interjected, “Jimmy almost caught us.”

Maddy said, “A robot and a blind waiter walk into a restaurant. There’s got to be a punch line here somewhere.”

Chase said, “We need a few modifications so that she functions at the highest level, but she’s really close.”

Billy confronted Chase, “Don’t ever do that again!”

“Do what?”

“You went off on your own with MY ROBOT in a direction we hadn’t discussed and nearly got us caught.” Billy was livid. “This thing is complicated enough without you freewheeling the test half way through.”

Chase held up his hands defensively, “I didn’t mean to stir your pot. I was just having a bit of fun.”

“Let’s make a plan, agree to it, and stick to it. Agreed?”

Chase was surprised at the emotional outburst, “Agreed. That little robot can do amazing things. Was there rebar in the restaurant’s foundation? I can’t remember.” He went back to his laptop and replayed the encounter.

Billy grabbed a piece of pepperoni pizza and tossed it on a paper plate. He sunk deep into the couch, thankful that he didn’t need to get up any time soon.

The roommates enjoyed the afternoon football game while they processed the morning’s underground adventure. After the first quarter, the Cyclones were up by a field goal.

Between plays, Maddy inquired about the various machinations of the robotic performance that they had witnessed. Her analytical mind stirred and after dozens of questions, she felt that he had a good handle on the performance of the machine. At halftime, the game was tied 3-3. Maddy turned her chair around and hunched over Checkers with fresh eyes.

Chase said, “Why don’t you see what we saw when she was at work?” He opened a pair of video files in side-by-side windows and pushed “play.”

Maddy watched the video of the dig, analyzing the moving images of ground penetrating radar and all the numbers dancing along the screen. She saw through the numbers and saw not only the robot’s activities and performance, but the constraints due to its current design. She easily perceived where it was strained and in danger of being pushed beyond its limitations. She stopped the videos and replayed various portions of each of them several times with special attention to the performance of the drill head and enjoyed every tiny detail of the robot’s performance.

She sat mesmerized as Checkers slowed its pace yet still penetrated through the boulder. She scrolled through the GPR readings several times and confirmed the felsic intrusive igneous rock being granular and phaneritic in texture with 45% alkali feldspar and 65% quartz with a density of 2.7 $g/cm^3$.

“You drilled through granite!” Maddy said. “Impressive!”

During the break in action, the three engineers hunched over their laptops running simulations of tinkering and modifications of the various elements of the robotic performance. Maddy was quick to add a handful of traditional cameras to the front and back of the robot. She chose strategic positions that would not interfere with digging or the scanning of the other sensors. Chase worked out possibilities for angling the transmission while Billy dreamed up options for a round cover.

A feverish pace consumed the diligent creative team and they continued working through the second half of the game. Half watching, and wholly thinking about the problems that each new modification would bring, he engaged with the new project like a dog with a fresh bone.

Maddy said, “If the tri code optimizers that feed into the nipple sleeve receivers perforate their lubricators then they will boil up tensions against their side walls and stop the activation retractor.”

“I know, but we need the pressure high enough to compress the calcium hypochlorite and aerosolized polyethylene –”

"I know but, picture a knee, but without any cartilage, bone on bone. There's a sheering effect when alloys of differing densities abrade. They become magnetized because of reverse polarization."

"We need to make the activators from a different material."

"Exactly."

Billy groaned, "That will put us back weeks."

Maddy said, "It will also make this thing perform for years."

Chase grinned, "Let's do it."

The Hawkeyes dominated the second half of the game. There were no Cyclone touchdowns in Iowa City that day.

For the next few weeks, Maddy and Chase continued to work with Billy on Checkers. Their work schedule seemed to slip into the distance as they slogged through the updates and modifications on the robotics. Various pumps, wires, and motors were ordered online. Each tiny part was modified to fit their specific needs. The robot was dissected and her parts and pieces were scattered across the various flat surfaces in the apartment.

Pizza boxes piled high and red solo cups and soda cans were scattered across the room as the work continued. Eventually, they had refined the miniature marvel to their satisfaction. The apartment had the stench from three people working in their 800 square foot existence without opening a window in weeks. Fresh air seemed foreign to Billy.

He picked up his iPhone and checked the time, well past midnight. He tapped on his Life 360 App and checked to see where Chase and Maddy were. Maddy was in the library and Chase was en route on Madison Avenue. He noticed something unusual on his iPhone. The apps were loading slower than normal. He checked the settings and there was nothing abnormal, except a marker on his VPN that indicated that someone had cloned his iPhone. He thought that was unusual. He checked the settings on his computer and noted that someone had gained access to his programs and memory. He was tired and confused with the new finding. He would have to track down who was accessing his computer later. He went to bed.

The following day, the trio had reassembled and checked the technological marvel. In the flurry of activity, Billy didn't inquire about who had accessed his files. They were thrilled and ready for another test. The motley crew ventured to the park looking like they were headed to the airport. Billy rolled the suitcase that comfortably held Checkers, Chase walked briskly next to him with the cooler in tow and Maddy came along as well. With her additions, the group certainly worked slower, but she foresaw problems they hadn't dreamed of. Though it's outward appearance was virtually unchanged, to a skilled eye, the new robot made the previous version look like an adolescent boy in a college football uniform.

They passed the picnic table where they had previously dug and traveled fifty more yards. Chase plunked down his cooler upside down over the new and updated robot. Across the street was Soldier Field.

Chase sat next to Billy on the picnic table. Next to him Maddy was firmly ensconced on the upside-down cooler. Each of them pulled out a laptop and started tapping on the keyboard. They had agreed to a visit to the outside of the school next to the Stadium. They would scan as much of the north end of the building as they could, then return to the cooler. Nothing fancy.

Billy looked at his friends and noticed that they were three people sitting far to close to one another for social norms. He got up and sat a dozen feet away on a nearby bench.

They didn't need to speak to one another. They modified their software allowing each of them to see every aspect of the robot. They could flip between screens and see what the other person was looking at, if time allowed. Each of them had specific duties: Maddy was the pilot, guiding the robot carefully and gently, without creating any incidents. Chase was the navigator, in charge of the subterranean GPR, thermal imaging, and the traditional video images. Billy was tasked with watching over the details of the robotic performance. His eyes would pour over data on drill speed, temperature, torque, performance of the compressor, tiles, et cetera. Everything that happens within the robot's small world showed up on his screen.

After the work was done, Billy took extra time to copy every file Chase and Maddy had created in the process. He uploaded the files to the Cloud every hour to be sure that he had all the work backed up.

The three of them each ran through a comprehensive predetermined checklist like a pilot before take off. Billy tested each of the sensors as Checkers sat within the cooler. The camera was black, as expected, with the dark confines of the space. He briefly entertained the thought of adding low light "night vision" technology.

After the checklist was complete, Billy sent a message to the other two that appeared on their screen in a small box in the top right of the screen, "Ready."

Chase replied, "Ready."

Maddy confirmed, "Ready, let's dig."

Billy looked up. From ten feet away he could see Chase and Maddy sitting shoulder to shoulder. They would be communicating through messaging on the laptop screen. He looked at his laptop and found the thermal imaging screen, then panned the image to focus on the two of them. From below, Checkers' view showed them sitting comfortably. He focused on their heartbeats. Chase's heart cruised along at about a comfortable 60 beats a minute, Maddy was a little more caffeinated at 85 beats a minute. Billy looked over at the image of himself - 120 beats a minute. For him, it was personal. He still didn't fully trust Chase and he was now leaving major responsibilities in the hands of Maddy who he didn't know very well yet.

As his precious robot disappeared into a potential sepulcher he took a deep breath and tapped out another message, "Commencing dig."

Checkers' head went down into the soft earth and she tunneled like a gopher into the ground. Maddy and Chase monitored every aspect of the dig while Billy guided it downward into the depths of the Illinois soil. The familiar view of the two large sewer pipes came into view on screen. Billy slowed and came to a stop. He scanned further and noticed the significant improvement in resolution from the previous test. They could easily see forty to fifty yards in every direction.

Maddy sent a message, "This GPR resolution is truly a landmark scientific achievement. You should get the Nobel Prize for this!"

Chase and Billy were intent on their analysis and didn't look up from their screens. Time for celebration would come later. Billy focused on the stadium. He programmed out a course to traverse the thirty yards between their position and the outer wall. He had it curve to avoid a couple of dense rocks, then come to the surface between two evergreen bushes as they had discussed. With the program set, he pushed the "Enter" key and Checkers set off more rapidly than ever before.

The drilling proceeded at a furious pace. Maddy confirmed that the tiles were being produced and placed without difficulty. Chase noticed that the thermal imaging was changing as they came closer to the school. However, there was a slight lag in the resolution as Checkers crawled farther away.

Billy was pleased that the robot maintained her course and was proceeding with ridiculous efficiency.

Chase saw a new structure appear directly within the position of Checker's trajectory. He typed in the message "Stop the robot!" By the time Billy read the message, a one-inch metal pipeline was clear only inches from the drill surface.

He gasped.

He knew that an iron pipe underground should never be touched.

Billy's fingers swept over the keyboard and he sent the message to stop, but it was too late. The swift motion of the drilling machine had proceeded into the metal, easily cutting through the outer surface and penetrated into the pipe before it received the order to halt.

As the drill head slowed, natural gas poured from the severed underground pipeline and within a few seconds, filled the tunnel. Maddy, Chase and Billy each flipped between screens on their respective laptops to assess the crisis. Within a few moments, Maddy smelled the gas emanating from the cooler she was sitting on and realized the predicament that they were it.

Chase looked up from his screen, "You're sitting on a bomb."

Billy said, "Abort."

Checkers remained within the tunnel, a submissive and obedient workhorse, and ready to do her master's bidding, regardless of the danger she was in. The drill had stopped a little less than half way through the pipe, with the drill head still engaged into the metal surface. Billy quietly said, "Let's get her out of there and seal off this tunnel."

He typed in the order for Checkers to reverse course. The wheels engaged the tunnel surface and the drill head released its grasp on the pipe and let off a spark. The gas filled tunnel ignited immediately. The flame shot through the tunnel and lifted the cooler off the ground.

The blast propelled Maddy from the cooler thirty feet into the air in an awkward body manipulation. Her lumbar vertebrae were crushed as she was forced upward. Her head struck the trunk of a nearby oak tree, and as her body wrapped around it, each of her limbs snapped. She descended, hitting a branch that spun her around and she landed awkwardly on the lawn.

Motionless.

Chase had been sitting in the socially awkward position next to Maddy and was similarly launched upwards. The bench he was sitting on was completely destroyed. His body flew directly into a large branch and his chest took the majority of the impact. He descended and landed a dozen yards away on his side on a concrete bench.

Time seemed to slow down for Billy as he watched the eruption engulf his two friends. He didn't even perceive his own body moving as he was thrown backwards. His final conscious thought was the visual horror of his two companions being treated as human projectiles as they were launched upwards as a plume of fire surrounded them high into the air. His body landed on a sidewalk on his posterior before his head made an impact on the ground.

# Chapter 10

---

***Ein Gedi***
***Israel***

Dolly Jane's phone blew up. She received texts from a friend in the states, then another and another. Each message was short and unintentionally cryptic, but piecing them together she quickly came to understand that her younger brother was injured and in the hospital. Had she not sworn off social media, she would have seen many more images, facial expressions of shock and alarm, and photos from the Internet report about the explosion.

She hadn't seen him since the previous summer when they were both home in Dubuque, Iowa from their respective schools. She read more and more messages. There had been in some kind of explosion although the details were far from clear. He had been taken to Northwestern Memorial Hospital, a level one-trauma center less than a mile away.

Dolly Jane was stunned. She sat alone in the medical tent with her right hand still loosely holding an ice pack on the back of her head, and her left managing her phone. When Janet returned she found Dolly Jane in tears.

Janet was surprised, "Is your head still hurting?"

"No." She removed the ice pack from her head. "I'm sorry, but I have to go home."

"Home? Why?"

"Well, home is Iowa, but my brother was in an accident and is in a hospital in Chicago."

"Oh my. What happened?"

"I don't have many details yet, but it certainly sounds serious."

"Absolutely. Get yourself on a plane today. It's actually not bad as far as timing. Both you and I need to get out of this dig site today anyway. You go home, and I'm going to Jerusalem."

"Jerusalem?"

"I've got a bank there with a safety deposit box. It's probably the only safe place for the relic."

"So I'm the only one who knows about it?"

"And it's going to stay that way. That thing would bring way to much attention. I'm also going to start the process of applying for digging permits to look for the Book of the Kings."

"Permits?"

"I'll start with Dr. Nahman Mavigad and also the Anglo-Israel Archaeological Society. They've been looking for the Book of the Kings for years. Hopefully they'll be open to some of my ideas."

"I'm sorry I can't help you."

"You need to be with your family. Can you absolutely promise to keep this discovery a secret?"

"Absolutely."

"Even if you tell one or two close family members or friends it can be dangerous. If anyone Google's it, alarms are set off on the seeker's computers. People would be handsomely rewarded for reporting it. News this volatile can spread like wild fire. There's no telling what people will say, online or otherwise."

"My lips are sealed," Dolly Jane promised.

Janet gave her a gentle hug and departed for her private tent. After she packed a bag, she disappeared into the parking lot and left without an announcement to the rest of the team.

Dolly Jane took her time. She no longer felt the need to rest, but she used the time on her iPhone to secure a ticket to

Chicago. She found a bus to Tel Aviv and after packing her bag she said a few good-byes to fellow students. Once on the Airbus 380 she closed her eyes and disappeared into the night sky.

Upon arriving at the Chicago airport, she took an Uber to Northwestern Memorial Hospital and followed the signs to the Intensive Care Unit on the eighth floor. She saw the double doors labeled "Intensive Cave Unit – Authorized Personnel Only" and stopped in her tracks. She looked to the left and noticed a bustling waiting room. Families of the injured and sick were lurking in various stages of information gathering and grief as they gathered around loved ones. Among the faces in the crowd, she saw her mother, Eliana and a large group of family members.

"They say he's got bleeding on the brain, but not bad enough to operate." The white haired matriarch announced when she saw Dolly Jane join the group. Dolly Jane gave hugs all around and as more and more people spoke, she was confused with the contradictory reports.

"Bleeding on the brain sounds pretty serious."

Suddenly it seemed that everybody was talking at once.

"Subdural hematoma," her uncle said with authority.

"65% chance of full recovery," Billy and Dolly Jane's cousin Eliana announced.

"Not nearly as bad as it could have been," another person she didn't recognize said. Clearly, she would have to make some introductions and spend some time there.

Another voice said, "I'm so glad you came." It was the warm, comforting voice of her father, Drew. The tall graying man showed his years and the exhaustion of what such a trauma to a loved one can bring. He embraced Dolly Jane and quietly said, "Did you just arrive?"

She nodded and gave him a hug.

He checked his watch, "You must have left Ein Gedi the moment you got our text."

"There was more than one text. Dozens, actually, I haven't had that much activity on my phone since Billy won the state football championship."

Drew chuckled at the memory. "We're going to have plenty of time for us to learn about what you've found at Ein Gedi."

Dolly Jane's face flushed instantly with his statement. Her stomach turned over with anxiety. Her family must have already heard about the find! Were they in danger? Had anybody been there at the hospital? Her mind was swirling with questions. She gathered her thoughts and whispered, "How did you know? I haven't told anybody."

He looked at her curiously. "How did I know what?"

She hesitated. Maybe he didn't know. Maybe it was a normal greeting that she had misread in her tired and anxious state. She tried to replay the words he had spoken, but with all of her questions, she couldn't remember exactly what he had said. She looked for clarification, "What did you say?"

"How did I know what?"

"No. Before that."

Drew was confused. He couldn't remember the words he had said. He rephrased his greeting, "When we have some time, I'd love to hear about your time in Israel."

She took a deep breath not confident that she was in the clear, said, "Yeah. Sure."

Drew held both of her hands and gently said, "Let's pray for Billy."

She nodded.

He held her hands and together, they bowed their heads and he said, "Lord Jesus, Billy is your boy. Thank you for giving him to us to raise for a time, but we know he is and always has been yours. You made him. You know every cell in his body. You know what is wrong with him right now."

All around the waiting room, the conversations died down. Heads were bowed and people were agreeing in prayer.

He continued, "In the name of Jesus we command the bleeding to stop and the vessels and traumatized tissue to heal. Complete restoration of his body, in the name of Jesus."

The entire family was nodding and whispering similar prayers under their breath.

Dolly Jane raised her head and asked her father, "When can we see him?"

He motioned to a sign on the wall. The sign clearly said that visiting hours were 8 am to 9 pm. "In the morning. Usually the young doctors in training start making their rounds around five, but the docs who can give us some meaningful answers come around six-thirty or so."

"Aren't there any doctors there right now?"

"Of course, but there are quite a few people in there that are much more critical than Billy, and they need constant attention. Those include Billy's two friends who were in the accident."

"What friends?"

"I don't know. The newspaper report mentioned two young men and one woman but they may have been covering things up. It might have been a terrorist attack."

Eliana said, "Apparently, there was a freak gas line rupture at a stadium. These three were nearby at some type of picnic and injured."

Dolly Jane was shocked, "Billy was at a Bears game? That doesn't make sense, were they playing the Broncos?"

Eliana said, "I know. The other families said the same about their kids. Engineers. These guys are each reclusive introverts who would rather be looking at spreadsheets than walking in a park."

"Just like Billy."

"Certainly they were friends."

Dolly Jane turned and looked at the other families in the waiting area, "But what were they doing in the stadium?"

Drew said, "We've got plenty to ask him. Until then, let's keep praying. The prayer of a righteous man is powerful and affective."

Dolly Jane smiled, "I love it when you quote James 5:16. But don't forget the rest of the verse: 'Therefore confess your sins to each other and pray for each other that you may be healed.'"

He gave a comforting smile and together they found a seat among the crowded waiting room.

Standing at the doorway with short brown curly hair was a slender man in his early forties. He wore jeans and a flannel shirt and bore a warm smile. He approached Drew and gave him a bro-hug. Then he turned to Dolly Jane and said, "My name is Brian Pendleton, I'm a friend of your father's."

She smiled, "I remember you."

He said, "I've been listening to the medical reports and I've been around medicine and healing long enough to understand most of it. Certainly your brother is in need of God's healing hand right now."

Dolly Jane nodded.

"Your dad always says that I pray for a living." Brian laughed. "So I guess I'm here to work."

They once again bowed their heads and joined together in prayer. While they prayed, Dolly Jane's mind drifted. She imagined her brother in the hospital bed. She had spent enough time in hospitals to know how he would look with multiple intravenous lines, and monitors beeping all around the room. With the vital signs and EKG rhythm being viewed at the nursing station, certainly he was alone in the room at that very moment, with a nurse checking in by computer ten times more frequently than actually looking at him personally.

Dolly Jane worried about him.

Then her thoughts drifted to the relic she had been sworn to protect. While it was simply a piece of bronze, it actually conveyed the healing power of God to the Israelites. The bronze relic had provided healing from the venomous snakes that afflicted the Israelites in the desert. She had found it. She had stumbled onto one of the greatest finds of the century.

She wondered, *Could Nehushtan be the source of healing they needed?*

# Chapter 11

## Northwestern Memorial Hospital
## Chicago, Illinois

Dolly Jane had greeted each of her family members and conducted introductory small talk about college, archaeology, and her time in Israel. Despite the late hour, none of them had departed for the comforts of a bed at a hotel. When their social rumblings had settled down, Drew instructed the family to stand and join together in the central area of the room. A circle formed as the dozen men and women, family and friends, joined hands. Drew said, "We are here for Billy to pray for him and support him. Let's just go around and pray, one at a time. If you don't want to say anything you don't have to. But if you would like to pray out loud for Billy, the rest of us can agree with you in prayer."

The family prayed quietly in their circle. Drew started with a simple prayer. Others waxed eloquently with impressive displays of silver-tongued spontaneity.

When it was Dolly Jane's turn to pray, she said, "God, make him better, Amen."

Instantly, she felt silly. The next person started speaking, and she was jealous of every word. She should have said something profound; she should have spoken longer and prayed harder with great emotions to show what she felt for Billy. As the rest of the family continued taking their turns, one of Dolly Jane's cousins recited the Lord's Prayer, and several simply nodded silently, never voicing anything.

When they had gone around the circle, and everyone had their chance to participate, Drew simply said, "Amen." He let go of the hands at his right and left, giving the signal for everyone to break up and go their various ways.

Brian looked at Dolly Jane and said, "Let's go grab a cup of coffee."

Dolly Jane agreed, "I could use a break." She looked at her watch, 3:12 AM. "My days and nights are backwards right now, and I'd love to get out of this room for a bit."

They headed down the hallway to the elevator and Dolly Jane pushed the button with the downward arrow. "So what does it mean to pray for a living?"

Brian chuckled, "What do you think it means?"

Dolly Jane said, "Well, I suppose you're a pastor or some type of minister."

"You could say that."

"Where do you live?"

"I live with my wife and daughter in Grandview, Missouri, just outside Kansas City. I work at the International House of Prayer. We call it IHOP."

They boarded the elevator and he pressed the button labeled 1.

Dolly Jane smiled, "So you make pancakes?"

"Absolutely. Saturday mornings are pancake time in our house!"

"Seriously, what do you do?"

Brian grinned, "IHOP is a Christian movement and missions organization that focuses on prayer and worship."

She gave him a blank stare. The elevator stopped and the door opened. They found signs for the cafeteria and headed down the hall.

"We were founded with the idea to have 24/7 prayer with worship. We have a prayer room with live worship music going all the time, ever since September 19, 1999. And there are many other ministries that branch off of that. One of them is healing rooms."

Dolly Jane asked, "IHOP has a group of rooms that are specifically designated for healing ministry?"

"Yes, we do."

Dolly Jane's eyes widened. "So I would imagine that you know a little bit about what the Bible says about healing?"

"Sure, I know a bit. The gospels are full of stories of Jesus healing people. Blind people. Injured people. Sick people - all kinds of people. I've found that we learn a lot about Jesus from the miracles, but our focus should not be on the miracles as much as on the people that were involved with them! God loves people, and if healing brings them closer to Him, then many times He heals."

Dolly Jane smiled.

Brian said, "I love praying for people to be healed. And I love it when God heals."

Brian and Dolly Jane found the cafeteria and were pleasantly surprised to see it open in the middle of the night. The lights were dimmed and most of the cafeteria was closed off. They found the coffee bar and poured themselves each a cup of energy-producing coffee into plain white paper cups. Brian laced his with flavored cream and sugar, while Dolly Jane added milk. They paid for the drinks and found a table by the door. Brian wiped a few crumbs off the surface and pulled a chair out for Dolly Jane.

She asked, "Does God still heal today?"

"Absolutely! I could tell you about several people who were healed of various sicknesses just this week in our healing rooms."

Dolly Jane was confused, "How do you know?"

"What do you mean?"

"Well, how do you know they were truly healed and not just faking it?"

"That's an interesting question. I've been there for over thirteen years. My ministry is primarily in the healing rooms. I spend at least twenty hours a week dealing directly with healing in some capacity. People come asking Jesus for healing. We point them to Jesus and pray for them. If someone has an elbow problem, for example, I'll ask for some details of what's wrong, how long has it been hurting, how bad the pain is. You know, kind of like a doctor does when you tell them what you are having trouble with."

"And they are healed? Just like that?"

"Many times, yes. Lots of people are healed right away. Sometimes we have to keep praying, and after more prayer we see an increase in the healing."

"How do you know they aren't faking it?"

"It can happen. People come in with the wrong motivation and they fake something. But I've been doing it a long time, and I think I know people well enough to tell when people are faking it."

Dolly Jane nodded. "I've heard Bible teachers say that healing doesn't happen today."

"Sure, I've heard people say that too. Where, in the Bible does it say that healing stopped?"

"Well, in I Corinthians 13 it says that prophecy, words of knowledge and healing will all stop. Then it did."

"Is that really what it says?"

"I suppose it does. That's what I've been taught."

"When you read it closely, you'll see that this is Paul's great poem on love. He speaks eloquently on love, saying all kinds of amazing things, it's a great treatise on love. Towards the end he contrasts love to other aspects of Christian life such as prophecy and knowledge, saying that those will pass eventually away. Then he says three remain faith, hope, and love, but the greatest of these is love."

"Okay."

"Sometimes, teachers take this passage and use it to back up the position that certain aspects of ministry don't happen anymore. They say that speaking in tongues, prophetic ministries, and even healing have ceased."

"I suppose that's what I've heard."

"When they say this, they are taking a small portion of the scripture out of context and misusing it." Brian gestured with his hands, "Listen, if you can prove to me that knowledge has ceased, then I'll listen to an argument that prophetic ministry has ceased. But even then, the passage doesn't even mention healing! But I really don't think that knowledge has ceased, at least not yet. Do you?"

Dolly Jane's forehead wrinkled as she considered what he was saying.

"A lot of people say things with certainty. They truly believe their positions, and they look in the scripture to find some words to back up what they believe."

"I suppose."

Brian said, "I look at it the other way around. I assume I know nothing, and only believe what the Bible says is true. If the Bible says that God heals, then God heals."

Dolly Jane took a sip from her coffee. It wasn't the fine dark roast she usually drank, but she appreciated it nonetheless and relished the caffeine. "I've got a few more questions. But I don't want you to be offended."

Brian said, "I don't think I'll be offended. Take your best shot."

"Well I have weird questions. Do you need to lay your hands on people? Do you have to anoint people with oil when you pray for them? What about the folks who pray over handkerchiefs and send them to sick people and they get well? I remember that Peter's shadow passed over people and they were healed." She was expecting Brian to have some type of expression, but he sat plainly swirling his coffee. She finished with her question, "So why doesn't God just show up at the hospital and heal everybody?"

"Those are all good questions. Where would you like to start?"

She continued, "When one guy died and was placed in Elisha's tomb, his body touched Elisha's bones and he was brought back to life."

"Wow. That's awesome. I wish we could have Elisha's bones right here with us!"

She wasn't impressed with his humor. Since it was a sensitive subject for her it was hard to tell if Brian was simply joking or if he was subtly mocking her.

He looked her in the eye and said, "Let's start with this: God loves you. He sent Jesus to take your place in sacrifice and you can have life through Him."

"That's awesome. I get that."

"Great. And it is through that same character that God wants the best for us. He always wants us to grow, to be closer to Him. When Jesus died on the cross for your sins, that was the atonement. His life for yours."

"Okay."

"Healing comes at the atonement. Jesus does the healing."

"I don't get it."

"There are lots of great scriptures about healing, both in the Old and New Testaments. I love them all. Psalm 103:3 is a great one, it says that He "forgives all of your iniquity and heals all your diseases".

He took a pen from his shirt pocket and grabbed a napkin from the table and started writing:

חֳלָיֵנוּ הוּא נָשָׂא וּמַכְאֹבֵינוּ סְבָלָם וַאֲנַחְנוּ
אָכֵן
חֲשַׁבְנֻהוּ נָגוּעַ מֻכֵּה אֱלֹהִים וּמְעֻנֶּה׃

She looked at the passage and read it slowly. "That's Isaiah 53:4.

"I'm impressed," Brian smiled.

She gave him a slight bow.

He then translated it into English, saying:

> Surely he took up our pain
> and bore our suffering,
> yet we considered him punished by God,
> stricken by him and afflicted.

Dolly Jane had heard the passage, but never studied it. Brian said, "The original Hebrew text uses very specific words. Unfortunately the words 'pain' and 'suffering' do not adequately translate the Hebrew."

He pointed at a word on the napkin, and said, "Holi, יְלֹח clearly means sickness or disease, as is evident from the number of passages in Deuteronomy 28, like in verses 59 and 61.

He looked up at Dolly Jane who was completely engaged in his explanation. "Similarly, make obh וּנֵיבֹאְכַמוּ is used for physical pain. In Job 33:19 we read, 'Man is also chastened with pain on his bed.' These same nouns Isaiah used in describing the Messiah as 'a man of sorrows' – make obh וּמַכְאֹבֵינוּ and acquainted with grief – holi חֹלִי. I like the marginal notes that I read when I use my NASB Bible, they render these words as pain and sickness."

Dolly Jane listened attentively.

Brian continued, "The Messiah is described in this way because in His death He took upon himself our sicknesses and pains. The verbs used in Isaiah 53:4 were nasa נָשָׂא and sabhal מֶלְבָס. Those words speak clearly to this point. Nasa נָשָׂא means to lift, carry, bear, take away. Later in the chapter we read that He Himself bore – nasa נָשָׂא the sin of many. In the context of Isaiah 53, this definitely conveys the idea of the Messiah dying for the sins and sicknesses of His people, and not only for them, but in their place. The imagery of the scapegoat captures this concept of substitution when we read that 'the goat shall bear (nasa נָשָׂא) on itself all their iniquities'. That was from Leviticus 16:22.

"The Hebrew verb sabhal מֶלְבָס speaks of bearing a heavy load. Like a yak carrying a heavy burden. It occurs in Isaiah 53 in the context of the Messiah bearing our pains (verse 4) as well as our iniquities (verse 11). So it's pretty clear that Isaiah is saying that the death of the Messiah was for both the sins and the sicknesses of His people."

Dolly Jane sat back and asked, "So I asked you a series of questions about how you actually do it. What technique or techniques you use as you pray for people. And you answer with some obscure passages from the Old Testament."

Brian nodded and grinned, "It's all about the atonement that Jesus did on the cross."

Dolly Jane was confused. She threw out her hands palm up in frustration and asked, "What does the atonement have to do with healing?"

Brian smiled broadly, "Everything! The scripture brings answers in places you wouldn't expect. This is one of the beautiful aspects of scripture. If you're not being surprised by it, you're probably not reading it critically. Isaiah 53 is all about the cross."

"Okay, so it's all about the atonement," Dolly Jane said flatly.

"Did you know that Isaiah 53:4 was quoted in the New Testament? Matthew quotes it as a narrator while he is reporting what Jesus did at Capernaum. After Jesus healed many people, including Peter's mother-in-law, He drove out the spirits and 'healed all the sick'. Then Matthew says 'This was to fulfill what was spoken through the prophet Isaiah'. And he writes it in Greek."

Dolly Jane was exasperated by Brian's response. She slumped in her chair and asked, "Greek?"

"Sorry, I don't mean to do a ninety degree turn at high speed here, but Matthew was written in Greek so that's the hand we are dealt."

He picked up his pen once again and wrote on a new napkin:

Αὐτὸς τὰς ἀσθενείας ἡμῶν ἔλαβεν καὶ τὰς νόσους ἐβάστασεν

"When we read Matthew 8:17 word for word we read: Autos tas astheneias hemon elaben kai tas nosous ebastesen."

Then he translated:

> He Himself took [lambano] our infirmities [astheneia], and carried away [bastazo] our diseases [nosos].

Dolly Jane took a deep breath, "I appreciate the Greek and Hebrew lesson. But I'm not seeing the connection."

"Hang on for just another minute. You'll see what I'm saying."

She shrugged and rolled her eyes.

Brian pointed to the various words on the napkin with the tip of his pen as he said, "Each of the words is important. The basic meaning of astheneia is that of weakness, but it is used often in the New Testament for sickness or disease like in Acts 28:9, Luke 5:15, Matthew 25:39, John 11:1-3, 6, and James 5:14."

He pointed to the next word, "Nosos is a synonym, meaning disease or illness. It is found with this meaning in passages like Acts 19:12; Matthew 4:23, 9:35; Luke 7:21. As for the verb lambano, in this passage it carries the idea of taking away or removing. One suggested meaning is 'to take in order to carry away.'

As his pen landed on the next word he said, "Bastazo means to remove, to carry away, or to bear."

He dropped his pen and looked at Dolly Jane.

Dolly Jane pointed her finger at him and wagged it back and forth. She said, "Just because you dropped the mic, doesn't mean you've made any sense."

He concluded, "Reading that passage really is like dropping the mic! In the Greek, the words that Matthew used convey the exact same idea of the Isaiah passage as he was doing the healing – healing is through Jesus' crucifixion!!"

She held up her hand in objection, "But that doesn't make sense! Matthew was only in chapter eight, the crucifixion hadn't happened yet. Isaiah 53 focuses on the atoning death of Christ. How then could Matthew say that Isaiah 53:4 was fulfilled at a time prior to the Crucifixion?"

Brian said, "That's an excellent point. Several points need to be made. Even though Jesus had not yet died, we have Matthew chapter eight as an anticipation of His death and its benefits. God is not limited by the trammels of time; it is we who live a time-space existence. Matthew's quotation of the Isaiah passage is proleptic, or anticipatory in nature. In a way somewhat incomprehensible, the benefits of the cross extend back to all men of faith. The salvation of the Old Testament saints, even though they could not have been aware of it, took place on the basis of the yet-to-come sacrifice of Christ on the cross."

"So you are saying Matthew was quoting Isaiah 53 knowing that it pointed to Jesus' death and resurrection?"

Brian said, "Absolutely! God, who may be said to exist in the eternal present, transcends time. Indeed, in His eyes Christ the Lamb was slain from the foundation of the world. The Apostle John talks about this in Revelation 13:8. Consequently, the benefits of the cross span the entire history of mankind. Divine healing is indeed mediated to us through the cross."

Dolly Jane's mouth dropped open. "Jesus died for our sins. Our salvation is through the cross. I get that. But you've made a pretty convincing argument that Jesus provided for our healing through the cross as well."

Brian said, "You've got it. Christ died to reverse the curse resulting from the sin of our first parents. I refer to Jesus as the Complete Redeemer. He redeemed us from the curse of the Law (Galatians 3:13). The curse was death – both physical and spiritual. He died for the whole man, not only for man's soul. His redemptive work includes salvation for all aspects of man's being, however one conceives the interrelationship of body, soul, and spirit. There is no part of our being that is untouched by His redemption."

"So the points you've made so far, by my count, are first, healing is for today. Second, healing was provided for at the cross!"

"Right!"

"What about my questions?"

Brian thought for a moment and said, "Yes, about the technique. Let me ask you this: is there a proper technique to share the gospel with somebody?"

"What?"

"Should they attend a Billy Graham-type crusade?"

"Huh?"

He continued, "Do they need to watch a movie where the gospel is presented? Should they hear the four spiritual laws? Should you place your hands on their head and pray for them?

"No. It's different for everybody!"

"Both salvation and healing come at the cross. Both have the same issues regarding technique."

"So it doesn't matter how you pray for them?"

Brian shrugged, "Not really! When I pray, it's Jesus who does the healing. Not me. So if you inquire about how I like to do it, yes I have a favorite way to pray, just like an evangelist has a favorite way to share the gospel, but the technique doesn't matter. It's Jesus who heals."

Dolly Jane laughed at his simplicity of the matter.

Brian said, "Physical healing occurs as a result of the atoning work of Christ, but at best it is only a temporary deliverance since all must die. The greater physical deliverance is the redemption of the body, which will not only undergo resurrection but also transformation, never again to be subject to sickness and disease. That's in Romans 8:23 and Philippians 3:20-21. Ultimately, the consequences of physical and spiritual death have been overcome by the death of the One who took upon Himself both our sins and our sicknesses."

Dolly Jane looked at her cup of coffee. The base was scattered with uninviting cold black granules. She whispered to herself, "Healing comes at the atonement."

Brian said, "We should probably get back to the group."

Dolly Jane got up from the table and together they headed down the hall. She thought for a moment and wondered, "I don't know if I should ask my other questions."

"What do you mean?"

"I'm tired, maybe I'll wait."

Brian pushed the button on the elevator and said, "No, go ahead."

She said, "I've heard that He doesn't heal everybody who gets prayed for. Does He heal everybody?"

"You have wonderful questions. I think we've backed up the trailer and dumped a theological load already. Can we tackle that one another time?"

# Chapter 12

---

## Jewish Quarter
## Jerusalem

Janet awoke to the alarm on her iPhone. She picked up the phone and turned off the sound. The image on the screen was a brilliant photo of a sunrise as seen from Mt. Arbel. The sky was a glistening pink and reflected off the calm Galilee waters in majestic beauty. She remembered the times she had climbed from the town of Capernaum up the steep goat trail to the precipice where the photo was taken. She paused a moment and thought about Jesus escaping early in the morning to that very place to pray. Of the many places where Jesus had walked, she knew that Mt. Arbel may be one of the only places that still looked identical to the way it did when Jesus had walked over those same rocky crags in the year 33 AD.

Janet's thoughts immediately drifted to the Book of the Kings, the key to the rest of the pieces of Nehushtan. The Anglo-Israel Archaeological Society held the keys to the permit she would need to dig in Jeremiah's well to find it. This was her task for the foreseeable future. Nothing else mattered.

She put her phone down and sat up in bed. She felt lightheaded and dizzy. She grabbed the end table for stability and sat there for a minute, hoping it would pass. Eventually, she stood and in two paces she reached the opposite side of the tiny bedroom in the diminutive apartment. Her belly screamed in pain.

She thought to herself, *It's getting worse.*

At the sink in the bathroom, Janet took three pill bottles from her purse. She laid out one of each and downed them with a single gulp of water. She was reluctant to admit that there could be something in her life that she couldn't master. She would overcome. Decades ago, doctors ran their tests and gave her the diagnosis of Multiple Sclerosis. She treated the disease like a project to master and had researched it and took the medicine religiously. At first, she shared the news of her diagnosis with family and friends, hoping to receive comfort and suggestions for healing and health. However, it didn't take long for the affects of the disease to outpace the help from friends. She saw specialists and traveled to far away doctors to hear other opinions. They recommended a variety of treatments, some cheap and easy, others were painful and damaging to her bank account.

Over the course of the past thirty years, her symptoms of pain, muscle fatigue, vision problems and trouble walking would come and go. Every time the monster abated, she hoped that she had overcome, but the nature of the disease was one of exacerbations where she felt terrible, followed by remission, where she could tolerate the symptoms. It was her personal struggle and she would overcome it.

She got ready for the day and sat down with a bowl of oatmeal and a cup of coffee in a fine porcelain cup lined with hints of copper and looked around the tiny apartment. In spite of how she felt, she thought, *I'll beat this.*

She was thankful for professor Nahman Mavigad PhD who allowed her to stay there. The history of real estate in the city, could have it's own library. Every square foot of the city has a story to tell that spans from Abraham's time through a dozen empires until Israel's independence in the present day. Buildings were constructed and torn down over and over again, until his modern day apartment sat on top of Cardo's Pizza. In the heart of the Jewish Quarter, this apartment had been in his family for five generations. While his family preferred their home outside the town, they would never sell the family property and she was pleased to have a place so close to the action.

The first time she stayed in the apartment, Janet was overwhelmed with appreciation and left a bouquet of flowers and a shopping bag full of fresh Iowa corn on the kitchen counter to say "Thank You." A few months later, she returned and was using it again, she found the flowers wilted and the corn dry and full of weevils. Since then, she didn't feel guilty about taking him up on the offer to use the apartment, but never abused the privilege.

Today, she needed the time in the heart of the city. She grabbed her satchel and packed her laptop. She held the bronze snake in her hand. She thought, *I'll open a safety deposit box this afternoon.*

She secured the relic inside a zippered pouch in her bag and headed down the narrow limestone staircase. Pain seared through her body and she felt dizzy. She stopped and bent over with her hand on the wall. After a minute, she continued down the stairs out the door into the street. One step at a time, she walked through the bustling foot traffic. Just two short blocks away she found a table at the Holy Café. To her amazement, she hardly noticed the Roman ruins of the Cardo, or the explosion induced excavation of Hezekiah's Broad Wall that she passed by on the way.

Janet made herself comfortable at the Holy Café under the maple tree with her back to the wall, facing the busy public walkway. She smiled at an orthodox Jewish gentleman at a table next to her. He wore a kippot and tsitsi. The kippot, more traditionally called a yamika. is a universal Jewish headwear. Occasionally a man sporting a shtreimel or traditional type of fur hat passed by in front of Janet. The tsitsit, a four-pointed garment with fringes on the corners, underneath their shirt, was symbolic and served as a constant reminder for them to obey the Ten Commandments.

Janet knew that the Torah says little about clothing, either descriptively or prescriptively. She enjoyed the verses in Leviticus nineteen that prohibit blending wool and linen in a garment, such garments are known as shatnez. The same verse forbids "mixing" different seeds and types of farm animals. While she understood this as the ultimate in metaphorical societal separation – encouraging the Jews to keep themselves separate from their pagan neighbors - she knew that her friends took it literally, and seriously. She enjoyed the unique cultural aspects that it brought to the traditional appearance of the Jewish Quarter of Jerusalem and had a deep love and appreciation for her Jewish brothers and sisters. She considered it a privilege to join them in their Synagogue worshiping the same God. She loved the songs, hymns and spiritual readings on Shabbat and loosely followed their diet.

She was well acquainted with the Hebrew concept of Tzniut, the character trait of modesty and humility. The term was frequently used with regard to the rules of dress for women within Judaism, especially Orthodox Judaism. While many Jews dress similarly to non-Jews when outside synagogue, many Orthodox Jews are recognizable by their distinctive garments worn for reasons of ritual, tradition, and modesty. The dress serves multiple purposes. Even the simple khimar or headscarf, not only covers their neck and head, it also speaks of their social standing or synagogue affiliation. Like the Orthodox women, Janet chose to wear plain colored dresses and skirts rather than pants whenever in public, and she was sure to always cover most of her body.

She opened her laptop and entered her password and checked the WiFi speed. At the table next to her, an Orthodox Hasidic man wearing a black suit sat down and enjoyed a cup of tea. She smiled at him and tapped away at her laptop. She noted that his outfit was reminiscent of the style that Polish nobility wore in the eighteenth century when Hasidic Judaism began and wondered about that time.

She pondered, *What would have happened if the Hasidic Jews had made the decision to wear the outfit of the aristocrats at another place and time? What if, instead of making the ruling in Poland in the mid 1800s, they had made the same ruling in Philadelphia in 1776? If that had been the case, then the gentleman sitting at the table next to her would be dressed like Benjamin Franklin and Thomas Jefferson with a waist-coat, tights and knickers!*

She chuckled at the visual image of men dressed in ancient foreign elegant outfits. Then surmised to herself that what she was seeing before her, in reality was nothing different than men in ancient foreign elegant outfits.

The bright pink image of the Mt. Arbel sunrise appeared on her screen. Her fingers struggled to navigate the mouse pad as she opened an Internet browser to begin researching the history of archeology permits that had been granted by the Anglo-Israel Archaeological Society.

She knew that of the various entities that archeologists look for, lost books were among the most difficult to find on purpose. By definition, the lost work is a document, literary work, or piece of multimedia produced some time in the past of which no surviving copies are known to exist. In contrast to a rare surviving copy of old or ancient works that may be referred to as an extant. Books may be lost to history either through the destruction of the original manuscript, or through the loss of all later copies of a work. If a document was known to exist but could not be found, it most likely had been destroyed.

She looked up as a rare Muslim passed by. Even this slight motion caused a wave of dizziness, which she ignored. She pecked away at her keyboard, her fingers moving slower and slower with each search as she researched the various quests for lost works that were underway in the ancient world. These included the lost book of Homer, (*Margites*, a book fabled to include the "Quarrel of Odysseus and Achilles"), and the various books of Socrates and Cicero. European and American University programs funded by large endowments and some high profile individuals were mainly performing these. She researched the Book of the Wars of the Lord. An obscure book, mentioned only once in the Bible (Numbers 21:14). While a few researchers had mentioned it in lists of missing books, none were actively looking for it.

She needed to dig. Her location was close to the temple mount. She pondered that site for a moment. She thought about the 1.8 billion Muslims, or 10 million Jews that would oppose any excavation there. Her mind went on a tangent for a moment, from an archeological standpoint, the site should be considered equally important for the 2.3 billion professing Christians in the world. They should be just as protective of the temple mount as the Jews and Muslims. It was there that God's presence remained. The people went up to Jerusalem to worship at the temple, which had been built to specific specifications given by God himself. The people would get close to the Holy of Holies, but only the high priest would go behind the veil, and only once a year, after atoning for the sins of the people. The whole city was built around the temple. Why did the Christians ignore it?

She recalled the words from the Bible at the time of Jesus' death: *At that moment the curtain of the temple was torn from top to bottom* (Matthew 27:51).

God tore the curtain.

He removed the separation between God and man. He allows us into the Holy of Holies, his direct presence, without the temple. She thought, *I can approach God confidently because Jesus' sacrifice on the cross has atoned for my sins. I can approach the throne of God because He lives in me! I don't need to go up to the temple to pray, I can pray anywhere in the world.*

She took a moment to close her eyes and pray, *Lord I want to find the Book of the Kings. Please provide a means for that to happen.*

She smiled, and took a sip of her *Türk* kahvesi coffee. Stinging pain shot through her arm and the cup felt heavy. She set it down and her whole body sunk into her chair. She felt like she weighed a thousand pounds. She knew she should go lie down, but persisted for a few minutes and went back to searching on her laptop.

The public record of active permits each contained the detailed description of the property under investigation and a long list of archeological relics and historical artifacts that they were actively searching for. She searched for books, lost books, and missing manuscripts, but came up empty. She refined the search and put in the title of every known lost book that could possibly be found in the Holy Land. She only discovered two active investigations that were actively searching for the book called "*The History of Nathan the Prophet*". These were sub-contracted to search within the city of David, an active archeological site with plenty of noteworthy discoveries of pottery and pieces of carvings.

She tried to imagine a way to piggyback onto this project, but the cistern was on the other side of the temple mount. Not close enough for her needs. She thought of Cardo or even the Broad Wall, but again, they were too distant, with precious structures between the existing dig site, and the cistern. She would continue searching for a dig nearby the cistern.

While she had several contacts on the Society's board, she was reluctant to submit a proposal for a dig until she had something they would certainly love. She closed her eyes and imagined what they wanted to see. The rare approval for a dig within the city walls was either for something that was already visible but would become a better attraction, or something that had historical value that validated dates within the Old Testament, or for a find that got Christians talking about the end times. Nothing got people more excited than news about Jesus' return. When would it occur? Where would he return? Would it be on the Mount of Olives? Would it be before or after the great tribulation? Janet imagined a search for something that could be related to the rapture.

Eventually she settled on performing a comprehensive review of the location of Jeremiah's cistern. She needed to know what happened there during every year of Jerusalem's long and storied history. If there was any other reason to dig there, then she could use it to get permission to find her book.

Suddenly, her fingers came to a halt. She willed them to move, to carry on. She insisted that her hands perform the tasks she requested of them. But no matter how much she wanted to influence the motion of her body, it refused.

She tried to turn her head, but couldn't. She knew that she needed to get her blood flowing. She tried to stand up. With all her might, she forced her torso to the side and insisted on rising from her chair. She tried to ask for help. Shifting her eyes, she looked at the gentleman at the table next to her. She could not make the request for help.

She felt the motion of her whole body heading downward. The world turned dark as she collapsed onto the concrete floor.

# Chapter 13

## Northwestern Memorial Hospital
## Chicago, Illinois

Brian continued praying throughout the night. He walked the halls and petitioned God. He sat quietly by himself and interceded. He read God's promises in scripture and proclaimed them. For many hours on end, he prayed for each of the victims of the accident: Billy, Maddy, and Chase over and over again.

The remainder of the group would pray for a few minutes, then drop into conversation with one another, unable to keep a fluidity of prayer for extended amounts of time. Dolly Jane connected with her family and shared stories from Israel, being certain to stay clear of any discussion of her recent finding.

She couldn't help but be drawn to the desire for the power of healing. If only she had something in her hands that God had empowered with healing power, she could have her brother simply look at it, and he would be able to sit up and be healed. But for her, waiting was almost destructive in its frustration.

The time was painful in its monotony. The family was desperate in their desire for Billy to live. They pressed on in their vigil.

Drew eventually got to know Charlie and Jim, the fathers of the other young folks in the accident, Chase and Maddy. Spending that amount of time in the same room, most of the family members grew to enjoy one another's company and they became friendly toward one another. They shared stories and recounted the girl's education and employment and pieced together how they had known one another. But they still wondered about the nature of the accident. How had a freak accident been directed at them so violently?

They had no answers.

Only prayers.

And more prayers.

Their new routine was waiting for reports from the doctors at various times of the day, and the occasional bedside visitation, limited to a few family members at a time.

A middle-aged trauma surgeon with short-cropped silver hair approached the family. His scrubs were nicely arranged, his white coat pressed and clean, yet the lines on his face showed the affects of the stress of the job. He announced, "I'm Doctor Fuller. Billy is doing much better today. He will not require surgery. He is going to be transferred to the medical floor today."

Quiet cheers went up from the family, being respectful of the other families in the vicinity.

"Thank God."

"Jesus!"

"Thank you, Lord!"

Everyone in the family breathed a collective sigh of relief as they thanked the doctor and hugged one another.

Charlie and Jim congratulated the family on their joyous news, but they remained cautious and were reluctant to be too happy.

Charlie asked Dr. Fuller for information on Chase. The doctor moved toward Chuck's collection of people and made eye contact with each one of them as he spoke. "His ribs are broken on each side and he has what we call 'flail chest'. He's still on a ventilator and needs assistance to breathe. Yet his collapsed lungs are showing improvement. Eventually, if he continues to improve, the orthopedic surgeons will be taking him to the operating room to deal with his multiple broken extremities. Hopefully this will be within the next few days."

Charlie collapsed into a chair. Every time he came to grips with the extensiveness of his son's injuries, he covered his face with his hands and wept. There was still plenty of hope, but the road would be long and painful.

Dr. Fuller sat down among the family members. Slowly he said, "Maddy is still fighting for her life."

Jim was motionless.

The doctor described her injuries one by one. He reviewed organ systems that were in peril and the processes by which the medical team were aggressively addressing each one. After a long pause, he slowly said, "I'm surprised she's made it this far. She's a very strong and healthy young woman, but with her injuries, she's barely holding on."

Jim said, "She was an All-American basketball player in college."

Dr. Fuller smiled. "That would explain her tenacity." When he was finally done with his report, he excused himself and exited the waiting room, his white coat flowing behind him like a royal robe.

Jim turned to console his wife. Together they were silent.

Brian, the prayer warrior, heard the whole interaction from his perch on a nearby padded chair. He prayed fervently for Maddy, Chase, and Billy.

Dolly Jane brought him a cup of coffee, doctored the way he liked it. She asked, "Are you doing okay?"

"Just praying."

"For a guy who prays for a living, does it ever get old?"

"I'm at the feet of the Father. There is no place I would rather be. I'm drawing closer to Him now more than ever before. He knows my inmost being and I'm learning more about Him. Only when I am in a position of humility, where I can genuinely listen to Him, I ask our God for healing for Billy, Maddy, and Chase.

"So you are doing what Jesus says in John chapter fourteen?"

"What do you mean?"

Dolly Jane closed her eyes and said, "Very truly I tell you, whoever believes in me will do the works I have been doing, and they will do even greater things than these, because I am going to the Father. And I will do whatever you ask in my name, so that the Father may be glorified in the Son. You may ask me for anything in my name, and I will do it."

Brian said, "That's a pretty powerful promise."

Dolly Jane retorted, "He will heal because He said He would."

Brian smirked, "What if you ask Him for a Ferrari? Is He going to give you a Ferrari?"

Dolly Jane laughed, "Of course not. That wouldn't be right!"

Brian continued, "What about, 'God, I pray in Jesus' name let this be the winning lottery ticket!'"

Dolly Jane shook her head, "That's not how he operates. He doesn't want us to get something for nothing. He doesn't want simply the life that we see as the best – our happiness. He wants much more than that."

Brian refocused, "What did David go through that made him write the words of Psalm 42?"

Dolly Jane asked, "What's Psalm 42 say?"

Brian quoted:

> "My bones suffer mortal agony
> as my foes taunt me
> saying to me all day long
> Where is your God?"

Dolly Jane answered quickly, "That doesn't sound very happy."

Brian agreed, "But he ends with:

> Put your hope in God
> For I will yet praise Him
> my Savior and my God."

Dolly Jane said, "Okay, that's fine. There are some times when God allows us to go through hard times."

Brian replied, "Some times? The Psalms are full of laments like this:

> Why, Lord, do you reject me,
> and hide your face from me?
> From my youth I have suffered and been close to death;
> I have borne your terrors and am in despair,
> Your wrath has swept over me;
> your terrors have destroyed me,
> All day long they surround me like a flood;
> they have completely engulfed me.
> You have taken from me friend and neighbor—
> darkness is my closest friend."

They sat in silence. The weight of the grief was crushing. After a couple of minutes, Dolly Jane said, "That's pretty intense."

Brian sat quietly.

Dolly Jane said, "I had no idea."

Brian asked, "What do you mean?"

Dolly Jane wondered out loud, "How hard it can be."

Brian stated, "We will never be able to trust what God is doing in our lives until we figure out and personalize His ultimate goal. His primary purpose is not to make us happy, healthy, wealthy, and wonderful."

Dolly Jane furrowed her brow.

Brian continued, "He doesn't promise to make our lives easy and guarantee that things go smoothly. Though he is eternally committed to providing the best for his children. That '*BEST*' may or may not coincide with what many of us consider 'making it' in life."

Dolly Jane looked at the tile floor, then suggested, "Let's grab something sweet to munch on."

Brian nodded, "I could go for something salty." Together they walked down the hallway. He continued, "God is good. He is sovereign. And even in a fallen world, we can rest in the assurance that He is actively working to bring about the best possible results by the best possible means, and in the end, to make you and me like His Son, Jesus."

Dolly Jane stopped at a vending machine. She scanned the choices, Brian pointed at the Doritos. She put a dollar bill in and pressed B7. A moment later a bag of chips fell to the bottom of the machine. She reached in, pushed aside the protective metal flap, picked up the bag, and tossed it to Brian. She began putting the money in the second time but paused.

She said, "I'm not putting my tithe into church, then pressing a button that says 'heal Billy'. I'm not expecting God to work because I pay Him."

"Of course not! To assume that He will act as a heavenly vending machine is inane and immature. He's not your employee."

Dolly Jane smiled.

Brian continued, "Life isn't always easy, but God in His wisdom always brings about the best possible results, by the best possible means, for the longest possible time. The truth and promise from God keeps us from giving up or giving in when life seems utterly impossible."

"So, what if He doesn't heal?"

"Then He is working out something else in our lives."

"But He wants healing! That's the best thing for Billy, for Chase, and Maddy."

"Of course! If you are looking only through our eyes, that's what's best."

"Our eyes?"

"God plays on a stage that is so much bigger than ours."

Dolly Jane shook her head.

"We can't pretend to know what He is doing on the grand scale of things. We pray. We love Him. We pray. We seek Him. We pray. We lay our requests before his throne. We pray."

"But we can never know for sure."

Brian's face was flat, "What we can know, is that what He decides to do will bring Him glory, even if we don't like it or understand it."

"I don't and I don't."

The day passed painfully slowly. Even though Billy was transferred to the skilled surgical unit, he was only able to have a few visitors at a time. Though she was there for Billy, Dolly Jane was also closely following progress for Maddy and Chase.

For Billy, other than the constant use of his morphine button, he had no activity whatsoever. He was comforted by gentle hand holding from his family, but he could barely smile. Even a slight laugh brought searing pain throughout his body.

A day passed.

Then another.

Chase and Maddy had no new updates.

The following morning Billy continued to improve. After a few minutes of greeting and encouragement, Dolly Jane went with Brian and the rest of the family as they headed to the ICU waiting room.

Charlie greeted them warmly, "Hey! How's Billy?"

Drew said, "Better, thanks. He's not much of a conversationalist yet, but he's awake. Any word on Chase or Maddy?"

Charlie said, "Not yet, they are a little late today. I'm hoping that's good news, for a change."

The family settled in to wait for Dr. Fuller to come in.

Eventually, Dr. Fuller appeared in the doorway. He recognized Drew, Dolly Jane, and the family and gave them a smile, then he faced Charlie and his group. "Good morning," he said to the families who huddled around in solidarity. "Chase has shown significant improvement in his breathing. His fever is down and his vital signs are improving. The multiple rib fractures have left him with a deformity in the center of his chest but his lungs are improving and we hope to be getting him off the ventilator soon."

Charlie gave the doctor a hug. Dolly Jane and the rest let out a few thankful prayers.

Dr. Fuller gave them a few more details then turned to Jim to talk about Maddy. Charlie continued listening as they spoke. Dr Fuller looked each of them in the eye and slowly said, "I'm sorry, but Maddy hasn't done well. Last night we talked about whether or not she was continuing to have cerebral functioning. This morning, an EEG was performed."

Jim gave his rapt attention to the doctor.

"It showed no brain function, she is only living with the assistance of the life support."

Jim's eyes filled with fluid.

"I'm sorry, but she's not going to wake up."

A hush fell across the room.

Jim asked, "Are you saying that she has been officially declared brain dead?"

The doctor affirmed with a nod and a comforting hand on his shoulder.

Charlie wanted to do something to help. He could build anything, repair just about anything, but there was no help to give.

The families were stunned.

Silence reigned.

After a few minutes somebody asked about the process of organ transplantation. Dr. Fuller gave them an overview of the process and discussed some of the details. He explained that Maddy's heart, eyes, kidneys, liver, bones, pancreas, and skin would help heal multiple people. In an odd sense she would be living on, extending life for many others. Even as he was saying this, Dr. Fuller knew that it brought little comfort to the family.

Dr. Fuller explained some of the paperwork and the fact that if the family does give their consent, the process would get started right away. A nurse handed Jim a clipboard with a stack of papers. Jim scanned the legal document in a haze, hardly noticing a single word on the pages. He somehow managed to control his shaking hand and signed the authorization for Maddy's organs to be donated. By the time he handed the clipboard back, it was wet from Jim's tears.

The families mulled around in silence for a long time. Eventually, Drew, Dolly Jane, and their family realized that even their presence in the room could bring feelings of anger, resentment, and jealousy toward the members of Maddy's family. They were symbolic of healing to a family who had just suffered the greatest loss they could imagine.

They quietly left the room and made their way to the cafeteria. Dolly Jane noticed that Brian was still with them. She grabbed him by the hand and gave him a squeeze. "You're a true family friend. You've stayed longer than I would have thought."

Brian smiled.

One by one, they plopped down in their seats scattered around a few disjointed tables. Dolly Jane sat next to Brian. She looked down at the table and whispered, "How does this make any sense?"

Brian looked down and sighed.

Dolly Jane looked directly at Brian and said, "There were three of them all in the ICU. We prayed for all three. Billy was healed. Chase is most likely going to be okay. But Maddy died. It doesn't make any sense. It's not like I prayed for one of them and you prayed for the other two, you prayed the same way for all three. You know about healing. Explain that to me!"

"My faith is in my loving God. He has already proven Himself by what He did on the cross, He does not have to prove Himself again. I don't like the fact that Maddy died. But it doesn't change my faith in God."

"I don't know. I remember when I was in the sixth grade, I prayed for a pony. Not just any pony, a fourteen-hand-high Arabian-Quarter horse mix. The next day, a friend gave my father a fourteen-hand-high Arabian-Quarter horse mix."

Brian smiled, "I love stories like that. Your prayer lined up with what God already had planned for you."

Dolly Jane smiled at the memory.

Brian added, "I imagine that your understanding of prayer grew through that experience."

She shook her head, "I think I need something more."

Brian inquired, "More than what?"

Her thoughts drifted to the bronze snake, "More than simply praying."

# Chapter 14

## Northwestern Memorial Hospital
## Chicago, Illinois

Billy opened his eyes as he lay perfectly still in his hospital bed. His head ached, but for the first time in a week he noticed that he actually felt hungry. He looked across the room and saw Dolly Jane sleeping in the recliner next to the window. He turned on the television and she awoke instantly.

She said, "You're awake!"

Billy remained expressionless. He had been in and out of consciousness each day since being transferred from the ICU to the skilled nursing floor. But before that moment he had not expressed clear thinking.

She arose from her position of somnolence and stood at the bedside. "How are you feeling?"

Billy looked around, pain crept into every part of his body and he reached for his morphine button, after a minute he said, "Foggy."

She grasped his hand and smiled warmly. "I'm glad you're doing better. You've given us quite a scare."

He gave her hand a gentle squeeze and she smiled, happy for the interaction. He let go of her hand and lifted his head off the pillow. He moved both hands back and forth and wiggled his toes. He was amazed at the amount of pain that could be generated from such a simple motion. “Everything hurts.”

“Take your time. You’ve been through quite an ordeal.”

“How are Maddy and Chase?”

“Chase should be getting out of the ICU soon. He took quite a blow to his torso but his progress over the past few days has been encouraging.”

“His torso?”

“He broke a bunch of ribs. They were able to give him the ventilation support he needed. But now, he’s off that.” She smiled, “You should see his chest, he has some sort of deformity now that he’s improved. It looks like a cave where his heart should be.”

“How’s Maddy?”

Dolly Jane shook her head.

“What do you mean?” Billy pressed.

Dolly Jane was slow to respond. She closed her eyes and her countenance fell. Finally, she said, “She didn’t make it.”

Billy’s head dropped back on the pillow. He dropped his hands to his side and closed his eyes. The impact of the event hit him all over again.

Dolly Jane watched from the bedside as a tear escaped his right eye. She looked at her watch. She knew that she would be alone with him for at least another hour before anyone would be back to the room. She took her time before she asked another question.

“How did we get here?”

“Ambulance.”

“Did Maddy die instantly?”

“Well, she was brought here, and placed on life support for a few days. But never woke up.”

“She didn’t suffer?”

“No.”

They sat in silence for a while longer.

## Hadassah Medical Center
## Jerusalem

Janet tried to sit up in the hospital bed. She was awake for the first time since being admitted. She noticed the familiar buzz of her phone in her hands. As she turned the phone toward her, she found that IV lines annoyingly tethered her arms. It was Dolly Jane. She thought about ignoring it, but realized that she couldn't ignore her forever. She imagined what she could say. Her last contact with Dolly Jane was hopeful and she had promised to find a dig site for the Book of the Kings. Now, she lay helpless in a medical ward at Hadassah Medical Center in Jerusalem. After she collapsed in the Holy Café, she had been transported to the Emergency department where she was given a blood transfusion and subsequently admitted to the medical unit for further care.

She held the phone in her hands as a nurse entered. "You're awake!" she said. "My name is Bethany. I'll be your nurse for the next ten hours."

"When can I go home?"

"First things first. The doctor will be by to see you later this afternoon. He can answer all your questions."

"I have to get out of here." Her thoughts drifted to the relic, "Where's my bag?"

"Your personal affects have been locked up in our safe. There is no need to worry."

"I need to see something in my bag."

"I'll have an orderly retrieve your items right away."

Janet wasn't happy with the relic unsecured, but didn't have much of a choice. She knew that bringing more attention to the priceless relic would be counter productive. She said, "Thank you. If you locked everything in the safe, why do I still have my phone?"

"You don't remember much, do you?"

"I suppose not."

Bethany grinned, "You've been wavering in a state in and out of consciousness over the past few days. I gave it to you yesterday."

Janet was shocked, *How did I lose track of time?*

She tried to sit up and was struck with pain in her belly. "I suppose they did some tests while I was unconscious."

"You're lucky to be alive," Bethany recorded Janet's vital signs and tended to a few details in the room then exited saying, "the doctor will be in soon."

Janet tapped her phone. The calming image of Mt. Arbel was the only thing familiar in the room. Within a few minutes, she was once again asleep.

## Northwestern Memorial Hospital
## Chicago, Illinois

Dolly Jane's phone vibrated. She checked it and was pleased to see a message from Janet. The text said, "No luck on obtaining a permit. Looking for creative solutions. Any ideas on your end?"

She put her phone away and sighed. She was disappointed that they couldn't dig where they wanted to. She wondered what Janet meant by "creative solutions."

She texted back, "I've got an idea. Will fill you in soon. Is everything okay there?"

Janet responded, "Fine."

After a few moments, Dolly Jane refocused on Billy. He was clearly saddened over the demise of his friends. She asked, "How did you know them?"

"Chase helped me at the science fair. We were working on a project together–" suddenly he realized that if he were to share anything more, he would certainly have to reveal the nature of the robot and the whole project. He'd be guilty of trespassing, and possibly murder.

"What were you doing in the park?"

Billy kept his eyes closed. He didn't know what to say so he said nothing.

She asked softly, "What can you tell me about the explosion?"

He opened his eyes. Nobody in the world knew him as well as his sister, yet she couldn't read him.

She thought, *What is he hiding?* She wondered if his silence was stemmed from shame, trauma, or fear.

He shook his head and remained silent.

She said, "I'm so sorry. You know we've always shared everything. We don't have secrets between us."

He looked her in the eyes and remained silent.

She pulled her chair up next to the bed and once again grabbed his hand. Her cadence picked up as she spoke, "Okay, I'll go first. When I got the news that you were in the hospital, I was in Israel."

His eyes reflected the fact that he was happy to think about something other than the explosion. He asked, "Ein Gedi?"

"You remember! Yes. It's the dig that I'd been looking forward to."

She told him about her time there for the first couple of weeks. The monotonous digging, her friendship with Janet, and how much she loved Ein Gedi. Then she recounted the finding of the cave, the skeletons, her falling back and hitting her head. Then she told him about Nehushtan.

His blank stare revealed a limited knowledge base on the subject. She filled in the gaps with a brief teaching about Moses, the Israelites, and Hezekiah. She ended with the Book of the Kings and that she knew where it was, but couldn't get there without a permit.

She told the story without alluding to any wrongdoing on her part and made it clear that they were stumped. She knew that digging without a permit was not only illegal, but would certainly result in being caught, especially in a high profile place like Jerusalem. Her mind drifted to Janet taking the relic away from the site. In this case, their safety overruled the governing laws. She wondered what other laws could or should be bent or broken in the pursuit of the ultimate healing power.

Billy inquired, “How certain are you of the healing power in the snake?”

She was firm, “Absolute! It’s documented in the Bible.”

Billy asked, “How certain are you that this book is in the well?”

She was pleased that he was taking interest in her archaeological investigation, “It’s not 100 percent, but it’s quite likely.”

“How big is the bronze piece that you found?”

“About ten inches long, two or three inches in diameter.”

“How big do you think the Book of the Kings is?”

She thought about it for a moment and said, “I don’t know. The Dead Sea Scrolls were in jars about two feet tall.”

“How much does each jar weigh?”

She answered, “I have no idea. What are you getting at?”

In his head he quickly estimated a two-foot tall pottery jar with a paper scroll inside to weigh between ten and twenty pounds. He calculated how much Checkers would be able to drag.

He closed his eyes and lamented that his precious robot had been destroyed in the explosion. He imagined the remnants of Checkers stowed away in a Chicago Police Department crime lab. He wondered if there would be an investigation of the explosion. It would certainly reveal a cut gas line, a tunnel, and a small robot. He shook his head, *There’s nothing I can do about that now.*

She squinted at him and said, “Those are pretty specific questions. What are you thinking?”

Billy took a deep breath and replied. “Okay. You’ve told me a secret. And I understand that it’s pretty important that nobody else knows. I get it. Now, it’s my turn.”

She leaned forward.

“What do you know about tunneling?”

She made an inquisitive look on her face.

He smiled for the first time since before the accident, “Let me tell you about Checkers.”

# Chapter 15

## Dubuque, Iowa

Upon Billy's release from the hospital, the family returned to his hometown of Dubuque, Iowa with the hope of convalescence and rest. However, on his first day back, he plopped down on the couch with a laptop. It only took a few minutes for him to retrieve his entire hard drive from the cloud. He reviewed the blueprints of the updated machine, with the exact position of each sensor, robotic arm, wheel and motor. He found the make and model of each part and quickly made a list of everything he needed to rebuild Checkers. He enlisted Amazon prime to help with his extensive shopping list and got started rebuilding the machine.

He built a new chassis and assembled the parts he needed from everything he purchased. The second time fabricating the unique parts was significantly quicker. Maddy and Chase had solved a multitude of technical problems. These were already built into the upgraded software. He knew exactly which sensors to install and exactly where to place them for the most effective outcome.

Billy found the work thrilling, but his body was still unable to handle a full day's work. He took frequent breaks and rested. Fortunately, there were no inquires related to the explosion. He wanted to complete the project because it gave him satisfaction - having Checkers back. Day after day he labored. Progress for making minor upgrades and took time to ensure that the machine functioned perfectly. With the memory of the explosion a lesson that he would never forget, Billy slowed the digging speed and put in a governor to ensure that the highest detail of GPR resolution had been acquired before any digging would take place. Never again would he put himself or any of his loved ones in danger.

Every bolt and wire on the new version of the robot was re-evaluated. Everything from the robotic arms, to the new drag sled was installed, tried, and tested. Then re-tested until perfection was certain. He modified a suitcase to protect and transport the robot. Stuffing some clothing into the empty corners of the suitcase ensured that this would be his only packed bag. Barring a manual inspection from a TSA agent, he expected no trouble in the transporting of the technological marvel.

After an uneventful test in the brown soil of his backyard, Billy was confident that he could help Dolly Jane retrieve the book, and soon afterward, the real treasure.

They checked through security at the Dubuque Regional Airport. Though the building was brand new and the appearance was that of a state of the art facility, the security was surprisingly lackadaisical. As their suitcases were being x-rayed prior to being loaded on the belt, Billy leaned over to Dolly Jane and said, "When we get there, we will have to make a quick stop at an auto parts store for a few supplies that we can't bring on the plane."

They watched as the TSA agents lazily viewed the monitors as the suitcase passed by. When they were assured that their bags wouldn't be further inspected Billy said, "Let's get moving."

The twenty-five minute flight to Chicago was just a warm up for the long flight through Zurich and on to Tel Aviv.

After lunch in the G terminal, they boarded the 767. After they stowed their carry-on bags and tucked their water bottles into the seatback pocket in front of them, they buckled into their seats. He found a plastic package with a felt eye covering with an elastic band and a set of ear buds. He stowed the eye cover and put his ear buds in. He tapped on the screen on the seatback in front of him. Movie selections came up and he began scrolling through them.

Dolly Jane said, “Really? You’re going to watch a movie?”

Billy huffed, “What I really want to do is sleep.”

Dolly Jane responded, “It’s a long flight, we’ll have plenty of time for that. But first, I need to know the limits of your machine.”

Billy scoffed, “Limits? My robot has no limits!”

Dolly Jane scolded, “That’s the kind of thinking that gets you into the Intensive Care Unit. Just tell me what it can do.”

Billy took out his ear buds. “It can see underground at least 50 meters in every direction. Drill, tunnel, and retrieve anything up to twelve inches in diameter.”

Dolly Jane said, “I don’t mean to be harsh, but I need to ask, can it see gas pipelines?”

Billy rolled his eyes. He brushed off the comment about his friend’s demise.

Dolly Jane apologized with a sisterly smirk.

Billy said to Dolly Jane, “Tell me more about Nehushtan.”

“I’ve told you the basics of the story. Moses held up the snake in the desert after the people of Israel were afflicted with poisonous vipers.”

“Why were they getting bit by snakes?”

Dolly Jane furrowed her brow. She opened her Bible app on her tablet and turned to the twenty first chapter of Numbers. She scanned the chapter and said, “So the Israelites were slaves in Egypt, God had just gotten them out of there using the ten plagues, and took them through the Red Sea, right?”

Billy nodded.

She said, “They were a large group of people in the wilderness and God provided them with Manna every day. After a while they got grumpy.” She looked at her tablet and read from Numbers 21:4.

> “The people grew impatient on the way; they spoke against God and against Moses, and said, ‘Why have you brought us up out of Egypt to die in the wilderness? There is no bread! There is no water! And we detest this miserable food!’ The Lord sent

> venomous snakes among them; they bit the people and many Israelites died."[1]

Billy interrupted, "That sounds like the theme of the Old Testament. God saves Israel, then Israel gets upset and lashes out against God, then He steps up and punishes them. Sometimes it was famine, sometimes a nearby king attacked. This time God sent the snakes as a punishment, right?"

"Right"

"What kind of snakes? Do we know anything about that?"

Dolly Jane said, "I love what Charles Spurgeon said about the snake bites." She opened another file on her computer and read:

> "These serpents when they bit caused vehement heat, so that there was a pain throughout the body, as if a hot iron had been sent along the veins. Those who had been bitten had a great thirst; they drank incessantly, and still cried for water to quench the burnings within. It was a hot fire, which was lit in the fountain, and which ran through every nerve and every sinew of the man; they were racked in pain, and died in most fearful convulsions.
>
> Oh, the shrieks, the yells, the screams! Oh, the face of anguish, the contortions, the misery. Have you never heard how men do bend their fists and swear they will not die; and how they start forth, and declared, 'I cannot, and I must not die; I am unprepared!' Starting back from the fiery gulph, they clutch the physician and desire him, if possible, to lengthen out the thread of their existence. Ay, many a nurse has vowed that she would never nurse such a man again, for the horrors would be with her till she died."[2]

Billy said, "That's some fire and brimstone preaching right there. I want to hear the rest of the Biblical passage."

Dolly Jane looked back down at the screen. She tapped a few times and continued:

> "The people came to Moses and said, 'We sinned when we spoke against the Lord and against you. Pray that the Lord will take the

> snakes away from us.' So Moses prayed for the people. The Lord said to Moses, 'Make a snake and put it up on a pole; anyone who is bitten can look at it and live.' So Moses made a bronze snake and put it up on a pole. Then when anyone was bitten by a snake and looked at the bronze snake, they lived."[3]

Billy pondered, "So God sent the snakes. That punishment was really harsh, and the people repented before anything else happened."

"Why does that matter?"

"The first thing that happened was their repentance, then God's forgiveness. Then his deliverance came when they looked at the snake, right?"

"Sure."

"Healing and restoration came to a repentant people, not a rebellious people."

"I've never thought of that before."

"Were there any people who refused to look at the snake?"

"I don't know. It doesn't say anything about that. The Bible only records what happened to those who did look at the snake. They got healed."

Dolly Jane thought out loud, "You know God can use anything he wants to use. The technique is not important. It's Him who heals. He could have required that in order for people to be healed of the snake bite, they had to jump up and down and turn around three times yelling Rumpelstiltskin!"

Billy remembered, "He made Naaman wash seven times in the Jordan River!"

Dolly Jane said, "This time the technique was the snake, but the healing was from Him, not the snake itself."

Billy wondered, "Do you think the snake was symbolic?

Dolly Jane declared, "It was certainly a real bronze snake, and it delivered a literal, real healing. It wasn't used as a symbol of healing until Jesus mentioned it to Nicodemus."

Billy asked, "Did it mean forgiveness? Did it mean restoration and healing in a complete way? Or was it just healing from the snakebite?"

Dolly Jane said, "I just want to have the rest of it so that people like Maddy could be healed."

Billy sighed, "Maddy was great."

They paused for a moment as they remembered. Then Dolly Jane said, "The hospital was full of people who needed healing."

Billy said, "What does Hezekiah have to do with all of this?

Dolly Jane answered, "Hezekiah. That's where the next stop in the story lies. Remember, this snake was carved by the hand of Moses!"

Billy added, "Actually, one of Moses' sculptors or artists probably made it. The same guys that he commissioned to build the tabernacle."

Dolly Jane smirked, "Right. That's true. After it was used for healing, it was carried with the Israelites possessions through the desert. Every single great man of the Bible from Moses to Hezekiah knew about it. They had seen it, held it in their hands. They knew the story. Imagine all the greats – Joshua, Caleb, Samuel, Saul, David, Solomon, Elijah, Elisha, and Isaiah – they all held it, honored it, and protected it."

Billy said, "Don't forget my favorites, Ehud and Eglon."

Dolly Jane laughed, "You like the story where the Navy Seal takes out the fat guy, don't you?'

Billy said, "Ya heard!" He laughed too, then said, "I always liked the story as a kid, 'cause the guards thought the king was pooping."

Dolly Jane cocked her head off to the side. "It's amazing how quickly an honest, serious discussion turns when you make a pooping reference." She continued, "It appears that in the temple, the bronze serpent of Moses ultimately became a symbol of worship in its own right. It sat right next to the Ark of the Covenant in the holy of holies for hundreds of years until our friend Hezekiah came along. He saw the worship of the bronze snake as an apostasy and it came to a violent end."

"Wait a minute. Hezekiah was the tenth king, right?

"He was the thirteenth king of Judah."

"Okay, smarty pants. It looks like you've been studying this. What made Hezekiah look at the bronze snake any differently than David, Solomon, or any of the other kings?"

"He got deathly sick."

"That changes people. I get it."

"There are essentially four parts of Hezekiah's story. He prepares for war, goes to war, gets sick, and is healed. He turns the whole country back to worshiping God.

"Sounds like a good king."

"One of the greats. In order to prepare the city for Jerusalem to be under siege he built a wall, dug a tunnel to bring water in, and he fortified the city with weapons and food."

"So what happened when the city was attacked?"

"200,000 soldiers surrounded the city! With the wall and the tunnel that brought in water, they could hunker down for a long time. After a short time, an angel of the Lord struck the bad guys one night and 185,000 of them ended up dead on Hezekiah's doorstep."

"Very cool."

"But when King Hezekiah became sick, he got really sick. Actually it's pretty likely that he had anthrax."

Billy was shocked. "Anthrax? The disease used in biological terrorism?"

Dolly Jane nodded.

He asked, "Where do you read that in the Bible?"

"The Bible also used the word Shehin when it talks about the sixth of the ten plagues in Egypt and when it references Job's sickness. Job suffered with painful sores from the soles of his feet to the crown of his head. He took a piece of broken pottery and scraped himself with it as he sat among the ashes."

"That's pretty awful."

"In the second chapter of Job we witness the scene where his friends saw him from a distance. They could hardly recognize him; they began to weep aloud, and they tore their robes and sprinkled dust on their heads."

"Okay, I get it. He was really sick."

"You kind of have to read between the lines on some of this. There is a rough description of his sickness. He was weak and lethargic, and his body had boils. This is typical of anthrax: fever and chills, chest pain, shortness of breath, confusion, dizziness, nausea, headache, and of course, the skin lesions which are small blisters with a black necrotic center. All in all, it's a pretty non-descript illness until you get to the skin lesions. Because of the boils on the skin, the disease can be identified as anthrax."

"Is that an official statement, or just another one of your guesses?" Billy teased his sister.

"The Jewish academic community has done plenty of research on the subject. The semantics experts teamed up with infectious disease doctors and they think it's the real deal. The Hebrew Language Academy has adopted the name of the illness in Israel, known as Shehin in the Bible, to be identified as anthrax."

Billy squirmed in his chair, uncomfortable not being the smartest person in the conversation. "Okay, let's get back to Hezekiah."

Dolly Jane agreed, "Right. The prophet Isaiah told him that he would die. The fatal illness occurred the same year as the Assyrian invasion. Isaiah basically told him to 'Put your house in order, 'cause you're going to die.'"

"That's a pretty staggering pronouncement."

"When Isaiah left, Hezekiah turned his face to the wall and prayed earnestly with tears. For the king to turn his face to the wall was very symbolic. He was in charge, whoever he looked at would listen and obey. For him to turn to a wall was humiliating for him. He agonized in prayer, not just because he was sick, but also because he wanted to live to bring the people closer to God. He wanted to protect the people of his kingdom. He also wanted to produce an heir to the throne."

Billy interrupted, "I'm no Bible scholar, but I do know that in ancient Israel, long life was symbolic for righteous living. Fear of death was pretty overwhelming in days before modern medicine."

Ignoring him, Dolly Jane continued, "Before Isaiah had even left the palace courtyard, God told him to go back to the king. 'Tell Hezekiah that I have heard his prayer, and I will heal him. In three days Hezekiah should go to the temple and I will add fifteen years to his life.'"

Billy said, "I can picture the king fist bumping and letting out a giant Woot!! Woot!!"

Dolly Jane waved her hands above her head. Then said, "Ya buddy! This would nearly double the years of his reign."

Billy chuckled at his sister's playful behavior.

"Isaiah had Hezekiah's servants boil some figs and make a poultice which they spread on the king's skin."

"So apparently, figs cure anthrax?"

"Well, no. Otherwise the CDC wouldn't recommend ciprofloxacin. This was a common home remedy for use on inflamed boils, pain, and scar tissues. Just like eucalyptus oil sooths insect bites, and willow bark tea eases pain."

Billy was silent.

"Hezekiah struggled with the proclamation and he still wanted a sign that he would be well. Neither God nor the prophet was angry when Hezekiah asked for a sign. The stairway to the temple worked as a sundial. A nearby structure cast a shadow on the stairway of Ahaz."

Billy interrupted, "Who?"

"Ahaz was Hezekiah's father, the previous king, not a good guy. Hezekiah was given the choice of whether the shadow should go backward or forward ten steps."

Billy nodded, "It's really no big deal for it to go forward like it always does. Make it go the back, that would be contrary to the laws of nature."

"The prophet Isaiah called on the Lord, and the Lord made the shadow go back the ten steps it had gone down on the stairway of Ahaz."

"How did that happen?"

"What do you think?"

"I think it was a metaphor. Just a story to get the reader's attention."

"Sure, that's possible. But if they put stories like that in there it doesn't take long for the book to lose credibility."

"The Bible is full of stories like that."

"And if you look at them closely, one by one, using good scientific methodology, you'll find that even the crazy stories, like a shadow going back ten steps, can have more than one answer."

"Was it some sort of sun-dial?"

"That's an interesting place to start. I found two different inventions of the ancient sundials in recorded history. Marcus Vitruvius wrote that Berosus invented a sundial around 250 BCE. Herodotus, the Greek historian in 440 BCE states that the sundial was invented by the Babylonians."

Billy asked, "What was Hezekiah's time again?"

Dolly Jane patiently answered, "Hezekiah's 29-year reign was from 727-698 BCE."

Billy thought for a moment and asked, "So what does that mean?"

"If there was some sort of sundial, it would have pre-dated all the other historical sundials."

"So, it was the shadow going down a series of steps."

Dolly Jane said, "Right. Let's look at the scientific explanation first. A parhelia or 'mock sun' is a refraction of the sun's light as it passes through the prismatic ice crystals at high altitude in the atmosphere. These actually occur commonly in winters in the Midwest as 'sundogs', but occasionally they are profound celestial refractors, which completely alter the course of the sun's rays. The appearance yields two suns, one on either side of the true sun. It's a strange thing in the sky, but it really does look like there are two suns, and they really mess with shadows. So if this occurred at that point in time, Hezekiah certainly could have seen the shadow turn back ten steps."

"Seriously?"

"Historical record shows this event took place on March 27, 1703 at Metz, France and again on March 28, 1848 over parts of Hampshire, England."

"Okay, that's possible. What are the other explanations?"

"Well, Hezekiah was completely dedicated to God. He tore down the worship places dedicated to Baal worship. The pagan god Baal was symbolized by the sun. He was a 'sun-god' so to speak. If you think about it from Hezekiah's perspective, a solar sign would indicate that his healing came from Baal, not the God of the Bible."

Billy wondered, "So, you're saying that it didn't make sense for the sun to appear to have healed him."

Dolly Jane said, "There is another way that light could have overpowered the shadow, in a manner that didn't have anything to do with the sun!"

"I'm stumped. Gimme a hint."

"Think about what happened to Nadab and Abihu in the tenth chapter of Leveticus. Then it happened again in Numbers sixteen at Korah's rebellion. Finally, in Isaiah six, we see it again. Can you guess what I'm talking about?"

"I would imagine that it has something to do with light and shadows?"

"Absolutely! A fierce light, the Shekinah glory of God, blazed out from the sanctuary on the hill. It blotted out the brightness of the sun itself, lighting up all of Jerusalem with its radiance. The shadow of the steps would have vanished in an instant."

"That's quite a light! It would have been an immediate drawing back of the shadow making it go back ten steps!"

"Or a slow progression, depending on how the light increased in its intensity and direction."

Billy was lost in his imagination, "Amazing." He pictured the glory of God shining in all of His amazing wonder.

Dolly Jane nodded. She pictured the veil that separated the Holy of Holies and what it could have looked like. They sat in silence for a few moments.

"So which one was it? What happened?"

"I dunno."

Billy laughed. "You've taken me pretty far into the weeds of Hezekiah's story."

"I love this stuff. Nothing gets me more excited than studying the Bible and everything around the scripture."

"Obviously."

"Not just the literary context, but a thorough understanding of the language, the culture, history, and specific geography of the region. When you put all of that together, the scripture opens up in a new way."

"But you haven't told me where he hid the pieces of Nehushtan."

She pointed to her screen and said, "Read this line."

He read, "The other events of Hezekiah's reign and his acts of devotion are written in the vision of the prophet Isaiah son of Amoz, in the Book of the Kings of Judah and Israel."

"That's what we are going to find."

"What?"

"The Book of the Kings!" Dolly Jane blurted loudly. She looked around, hoping they weren't attracting too much attention.

"What's in the book?" Billy responded quietly, picking up on Dolly Jane's apprehension.

"The answers to where he hid the pieces of Nehushtan. The Kings recorded all their activities. I have no doubt that Hezekiah recorded what he did with the pieces of the snake."

"Okay, is that in a library somewhere?"

"No."

"Then where is it?"

"Nobody knows for sure and the search for it has pretty much died down."

"So, how are we going to find it?"

"Thanks to you, we have a technology that nobody has ever had before. We are going to look for a place called Jeremiah's cistern."

"Excuse me?"

Dolly Jane explained, "The prophet Jeremiah had a pretty tough life. He witnessed a lot of setbacks during his long career. He endured the death of King Josiah in 609 BCE at Megiddo. Then there was a meaningless revolt and the death of his son Jehoiakim in 601. This was followed by the occupation of Jerusalem by Babylonian soldiers, and then finally the exile of the Jewish people in 597."

"It sucks to be a prophet."

"One of the weirdest things that happened was something that occurred fifteen years earlier. As King Jehoiakim read what Jeremiah had written, he burned his scrolls, one strip at a time. All the things Jeremiah had written, the words God had told him to write down, were read before the king and burned, right in front of him."

"For a writer, that's a type of torture."

"It's not like he had a couple of copies lying around. Just imagine, Jeremiah had to re-write the entire prophetic book. He did it, but you know that event must have changed him."

"Changed him how?"

"He became very protective of the written word."

"Okay, but why does that matter?"

"Later on, he was thrown into a cistern. Sadly, that was meant to kill him. The king's advisors had permission from the king to kill Jeremiah. They threw him into the cistern and left him there to die."

Billy slumped in his east, "And people say the Bible is a story of happy stories and righteous teaching."

"Imagine what went through his mind as he wallowed in his personal prison cell. It was as if the rope had been placed around his neck and he was pushed off the platform and he was swinging from his neck, waiting to die. Only, in the cistern, he would take longer to die of thirst."

"Terrifying."

"Down in the pit, he gave up his life to God. He had plenty of time to think, time to pray. He was a prophet and knew how to hear from God. He certainly was able to listen deep within a cistern."

"When Ebek-Melek the Cushite took thirty men and lifted him from the cistern, Jeremiah must have been relieved."

"That's quite a story."

"And it made quite an impression on his life. Jeremiah wrote about it in Lamentations 3:53-55. He said,

> They dropped me alive into a pit and cast stones at me.

Dolly Jane continued, "Later he talks about being in 'the low dungeon.'"

"So I think I get what you are saying. Jeremiah's experiences caused him to emphasize protecting the written word. He knew that the enemy was coming and his people would be taken into exile. And he had an intimate knowledge of a fantastic place to hide books so he hid the most important books there."

"Bingo."

"The bottom of a dry cistern in the courtyard of the guard in Jerusalem. It would have been the most likely place that Jeremiah thought of to hide books and the last place that the Babylonian forces would have thought to look for treasure."

Billy sat back in his seat. He was skeptical of the plan, but not his sister. If she had faith enough to fly 11,000 miles to investigate a dry cistern to find a book that would lead to a piece of metal, that was enough for him. He said, "And you know where the cistern is?"

Dolly Jane said, "It was called the cistern of Malkijah, the king's son which was in the courtyard of the guard."

"What is it called now?"

"Really, it doesn't have a name. It's just a part of the courtyard."

"That sounds promising, but where is it?"

"Fortunately, we know the general region of where it is. West of the temple mount, just outside where they built Antonio's Fortress many years later."

Billy pictured the area in his mind's eye. "I remember that area from my visit when I was younger. That's a pretty closely watched public area."

"Which is why we are having trouble getting a permit."

"And why you need Checkers."

"This area has never been excavated and anything that was hidden in the depths of the cistern at the time of the Israelites exile to Babylon is certainly still there."

"So our first quest is to find Malkijah's cistern."

Dolly Jane concluded, "When we find Malkijah's cistern, we find the Book of the Kings. That will lead us to Nehushtan."

Billy looked at his watch. He yawned and sat back in his seat. He took a sip of water and pulled a blanket up to his chin and said groggily, "We'll see what Checkers can dig up for you."

Within a few minutes he was fast asleep.

# Chapter 16

---

## Tel Aviv International Airport
## Israel

With a long layover in Zurich, their total travel time was over 26 hours, resulting in a complete reversal of their circadian rhythm. Dolly Jane expected the profound daytime somnolence. Even though she had prepared for it by attempting to modify her sleeping patterns and imbibing caffeine at strategic points, she was still struggling to stay awake.

The culinary choices on the plane had left both Dolly Jane and Billy longing for something familiar. Billy had eaten nothing but bread for the last day, and expected nothing beyond that until he returned home.

The two of them looked like tourists as they waited for their luggage. Dolly Jane's bag was brightly colored and easy to identify on the turnstile among their large group. Neither her bag, nor Billy's plain black roller suitcase appeared on the belt. Eventually, all of the luggage had been claimed and they were the only two left from their particular group of passengers.

Dolly Jane said, "Let's find the Swiss Air customer service representative."

Billy saw a sign labeled "baggage claim desk."

Billy's eyes widened as the reality of the situation hit him. He spoke quietly to the agent at the desk. "It seems that my bag has been lost."

Like a teenager whose rapt attention was occupied by an iPhone, the uniformed Swiss Air agent sat slumped over and didn't look up from his desktop screen. He simply said in a strong German accent, "Name?"

"My name is Billy, and this is my sister, Dolly Jane" he handed his boarding pass across the desk.

The agent struck a few keys on his computer. Something on the screen grabbed his attention. He sat up and tapped a few more keystrokes. "Your passports and cell phones please."

"What?" Dolly Jane was shocked. "Why do you want our passports?"

Billy added, "What are you going to do with our cell phones?"

He spoke not a word, simply extended his hand with palm facing upward and waited.

Billy looked at Dolly Jane, "Can they do that?"

The officer touted, "This is not the United States. Your passports and cell phones please."

Reluctantly, they pulled out their two most precious possessions and placed them on the table. Dolly Jane felt naked and afraid.

Without a word, the Swiss Air agent grabbed their property and pushed away from the desk. He briskly rose from his chair and disappeared around a corner.

Billy looked at Dolly Jane. "What the heck is he doing?"

Dolly Jane spoke quickly, "Just relax. They'll find the bags. I had my luggage lost in Delhi once. It took a phone call from a friend in Chicago who had a cousin who worked at the airport to get my bag back. The gal's cousin was amazing. She brought us clothes to wear that were even our size! Eventually we got our bags just before the trip home."

Billy wasn't listening. He saw through the office windows as the agent spoke with a uniformed police officer. The young police officer took their passports and boarding passes and walked down a long hallway away from them. The agent returned to his desk and typed into the computer once again.

Billy tried to be polite, "Have you found our bags?"

"They are working on it."

Billy confronted him gently, "I don't think that's true. You just gave our passports to the police and they left with it. What's going on?"

The agent looked back at his computer screen and ignored him.

Billy's mind was racing. He wondered if the explosion he had caused had been traced back to him.

*Was he under investigation in Chicago?*

*Could he be labeled as a terrorist?*

He had made it through the TSA screening in the states, but Dubuque's security was minimal in comparison to Israel's. Was it possible that they had found something connecting him to the explosion? He wondered about fingerprints, or even his laptop. He had watched too many CSI episodes to think that he could get away with something like that.

They hadn't said anything while he was in the hospital. He was discharged without any contact from the police. He was confused. Could it have been investigated and reported to TSA while they were in transit? Why would they report it to the TSA or Interpol? He had no business being overseas. He wasn't even a frequent flyer.

He started to sweat.

The agent interrupted his internal panic, "Please wait in the chairs over there."

Dolly Jane grabbed Billy and they made an awkward shuffle over to the area the agent indicated. Billy was almost paralyzed, moving only with the assistance of his sister.

She hissed at him, "What's wrong with you?"

He shook his head. In all of his discussions of Checker's abilities, he never told her about how their illegal digging was considered trespassing, or even terrorism. He wondered if he needed to tell her what he had done. He looked up at the ceiling. Cameras were prevalent, he was certain that if he confessed his crime, his confession would be caught on camera. Even if they couldn't hear him, with as many camera angles as they had at their disposal, they would be able to read his lips and get everything they needed to turn an accident into an international terrorism incident. His guilt was like a lighthouse, his facial expression revealing his past. He stared at Dolly Jane blankly as sweat built up on his brow.

She squared up to him, "You look like you did when we were kids and you got caught Face timing your girlfriend at two-o'clock in the morning."

Billy remembered the incident. He felt the instant knowledge of crime and without a word, offered his phone up to his mother for a week as punishment. They had referenced this semi-innocent infraction numerous times in the past, yet this time he didn't crack a smile.

Dolly Jane asked, "Have you done something I need to know about?"

He remained silent, looking into the distance, searching for a remedy to his atrocity.

"Listen," she said. "If you're guilty, then I'm guilty by association and that's not acceptable."

As the words escaped her lips, she was suddenly aware of her own transgressions. Her verbal assault of Billy halted as she remembered that the last time she was in Israel, she helped Janet break numerous laws. She understood that every relic found was the property of the people of Israel and theft was a serious crime. She counted on her fingers one by one as she imagined the handcuffs being placed on her wrists and charges being levied to her: desecration of an archeological dig site, failure to register an archaeological find, grave robbing, and theft of a priceless relic. She wondered if this was a complete list or if there were even more charges that could be brought against her.

Her face turned pale as her mouth dropped open. In all of her discussion of Nehushtan with Billy, she had never revealed that they hid the find and the criminal nature of their lack of reporting.

Her thoughts were far from the cameras and she blurted out, "It's me! They want me!"

Billy saw the guilt in her eyes that he felt himself. He was utterly shocked. His sister had never even gotten a speeding ticket. She was the most forthright and innocent law abiding person he had ever known. What could she have done to create a response like that? He saw that she was going to confess and jumped to her protection.

His expertise in legal matters was limited but he did know one thing for sure. He warned her, "Don't say anything. Don't confess anything. Everything you say is being recorded right now. Wait until we get a lawyer."

She dropped her face into her hands and wept.

A few minutes later a pair of young female police officers approached them. The taller of the two said, "Dolly Jane and Billy?"

Dolly Jane nodded. Her face was a blotchy conglomeration of erythematous patches and streaked mascara. Billy's mind was spinning as he thought about how he would handle whatever type of interrogation they might encounter next.

She said, "Follow us." They turned and took a few steps down the hallway. Dolly Jane and Billy were escorted down the hall, one police officer in front, the other behind the criminals. They marched slowly and made sure the two of them were keeping pace.

Dolly Jane's thoughts were blank. She felt nauseated.

# Chapter 17

## Tel Aviv International Airport
## Israel

Billy and Dolly Jane followed the soldier through a glass double door and headed down a hallway. They turned right, then left, and proceeded through a heavy steel door. In another hallway, the officer opened the second door on the right and stood at attention, waiting for them to enter.

The twelve-by-twelve foot office was plain white except the black file cabinet in the corner, the black bookshelf on the back wall packed with files and folders of various sizes, and the grey metal desk symmetrically positioned in the center of the room. There were no pictures on the walls. No decorations, flags, or awards of any kind. Next to the desk sat two suitcases. Both had clearly been opened. Dolly Jane's sat against the wall, the zipper still undone. Billy's was open in the center of the room and Checkers was clearly exposed within it. Billy gave a cursory visual inspection and was pleased that while it wasn't in the exact position he had originally packed it, it didn't appear to have been tampered with. The other contents of the bag were neatly placed outside the bag on the tile floor.

Behind the desk was a mountain of a man. A large placard faced the visitors and announced his name and rank:

# מאקס רד'ריצ קולונל
# ماك ريتشارد العقيد
# Полковник Ричард Макс

Dolly Jane recognized the Hebrew, Arabic and Russian lettering. She quickly translated it and whispered, "'Colonel Richard Macks sounds like a very American name."

His presence seemed to consume the majority of the room. His muscular frame bulged the pockets and patches on the operational camouflage pattern of his Army Combat Uniform. His arms were like tree trunks with veins. His short-cropped blonde hair minimized the potential for future graying and provided a thin frame for ruggedly handsome facial features. His nose, though broken on many occasions, both in sports and combat, gave him an unrefined attractiveness that complimented his position and status. His piercing hazel eyes revealed nothing as he examined the two new guests in his office.

Dolly Jane was nervous about her potential conviction for crimes against the people of Israel. Yet, something about the man behind the desk calmed her. She was reminded of the many division-one football players she had dealt with during her collegiate experience at Iowa State University, and was comfortable ordering them around in spite of their physical prowess. She smiled warmly at the officer, but got no response. In spite of the military nature, and her submissive position, she saw him as a firm intimidating man on the outside, yet a joyful and playful young boy on the inside. She also understood that it might take some time to break through his exterior shell.

Billy remained focused on Checkers. He gave the officer a few quick glances, but concentrated on his pride and joy that sat exposed and vulnerable inside the suitcase.

The desktop was well organized with a ten-inch black metal fan in the corner, a desk light in the other corner and two passports, belonging to Billy and Dolly Jane in the middle, under the officer's hands. He tapped his fingers on the passports.

It was clear to Billy and Dolly Jane that they had just walked from the airport into another sector of life altogether, a military zone in which one man was in charge. In his mid-fifties, yet having the build of a man in his prime, the officer sat still, while his guests shuffled about. Billy didn't know whether to stand at attention, or to sit in the padded metal chair. But since there was only one seat available, he certainly wouldn't take it with a lady present.

He motioned to Dolly Jane to sit but she was motionless. Billy, on the other hand was annoyed. With the exposure of his invention, he tried to think of a way to explain why they brought a tunneling robot to Israel. He came up blank.

Colonel Macks spoke in perfect English with a Mid-western accent, "I've got a few questions for the two of you.

Billy was visibly sweating. Dolly Jane said, "I'd love to chat, what would you like to chat about?"

"What is the purpose of your visit to Israel?"

"We are re-joining my team in Ein Gedi for our Archeological dig."

He was silent, expecting more.

She continued, "How about you? You're obviously not from here. You sound like you're from the Mid-west "

Colonel Macks relaxed his posture and smiled, "I was born in Wisconsin, but raised in Iowa where I excelled in football and track. I enjoyed my time at Annapolis, and then joined the Navy. Back when I was in high school, my family took a trip to Israel. We were part of a group of twenty-three tourists, family and friends. It was an amazing experience. I had the privilege to visit the famous holy sites and literally fell in love with this place."

Dolly Jane sat down in the chair and smiled at him. He continued, "The Bible stories I had grown up with from infancy had always seemed like fairy tales until I walked the ground that Jesus walked on. In Caesarea Philippi, we toured the temple to the Pagan god Pan, and witnessed the historical significance of the human sacrifices that took place there.

That place was called 'The Gates of Hell'. It was in this location that we read the scripture where Jesus said, 'I will build my church and the Gates of Hell will not overcome it.' Suddenly, this had real meaning to me."

Dolly Jane chimed in, "I know the place well. It completely changed how I read the Bible!"

Colonel Macks agreed, "Absolutely. Every story in the Old and New Testaments seemed to come to life after I had been here. When we toured the tunnels outside the Temple Mount, I was amazed with the architecture and building techniques the ancient Romans used. Herod the Great did some truly incredible things. You know, it's easier to stomach his accomplishments when you ignore the genocide."

Dolly Jane nodded in agreement, "Killing every newborn in the country is pretty horrible."

Colonel Macks smirked, "They even gave me a Yakima. I wore it every day under my baseball cap for months when I got home."

"Did you feel comfortable here?"

"Absolutely! I think I was born in the wrong country. I belong here."

Dolly Jane laughed in agreement.

Colonel Macks continued, "On one evening that we had off as a group, about twenty of us went through downtown Jerusalem. It was an eclectic group of teenagers, moms and dads, looking at stores and just having fun. But I assumed the position in the back of the pack as the security officer. Not because I was bigger, in comparison I was tiny – only 6' 3" – and a measly 220 pounds back then. It was just because I wanted to protect every member of the team, a perfect way for me to serve. I remember my dad was trying to do security checks for the group. He would scan over the group then do a little window-shopping. Every time he looked in on people, I saw that he was checking late, because I was constantly watching everything the team was doing. I relieved him of his duty and he got to enjoy window shopping."

"So security was in your blood?"

"I suppose. It just came naturally for me."

Billy asked, "Is that why you joined the military?"

"I had never felt so comfortable, like when I visited Annapolis and West Point. I had always excelled in athletics and school, but there - valedictorians and team captains constantly surrounded me. It was very humbling."

There was a knock on the door. Colonel Macks said loudly, "Enter."

Three soldiers entered the room behind them and stood at attention. Colonel Macks looked up at them. They were each in a slightly different uniform, but the thread of security and respect was clear. The first spoke quickly in Hebrew. The second made rapid fire in Russian for two quick sentences and the third said two words in Arabic.

Colonel Macks made eye contact with each in turn as he answered them in their respective languages. They performed a military turn around and exited the office immediately.

Dolly Jane asked, "How did you become fluent in so many languages?"

The large Colonel placed his hands behind his head and sat back in his chair. "While I was in high school, I took Spanish. I found that I had a knack for it. Then when our family took a trip to Israel, our tour guide's name was Olga." He smiled and motioned with his meaty hands as he spoke. "You guessed it, she was from Russia, and I picked up a Russian Bible while I was here. I learned a few words and phrases from her and loved it. I learned Japanese and Russian in college, then got a master's degree in Russian at the Monterey Language Institute. Later on, I couldn't wait to dive into the Hebrew language, mostly to understand the Bible. You know the Bible really takes on another dimension when you read and understand it in the original languages. That's why I learned Biblical Greek. But when you're living in the Middle East, it sure comes in handy to know some Arabic too."

Dolly Jane said, "You know, I love this place too. I could live here if I could find a way to do so. As an American, how did you end up here?"

The Colonel replied, "After my career in the navy, I had all kinds of opportunities. I had buddies in the force who went into sales, management, or back to graduate school to get advanced degrees."

"Did you go to more school?"

"I thought about it, but instead I volunteered with the IDF."

"The Israeli Defense Force?"

Colonel Macks nodded, "They have an amazing program that they offer to American citizens. You can come on a work Visa and help on one of their bases. They pay your way and you get to see the country as you help their army. The minimum stay is twenty-three days, and that's what I had planned for."

Billy chimed in, "With your military training and experience, you certainly had a lot to offer."

"At first they had me training their recruits. After a while, I trained their special-forces guys and then worked up the ranks of their defense force."

"So you stayed?"

"Like I said, I should have been born here. After two years I became a citizen. I have dual citizenship. Now, I can't imagine living anywhere else!"

Dolly Jane and Billy felt so comfortable with their host that they almost forgot why they were there.

"Right now, they have me between posts. So I'm stationed in various positions here and there, this week it's the airport!"

"Well, I hope you're enjoying the time here."

"So, do you know why you are in here with me, instead of being off to your destination?"

Billy said, "Search me, sir."

The Colonel laughed, "I have no intention of searching you."

Billy corrected, "It's merely an acknowledgement meaning I have no knowledge of the answer to the question at hand."

The Colonel said, "You know, when you look at the English language in comparison to other languages, you'd think that there are no rules at all and idioms run rampant."

Dolly Jane asked, "So how would you fix the language?"

The Colonel looked at the ceiling and said, "It would be hard, since so many people speak it so poorly. Irregardless of that, we should talk about what you are doing here."

Dolly Jane said, "Regardless."

The Colonel questioned, "Excuse me?"

"Irregardless isn't a word. You meant to say regardless. The insertion of the 'ir' at the front of the word actually reverses the meaning of the word."

The Colonel smirked, "My point exactly. English needs to be fixed."

Billy was confused, "Then it wouldn't be English at all."

The Colonel said, "Would that be so bad?" He paused for a moment, and then continued. "I get to see all kinds of unusual things that come into our country." He pointed at Checkers and said, "Like this little guy. It looks like some sort of drilling device."

Billy's heart sank. His throat rose within him and he couldn't breathe.

"Tell me about it."

Billy collected himself and said, "We call her Checkers." Then he was still. Motionless. Dumbfounded.

The Colonel looked at him expectantly.

Dolly Jane had to think quickly. It was obvious that she would have to pinch hit for Billy. She knew that the best lie was like a small drop within a sea of truth. She thought for a moment then chimed in, "This is one of the many tools we are using at our dig site." She dug into her backpack as she spoke and pulled out the official Ein Gedi site permit and handed it to him. "For years, we have dug with a spade and a brush and progress is painfully slow. Now we have a mechanical drill to do the same thing, just quicker. I'd be happy to explain how it works."

"A mechanical drill?"

"Certainly. Have you ever been to an active dig site?"

He stared at her.

"I'm sorry. Of course you have. You can't swing a dead cat around here without coming across a dig site. When you dig, you are careful to preserve everything, you dig around the edges, taking years to unearth even the smallest site.

"Like Magdala."

"Excellent example. With this little contraption, that excavation would have taken a fraction of the time."

He stared at Checkers. Other than the black and white checkerboard and the obvious drill head, there were no other identifying features. He had no evidence to contradict what she was saying.

She continued her improvisation, "I'm majoring in Archeology at Iowa State, and am a part of the most exciting dig we've ever seen. In an Ein Gedi cave we found a whole series of skeletons at Christmas time. Now, we are hoping to explore the edges of the cave, using this machine to dig around to see if there are any undiscovered relics there."

Colonel Macks looked them over. He had read about the discovery in the local papers, and wondered about the importance of finding skeletons in a cave. He opened his laptop and struck a few keys. Within moments, he found the article he had read. He scanned it, confirming the presence of Iowa State University. He found a name and said, "What can you tell me about professor Janet Zimmerman?"

Dolly Jane's face lit up. "Janet is great. She holds the title, 'Professor of Anthropology' at Iowa State University, but I consider her to be a friend and mentor."

Dolly Jane continued, "I met her my first year when I took her class 'ANTHR 128: Archaeological Methods and Techniques' and have been on several digs with her. She specialized in studies on or around the Dead Sea and leads teams of students to study various dig sites."

While she spoke, he pulled up her bio and confirmed the classes she taught and her interest in the Dead Sea. As he stared at his computer screen, Dolly Jane dove into the story of their first lecture where she taught them that archaeology was about putting themselves in a different place and time. She described how she had fallen in love with the study of ancient cultures. Her story took quite a while.

Colonel Macks closed his laptop and picked up the phone on his desk. He uttered a few words in Arabic then set the phone down. Instantly the door sprung open and an olive skinned Lieutenant appeared, set a pair of phones on the Colonel's desk, and quickly exited the room.

The Colonel motioned to the robotic drilling device and the suitcases and said, "I'm impressed with your creativity. The only thing I would change is the drill's name. Checkers is pretty plain for such a complex device. I look at that, all of it's capabilities, and what it will bring to your team and it reminds me of a great religious party like Mardi Gras. Have you ever been to New Orleans on Fat Tuesday? That's a party!"

Dolly Jane and Billy smiled politely.

The Colonel smacked his hands on the desk and shouted, "*Şeker Bayramı!*"

Billy said, "Excuse me?"

"That's what you should name the drill!"

Billy looked at him blankly.

He grabbed a pen and wrote on a piece of paper "Shecker Byron" then turned it to face his guests. "Pronounce it however you like. But that's her name!"

Billy placated the officer, "I'll consider it."

The Colonel was pleased with himself. "We don't think of Muslims as party animals, but that's because the world doesn't focus on Turkey after Ramadan. *Şeker Bayramı* is the three-day festival to celebrate the end of the thirty days of fasting. There's plenty of religious intonations as well, but it's mostly about being able to eat during the daytime again."

Dolly Jane said, "I don't know much about Turkey, except a few Turkish words."

Colonel Macks said, "My father spent some time there when he was a child. I could tell you some wild stories about that guy. He was a character!"

Dolly Jane tried to be polite. "I'd love to, but we have a schedule to maintain."

"Of course." The Colonel slid the phones and passports towards his visitors and said, "You two be safe and enjoy your stay in Israel." He stood and extended his enormous hand across the desk for a handshake.

Billy shook the meaty hand with his own impressive grip. Billy wondered how many people that hand had taken down, killed, and secretly buried in the desert over the years. The two mighty men locked eyes. Billy was confident that he could take down the Colonel in a wrestling match if it ever came to that. The handshake lasted far longer than necessary. The testosterone in the room was boiling over.

The Colonel released his grip and retrieved the passports and phones. He handed them back to their owners. Dolly Jane tossed the phone and passport into her purse then grasped the Colonel's mighty hand with both of her hands and shook it heartily. She felt comfortable with the giant of a man and wasn't overstating her joy when she said, "It's truly been a pleasure to meet you, sir."

They packed Checkers and exited the room. The hallways were like a maze; they traversed it quickly and made their way to the shuttle, which took them to their hotel in Jerusalem.

Colonel Macks opened his laptop and a map appeared with two blue dots side-by-side moving down the freeway. He suspected that they were going to use that drilling machine for something illegal. *It's just a matter of time before they show what they are up to.*

He addressed his Lieutenant in Hebrew and instructed him to keep an eye on them.

The Lieutenant saluted and departed.

# Chapter 18

## Jerusalem

Billy and Dolly Jane took a shuttle from the Tel Aviv Airport to the Dan Jerusalem Hotel on Lehi Street in Jerusalem. Though unassuming from its outward appearance, the hotel facility was first rate. A few visitors scattered around the vast expanse of the lobby and lounged on the comfortable square leather chairs and ottomans. Fountains scattered through the lobby created a subtle ambiance that Dolly Jane found calming and relaxing. They passed by a pair of elevators on the left and proceeded to the black granite check-in desk.

The immaculately dressed guest service liaison said, “We’ve got you checked into rooms 223 and 225, next door to one another in section A.”

Section A? Does that mean there is a section B?”

“Certainly,” he said. “The elevators to section A are past the front door and past the bank of elevators which go to the elite suites. The section B elevators are this way to your left,” he motioned with his hands as he spoke. “This bank of elevators takes you to the other half of the hotel rooms and the dining centers, on the first and sixth floors.”

Billy said, “Sounds like a maze.”

Dolly Jane took the keys and gave one to Billy. She looked at the liaison and said, “Thank you.” They spent the next fifteen minutes traveling on elevators and looking for their rooms. She checked her watch, it was 4:00 PM. Exhausted from jet lag, their time in the interrogation, and now with the confusing hotel, they were both frustrated by the time they found their rooms. They were both asleep as soon as their heads hit the pillow.

## Chicago

In his apartment, Chase focused on taking one deep breath after the next. It was all he could do to boil oatmeal and spoon it down along with his multiple medicines. His neck, chest and extremities screamed in agony, redefining pain for him. The occasional trip to the bathroom took nearly all his energy.

Thankful to be out of the hospital, he was surprised at how much pain he was in. Leaning over the sink in the bathroom, he took off his bathrobe and examined his chest. He didn’t recognize his own torso. The multiple broken ribs had healed with an embarrassing anomaly, a hole in the middle of his previously athletic chest. He considered calling a friend or his parents for help, but he knew how to recover from injuries and was certain that he could manage on his own.

He sat in his recliner. Though moving around was difficult, his mind was clear and he could work on his laptop. He checked his email and social media, and responded to all the well wishers and gave them a glowing update, far better than he actually felt. He wondered what had happened to his friend Billy. He tracked his cell phone and saw that he had made a trip.

He thought, *What are you up to?*

# Jerusalem

The following morning, Billy and Dolly Jane awoke at 3:00 AM. They spent time reading and trying to go back to sleep but eventually acquiesced to the fact that their day was underway. When the sun came up, they indulged in a hearty breakfast and boarded a taxi to the Old City. Billy enjoyed riding in the sleek silver Mercedes. He appreciated the quality vehicle and took a few moments to feel the fine leather seats and listen to the minimal road noise as they cruised the smooth clean Jerusalem streets. He wondered if American Uber drivers would upgrade to such nice wheels. Dolly Jane gave instructions to the driver to take them to the Lion's Gate.

Despite the early hour, foot traffic was prevalent and busses occupied the streets. They made it to Derekh Yerikho Street on Highway 417, once they past by Derech Sha'ar HaAryot street they stopped at a vacant bus stop.

Billy reached into the trunk and retrieved his small black suitcase as Dolly Jane admired the scenery. From her vantage point, she could see some of the major tourist destinations in Jerusalem. Just across the street and across the valley was Gethsemane and the Church of All Nations, also known as the Basilica of the Agony. This Catholic Church was built on the foundations of a crusader chapel and fourth century Byzantine basilica with funds from twelve different nations, thus the name. The church provided a beautiful place for tourists to remember and worship Jesus in the Garden of Gethsemane, where Judas betrayed Jesus and brought about his unjust arrest.

She looked over to the Mount of Olives and imagined all the teaching that Jesus did there during 30 to 33 AD. She imagined him after his resurrection, surrounded by his remaining disciples and friends. This is the very place where Jesus said the words, "Go and make disciples of all nations, baptizing them in the name of the Father, and of the Son, and of the Holy Spirit." Then, in her mind's eye, she saw Jesus ascending to heaven from that very site.

She imagined the angels speaking to the disciples saying, "Men of Galilee, why do you stand here looking into the sky? This same Jesus, who has been taken from you into heaven, will come back in the same way you have seen him go into heaven." Her eyes drifted from the top of the hill to the sky. Looking for any sign that Jesus was descending.

She wondered, *When would He return? Would it be today? Tomorrow? Next year?*

The powerful implications of how we live our lives was not lost on her as she gazed at the last piece of earth where Jesus' foot walked before his ascension.

She took a deep breath and turned back to Billy, he was waiting on the sidewalk with his suitcase. They backtracked a dozen yards, then turned left and headed up the hill two hundred yards, towards the Old City and as they approached, the colossal beige limestone gate came into view.

The Lion's Gate at El-Ghazali Square was the least ornate of the seven open gates in Jerusalem's Old City Walls. With the exception of a pair of lions subtly carved in relief on the walls surrounding the Gate, the entrance remained unadorned. Nothing about this entrance was attractive. There were no shops, green spaces, or places to gather, it was merely a guarded entrance to the ancient city. Ironically, this gate, though it lacked visual appeal, was the entrance to the Via Dolorosa, the path of the traditional Christian observance of the last walk of Jesus from prison to crucifixion. In spite of it's apparent desolation within the city, thousands of tourists traversed the gate every day.

Billy looked at Dolly Jane and sighed, "It feels like we came through the servant's entrance of a magnificent hotel. There are other more attractive entrances, you know. There's even a gate called the beautiful gate, that's what they called it in the Bible, but you chose the Lion's gate."

"At least I didn't take you through Dung Gate," Dolly Jane smirked. "We need to be as inconspicuous as possible. Today, we're just a couple of American tourists."

They passed several police cars and a handful of blue barricades stacked off to the right side as they officially entered Via Dolorosa Street. The narrow ancient cobblestone road attacked the wheels on his suitcase like miniature landmines. Intimidating light brown limestone walls towered on either side, like a desert within a city. They joined the constant flow of Muslim men and women as they made their way down the road.

After a short distance, they entered the Lion's Gate Bazaar where several small shops sold souvenirs and various antiquities. Billy noticed mostly Muslim garb and trinkets. He smiled when he saw an old sign on a gift shop on the right advertizing Kodak film. A decade earlier, Kodak filed for bankruptcy amidst changes in the digital imaging market. Billy wondered how many years had passed since that store had actually sold any Kodak film, and wondered why they hadn't updated their advertisements. They passed through a tunnel and down another two hundred yards of cobblestone urban wasteland. A dark tunnel formed by overhead connection between buildings. Persian rugs lined the walls and Billy suddenly felt as though he was inside an Iranian carpet shop. A large bronze sign emblazoned with the words "The Palace" hung over a store on their left. Billy thought that it wasn't much of a palace since the bronze showed it's age and looked as if it hadn't been polished in ages.

As they proceeded through the street, they passed an awning held up with a wrought iron railing; this was turned into a Muslim shopping center, selling everything from women's apparel to frozen orange drinks, Billy smirked and asked Dolly Jane, "Is that the Wal-Mart of the Old City?"

Dolly Jane didn't answer. She was focused on her destination. Malkijah's cistern was close to the Anotonio Fortress and the Temple Mount, but she was looking for places nearby to do their initial scanning. As they got deeper in the city, it was crowded with Muslim men in plaid shirts, covered heads, and loose fitting slacks. The women were covered much more. A group of women with dark dresses and veils partially covering their faces walked by slowly.

They passed the Greek Orthodox Patriarchate of Jerusalem Prison of Christ on the right and across the street was the Christ Prison Shop for gifts and souvenirs, full of Greek orthodox icons and Persian carpets. The sign on the outside of the store revealed that the shop was recommended by the ministry of Tourism and included the services of money changing and a garment store.

A group of tourists passed by them with the leader carrying a worn cross over his shoulder. Group members wore a radio receiver into which the tour guide whispered, allowing him or her to stay in constant communication with their leader. The group stopped at each of the nine Stations of the Cross until they arrived at the Church of the Holy Sepulcher where they observed each of the last five.

Billy found the Muslim quarter oppressive and uninviting. "Today, I'm not concerned with the places where Jesus fell. Let's get to a spot where we can look underground."

They traversed another hundred yards and turned left on El-Wad-ha-Gai St. They saw Basti Restaurant and Café and advertisements for such comforts as Armenian Pizza, Kubeh, hot dogs, and free Wi-Fi.

Billy noticed the eight heavily armed police officers across the narrow street with riot gear at the ready. He wondered about the heavy security in this place as opposed to the other blocks they had passed through. He looked back towards the Muslim Quarter; then looked around the Basti Restaurant and the street ahead of him, it was packed with Jews, Muslims, and a spattering of Christians. Overhead, the second story apartments were lined with a dozen Israeli flags. He recognized this corner as the junction where the Muslim and Jewish Quarters converge, a potential powder keg. He was thankful for the show of force presented by the Israeli Police clad in riot gear – a clear effort to keep the peace.

They walked a few more minutes until they came to the Panoramic Golden City, a Hookah bar across the street from the church of the Holy Sepulcher. Dolly Jane quickly found a booth and Billy stowed the suitcase by his feet. They each ordered cappuccino and Billy placed his laptop next to the napkin on the wooden table. Before he looked at the computer screen he looked around the bar and noticed the garb worn by the ladies. He motioned with his forehead towards a woman walking by with her face almost completely covered, only her eyes and less than an inch of her forehead exposed. He quietly asked Dolly Jane, "Is that a hijab?"

Dolly Jane whispered, "Actually, she's wearing a Niqab. The word hijab in the Qur'an actually refers to a spatial partition or curtain, but really means separation. Islam says that believing women should guard their modesty and not display their beauty and ornaments."

He asked, "I thought it was just a type of outfit."

She looked at him and saw that he was listening intently but shaking his head. She continued, "The Qur'an speaks of it in Surah twenty-four, verse thirty one. It says, 'That they should draw their veils over the bosoms and not display their beauty except to: their husbands, their fathers, their husband's fathers, their sons, their husbands' sons, their brothers, their brothers' sons, or their sisters' sons—"

Billy interrupted, "Are you kidding me?"

Dolly Jane said, "What?"

Billy said, "That sounds more detailed than Leviticus!"

Dolly Jane continued, "Yes it is. The passage goes on in much more detail."

Billy laughed.

Dolly Jane said, "The Hijab applies to both men and women in terms of protecting both their private lives from outsiders and preserving their honor. Metaphorically the Hijab also applies to their behavior."

Just then two women passed by outside the bar, completely covered from head to toe in a black dress. A small area of mesh in front of their eyes gave limited visibility.

Billy motioned subtly, "Tell me about that."

Dolly Jane smiled and whispered, "I'm not a fan and don't plan on wearing one of those myself, but a lot of Muslim women wear them. According to a fatwa written by Muhammed Salih Al-Munajjid, the woman's face is 'awrah which is the most tempting part of her body, because what people look at most is the face. Therefore, the face is the greatest 'awrah of a woman. So he concluded that women must wear a Burqa in public."

Billy rolled his eyes, "I don't get it."

Dolly Jane whispered, "You don't have to. Just respect that they are doing what they understand to be most appropriate behavior."

Billy shook his head.

Dolly Jane looked at him and snapped, "Are those two women hurting you in any way?"

Billy was surprised. He scowled and shook his head.

Dolly Jane said, "Then show them respect. They are doing an honorable thing. They think that I'm disrespecting men by wearing what I'm wearing, but they would never be offensive and tell me that. They just live their lives."

A waitress wearing a dark dress and an Al-Amira two-piece veil skillfully draped over her head approached with an orta for her and a sekerli for Billy. He looked up and smiled, "Sukran Jazeelan."

Dolly Jane also smiled. Billy opened his laptop and started as the waitress departed. Dolly Jane said, "I'm impressed. You're learning Arabic."

Billy said, "Just a few words. Hopefully I'll be able to ask where the bathroom is later on."

Dolly Jane asked, "If we find something, I believe the bathroom in this fine establishment is a spot where we can tunnel from."

Billy raised his eyebrows, "Let's not get ahead of ourselves. From what I can tell, scanning this area can be a nightmare."

"What do you mean?"

He tapped the keyboard as he spoke. Inside the suitcase, Checkers came to life. The drill head remained still, but the Ground Penetrating Radar sprang into action. Four windows appeared on Billy's screen. He could monitor the robot's performance, view the actual inside of the suitcase, and scan all around with thermal and laser imaging. He clicked a few boxes and the unused windows immediately minimized, making the underground images larger and more precise.

He scanned directly below their booth. Below eighteen inches of dolomitic limestone was a basement. Billy viewed the large bags of coffee stored on shelves, and smiled at the broad variety of Hookas to choose from. He looked deeper, through the basement floor and waited for the resolution to clear. Another eighteen inches of limestone covered a cistern.

"That didn't take long," Dolly Jane said. "You've already found a cistern. Is it full of water?"

Billy scanned the cistern back and forth. The thermal imagery showed that everything was 55 degrees. He checked the densitometer readings and the numbers revealed that the cistern was full of water. "Yes, see?"

Dolly Jane looked at the screen and saw nothing that she could interpret.

Billy said, "Just a minute." He closed the window and changed a few settings within the program to bring the densitometer readings onto the screen in a visual format then reopened the scanning window. A view of the cistern with water inside came on the screen.

Dolly Jane said, "Much better."

Billy panned to the right and through the wall into the earth. There were pipes and wires traversing the ground in every direction. He went farther and saw a few yards with nothing but solid rock, then another cistern on the other side of the underground tank was more wires, and rock, and another cistern. Then the image quality became pixilated.

"It looks like we reached our limit. That's about seventy five yards."

Dolly Jane was impressed, "So you'll be able to see seventy five yards in every direction?"

Billy scratched his chin, "I thought it would be better. I apologize." He spent a few minutes and looked in every direction then said, "Every cistern we see here has water in it. And there are very few places we could tunnel if we wanted to."

"How about going deeper? What is below the cisterns?"

"Below them?"

"This city is ancient. The cisterns we are looking at now simply collect rainwater. They aren't wells. The Pool of Bethesda was excavated 45 feet below the surface. I wouldn't be surprised if the cistern we are looking for is at that level."

Billy tapped the screen and scanned the entire region going deeper and deeper. He reached seventy-five yards directly beneath them, and shallower as they moved out in every direction. They saw two more cisterns at 45 and 60 feet of depth, one of them contained water while the other was dry. He looked closer at the dry one, looking for any remnants or contents, but it was empty.

Dolly Jane smiled. "This is amazing!"

Billy shook his head, "Disappointing, really."

Dolly Jane exclaimed, "You don't understand. We've been at this for about ten minutes and already have mapped out underground structures within the Old City of Jerusalem that have never been described before!"

Billy smiled.

Dolly Jane continued, "If you can make a 3 dimensional map of what you just scanned, then we repeat the process at more locations, we can overlap the edges and scan the whole city!"

Billy said, "Probably. But that's not why we are here."

Dolly Jane agreed, "Right. Let's focus on Malkijah's cistern. It's got to be near the Antonia Fortress."

Billy said, "There are plenty of places that we can hunker down and have a cup of coffee while Checkers scans away."

The pair spent the morning sipping various kinds of coffee and admiring the variety of Hookahs in bars in the Old city. Every fifty yards they stopped and scanned. They found a maze of plumbing structures, modern enclosed pipes, and ancient drainage tunnels. Interspersed were electrical lines and cisterns, both full and dry. The only time they spent time going over anything on screen was when they stumbled upon a dry cistern. But each was empty.

Dolly Jane looked closely at the map and realized that they had gone all around the western wall but were missing the section next to the wall itself. She looked at Billy and said, "You're not going to like this, but you have to dress like a woman for our next scan."

Billy asked, "Do I have to wear a Burka?"

"Absolutely not! They'd never let you near the holy place in one of those! You're going to wear a skirt, leggings, a sweater, and a head covering like the rest of the Jewish women who go to pray."

Billy shook his head.

Dolly Jane smiled, "I've got a little shopping to do."

Billy said, "There are no shortage of places to shop around here. Have fun."

Billy stayed where he was, tapping on his keyboard. He digitally stitched the previous scans together and prepared to overlay the image onto a street map of the Old City. After about half an hour, Dolly Jane returned with a shopping bag.

"I had to guess your size, ma'am." She chuckled. "Put these on." She tossed him a bag and he peeked inside.

"You have very conservative taste!"

"I think you'll look great."

He got up from the table and headed to the restroom. In the men's room, he donned the black blouse that she had picked out for him. When he put on the grey wool skirt it reached down and covered his ankles.

As he returned to the table, Dolly Jane saw him from a distance and teased, "Swing your hips more. You're not looking very ladylike."

He pointed back at her and scolded, “No pictures.”

“I’m just teasing. You look beautiful.”

“How badly do you want this scan? I’m thinking this trip might be shorter than you’d imagined.” He leered at her.

She smiled playfully and held out a mirror for him to look at his face. She manipulated her own scarf into three different positions and had him emulate her. As a young girl, playing with hair and scarves was a practiced routine and came easy to her. For Billy, other than a year of long hair experimentation in fifth and seventh grade, he had no experience managing this sort of thing.

He struggled to get the fabric into place. “Football and hockey helmets just plop on the head and you strap them on. This is different. It might take some practice.”

They took their time. A few young women at tables next to them looked on in curiosity as Billy received instructions on scarf wearing while in public. Then she had him simulate how he could monitor his laptop in privacy with the scarf as cover. Eventually he got the hang of it, and before the women at the nearby table made any serious inquiries, they exited the shop.

They turned on Ala’ e Din Street and walked through a series of narrow corridors into the deep recesses of the past. Billy was forced to duck numerous times as they passed under arches and through areas under construction going farther into the depths of the ancient city.

Dolly Jane knew they had reached the Western Wall Tunnel when she saw groups of Jewish women in prayer. Several of the older women sat on white plastic stackable chairs, wearing black skirts, white blouses and a variety of head coverings. They were content to be so near the most holy of places. It was the closest place possible for women to get to the temple. The devout women read prayers from their tiny books and swayed back and forth as they silently cried out to God.

Dolly Jane pulled out a plastic chair from what appeared to be a cave where they were stored. She settled into the chair a few yards from any of the other women, partially blocking the path. She brought her head covering up over her head, pulled out her Bible, opened it to Psalm 122, and read, “Jerusalem is built like a city that is closely compacted together.” She chuckled under her breath and began praying,

“God you really do have a sense of humor.” She closed the book and bowed her head, “Father God, please show us where we need to look.”

Meanwhile, Billy sat down next to her and kept his scarf in a traditional position. An older woman noticed his shoes as he settled the suitcase under his seat. She looked up from her prayer book and glared at him. Billy quickly brought his head covering all the way over his head like a tent and opened up his laptop. He could feel the Jewish woman’s gaze penetrating him as he turned on the computer and silently began his scan of the region. His previous scans gave him the experience he needed to be efficient. He scanned the entire perimeter fluidly. He saw three dry cisterns in the region. Two were very deep and fairly distant from their location, just at the limit of the scanner’s resolution. He looked at them closely and saw that both of the dry cisterns had irregular flooring, which may indicate that they held something.

He pulled his scarf down and glanced at the woman who had been staring at him. Instead of one, five Jewish women stared in his direction.

He tapped Dolly Jane on the shoulder and motioned in their direction. She brought her prayers to a close and got up from her chair. She approached the women while he finished the scan.

“Shalom,” she said.

They didn’t respond. Their books were closed and they squared up to Billy. She held position between them and him and said, “שהשלום יהיה עימך.”

The leader of the group was clearly offended by the lack of respect shown by a man in their Holy place. The women put away their books and stood up.

Billy pecked at the keyboard as fast as he could. He scanned the area twice and verified that the digital image was complete and accurate but didn’t take time to look it over. He glanced at the interaction going on between Dolly Jane and the women and held his breath. In fastidious fashion, he closed the laptop, stowed it in his satchel, and stood up. In the process, his head covering fell off. His head exposed, he didn’t know what the women would say or do. He looked in their direction and saw nothing but empty chairs.

Dolly Jane said, “Did you get what you needed?”

Billy nodded.
She said, “Let’s go.”

## Tel Aviv, Israel

From within his plain white office, the Colonel’s enormous body hunched over the computer screen on his desk. He read slowly:

私たち全員
私の人生のうちで
イエス
私たちはあなたを愛してます

He clicked the mouse a few times and the English lettering appeared:

Watashi tachi mina
Watashi no jinsei no subete□
Iesu-sama
Anata o aishimasu

He clicked again and the translation came up

All of us
All my life
Jesus
We love you

Suddenly, an alert came up on the screen showing Billy and Dolly Jane's movements within the Old City. He thought, *Japanese worship songs will have to wait until another day.*

He pulled up Dolly Jane and Billy's movements and tried to make sense of their steps all across the Old City.

He said, "You are far from Ein Gedi, my friends."

He picked up his phone and in Hebrew he ordered his Lieutenant to place cameras inside their hotel room.

# Chapter 19

## Old City, Jerusalem

“Follow me,” Dolly Jane said as she walked briskly through the tunnels beneath the Western Wall. She dodged a few Jewish women and a handful of tourists as she exited the tunnels into the open air. When they reached the open street, they stopped and took a deep breath.

“Are we in trouble?” Billy asked.

“Not really,” Dolly Jane answered.

Billy asked, “Why are you so upset?”

She looked down at the ground and sighed, “Those women were deeply bothered by you being there. I shouldn’t have done that. I never want to disturb other people’s worship experience.”

“But we technically haven’t done anything wrong. Right?”

Dolly Jane nodded. She agreed that they were innocent but still felt guilty. “We need to find a place to sit and talk about what’s on your computer. I don’t want to go all the way back to the hotel.”

Billy said, “I think we’ve had enough coffee already.”

Dolly Jane looked around. “If there was a park bench or any place like that, it would be fine.”

"I know where to go," Billy said. He lumbered his suitcase behind him over the cobblestone streets that worked like thousands of tiny speed bumps. He walked with the flow of foot traffic around a few corners, past the pool of Bethesda, and up to the Church of St. Anne. As they approached the entrance of the church Billy said, "People sing in here all day. We can sit and listen."

Dolly Jane smiled, she hadn't seen this church before. She followed Billy through the ornate front doors and saw a group of tourists huddled in the central aisle between the rows of oak pews on either side. They slipped between two groups and found a place to sit on the right side. Billy slipped his suitcase beneath the seat and said, "This is the Church of Saint Anne, dedicated to the memory of St. Anne, the mother of Mary, Jesus' mother."

"I haven't heard of her. Is she a fictitious character or is she real?"

"Everyone had a mother. Even Jesus' mother, Mary."

"Okay, she's real. What I'm asking is whether she is a person with historically cited information."

"Well, no. I suppose the information we have of her is more folklore than historically validated fact. But certainly she was an important person. She raised Mary, the mother of Jesus!"

Just then one of the tour groups gathered at the front of the church like a choir. With a single person standing in front of the group, they sang in unison a glorious rendition of "How Great Though Art." Billy and Dolly Jane watched and enjoyed the amazing acoustics of the church. Billy looked up and saw Romanesque architecture. Grey stones stacked thirty feet tall made clean lines and were almost completely unadorned, with nothing to dampen the echoes. The walls arched as they reached the vaulted ceiling making the perfect building for acapella singing.

Billy said, "They call it the church of St. Anne, but I like to think of it as a church of ironies."

She furrowed her brow.

Billy whispered, "First, even though it is located in Israel, the country of France owns the church." He pointed to an elderly gentleman in a white robe who was teaching a group of Americans about St. Anne's statue and continued, "Second, an Irish priest oversees the site during the open hours. Third, this Christian church is right smack dab in the heart of the Muslim quarter of the Old City."

Dolly Jane nodded, "The Church of Ironies indeed."

"A more international conglomeration would be hard to find."

With the attention of the crowd on the singing, Billy opened his laptop and began the process of stitching together his recent scans with the others of the morning. The computing power of the laptop was pushed to its limit as thousands of images were compiled into a massive file. While it worked he quietly asked, "This is so much information, I'd love to delete anything that we don't need."

Dolly Jane quickly said, "No! Please don't."

Billy complained, "It's just that the file size is..."

"You don't understand." Dolly Jane interrupted, "This information has never been acquired before. This is groundbreaking research without breaking ground!"

Billy continued in a hushed tone, "It's just a scan."

Dolly's eyes were wide, but her voice soft. "Not at all! The ground under Jerusalem is considered to be holy by Christians, Jews, and Muslims. Most of what we've seen today has never been seen before and could never be seen any other way. After we retrieve the book, this subterranean map will provide very valuable archeological data."

Billy's laptop continued silently calculating and stitching. He asked, "You think of this as research?"

She whispered, "Absolutely. This is so incredible I could use it as a Master's or PhD thesis if I ever get that far."

She thought about how this find could catapult her career like Janet had done with the Dead Sea Scrolls. She couldn't wait to tell her about all of this. But then, she considered the legality of it all. Thoughts of Janet brought her back to the search for the Book of the Kings. That book was the key to finding the rest of Nehushtan. She had to stay focused. The pieces of the snake were out there. As she sat in the beautiful church, listening to a choir of tourists, she understood that she just might have the technology to find them.

She looked at Billy and said, "Let's not worry about all of that right now. Let's just find the Book of the Kings."

Just then the computer opened a box and gave Billy the option to delete or save the work.

He quickly saved the files and opened the scan. Dolly Jane was amazed at the detail within the images. They scrolled back and forth looking at power lines, tunnels and cisterns. Within a minute, Dolly Jane was lost.

She held up her hands defensively and said, "Wait. Which way is north?"

Billy tapped a few keys and a compass appeared on the screen.

Dolly Jane oriented herself and said, "Good." She pointed at the image on the screen and asked, "Where is that?"

He tapped a few more keys and the image rose above the surface onto a map of the city.

She whispered to herself, "Amazing."

"Gotta love the geeks. We are good for something!"

She smiled, "Let's go to the Western Wall. Show me the dry cisterns over there."

They found the Western Wall and looked under the Antonio Fortress at the cisterns nearby.

"Is there anything inside the dry cisterns?"

As Billy began the process of scanning, Dolly Jane put herself in the mindset of the Jewish worshipers. *This was the closest they could get to the Holy of Holies to worship God. The Six Day War opened up the Western Wall to the Jewish people and for the first time in hundreds of years, they were able to worship there. They would some day rebuild the temple.*

Billy brought up the first cistern. Rocks and debris were scattered along the floor of the vacant room.

Dolly Jane explained, "I'm hoping for a series of large ceramic canisters that look like those that were in the caves of Qumran."

Billy said, "The Dead Sea Scrolls?"

"Yes, jars were a common way to store things, but they also give clues to who owned them. At more than a dozen sites throughout Israel over 2,200 engraved jar handles have been recovered. The handles belonged to large ceramic storage jars that likely served as containers for wine, oil or wheat, the main agricultural products of the land. Stamped on the handles are seal impressions with two Hebrew words: the first word is 'Belonging to the King' the second is the name of the Judean city it was from."

While she spoke, he continued looking through the images.

She continued, "The date of their manufacture can be determined by the site of their discovery, especially from Lachish where over 400 were discovered, and the names on the handle. Sometimes a King's name or his seal is on the handle."

Billy asked, "What symbol are we looking for?"

"A couple of symbols. LMLK jar handles mean they belonged to a king."

"Excuse me?"

"Sorry, LMLK is merely transliteration of four Hebrew letters on the seals - lamed, mem lamed, laph, which are shorthand for 'belongs to the King'.

"So we are looking for Hebrew lettering?"

Dolly Jane affirmed, "Yes, and the seals of Hezekiah and Zedekiah."

"Refresh my memory. Who was Zedekiah?"

Dolly Jane said, "Zedekiah was the King of Judah when Israel was taken into exile."

"Okay. We are looking for their seals? What do they look like? "

She pulled out a piece of scratch paper and a pen as she spoke, "Hezekiah used a four winged scarab beetle, this was a common motif known in Egypt, or a two winged sun disk. Or..." She drew the symbol:

Billy looked at what she drew and scoffed, "You're kidding!"

She looked at him blankly.

"I know that symbol. It's called the Ankh. It is ancient Egyptian symbol that represents the deities of the afterlife. A few of my 'new-age' friends wore that symbol on pendants around their necks."

She smiled, "You're right, the Ankh was used in Egypt, it is a pretty major hieroglyph that was found in a lot of their tombs. But this symbol was so prevalent that it has been found in digs as far as Mesopotamia and Persia. It's even on Hezekiah's seal."

Billy said, "That doesn't make any sense. Why would an Israeli king use the symbol of an Egyptian god?"

Dolly Jane thought for a moment. She remembered this type of discussion in Janet's anthropology class. She said, "Professor Zimmerman would have said, 'Why would a Judahite king's seal have a lotus or Ankhs especially as the lotus symbol was associated with the goddess Ashera?'"

"Isn't that what I just said?

She laughed as she drew out a second image:

She asked, "What comes to mind when you see this?"

Billy stopped what he was doing and said, "The US Air Force."

Dolly Jane agreed, "Absolutely."

Billy asked, "What's your point?"

Dolly Jane said, "It's just a star, circle, and a few lines on the side. It used to symbolize the worship of stars. Does that mean that the country of America worships stars? A lot of the USA symbols have an eagle on them. Do they worship eagles?"

Billy turned back to the comfort of his computer screen.

Dolly Jane concluded, "Over centuries of use in the region, these symbols assumed generic meanings. The Ankh symbol – the one you called the Egyptian symbol – was so ubiquitous that it came to have meaning beyond the Egyptian use, just like the star symbolizes the USA, the Ankh was on Hezekiah's seal. Later in his life, it represented long life and God's protection."

Billy continued scanning the underground cavern deep underground.

He went on the look for the next cistern when Dolly Jane said, "Go back!"

"What's wrong?"

"Take a look under the floor."

"Under the floor of the last cistern?"

"Yes, look below the floor. Take your time this could be a false bottom."

Billy looked through the floor and as he explored deeper, he found only rocks for another 20 yards. Then he brought into view another dry cistern and repeated the process. Once again, the floor was irregular with a few rocks scattered around. Then he dove through the floor. It took a moment for the computer to adjust to the density changes and as it brought up the image Dolly Jane brought her hand to her mouth.

"My God."

Billy was surprised to hear her take the Lord's name in vain.

She repeated, "My God, he protected your name."

Billy remained quiet, realizing that she was speaking to God. He zoomed in and clearly saw that inside the cistern was a series of ancient jars. These were no modern pieces of pottery, they were not pieces that would have typical kitchen use, except for storage of grain or flour. Or, more importantly, they were designed by the king to store something valuable.

He panned over the whole space and saw jars lined up with as many as possible being stowed in the tight space.

Dolly Jane said, "This is it. We are in Jeremiah's cistern."

Billy asked, "I thought it was Malkijah's cistern?"

Dolly Jane said, "The King's men threw Jeremiah into the closest dry cistern as punishment for all of his harsh statements. Malkijah owned it. He was a goldsmith, a member of the royal family, and one of the family leaders who was credited in the rebuilding of the city wall. Call it whatever you like, this is the spot where Jeremiah hid the books prior to the exile."

Billy beamed with pride.

Dolly Jane said, "Look closer at the handles. Is there an inscription?"

He zoomed in to the handle on the right and saw a smooth surface with a few lines on it. They looked closer and saw that the lines made the inscription:

צדקיהו

Dolly Jane watched with her mouth open.

He moved on to the next jar. She grabbed his arm and said, "Wait, go back!!"

He panned back and focused on another jar and stopped.

She sat motionless.

Billy snickered, "What do you see? Is it like a bar code or something?"

Eventually she said, "Well, kind of. These aren't simple bar codes saying that the jar was made in China, but these markings were Zedekiah's personal mark. This jar was from the King's personal collection."

Billy said, "Jackpot!"

"Take a minute and let's look at each one of these handles." Every handle had Zedekiah's name on the right handle. The left handle showed a different symbol on each jar.

Dolly Jane opened her iPhone and while she did a quick search she explained, King Hezekiah's seal was unearthed not far from here in a trash heap near the wall of the Temple

Mount in 2015. She found the image she was looking for and brought it up to full screen.

She explained, “We are looking for something that looks like that. It’s about half a inch across.”

Billy leaned over and looked closely at her phone. He inspected the image. “I recognize the Ankh, and the winged sun, like you mentioned. Let’s look closely.”

He continued to look at jar handles, one by one. Dolly Jane looked up at the front of the church. The line down the center aisle continued to move. Each group sang one song, then moved on. The tours were like a constant flow of bodies through the church, yet the singing was incredible. The acoustics augmented the singing ability of each participant and it was as if a group of professional choirs visited one after the next.

Billy continued scanning jars. After the first row, he panned back and saw that there were four rows of jars, each with three jars. He whispered to Dolly Jane, “Twelve jars! One for each tribe?”

She shrugged her shoulders, “It was during the time of the split Kingdom, but Israel was always twelve tribes. Or it could be Jeremiah’s twelve most favored books.”

He moved in to the second row and read the handle with the following inscription:

יהדה מלך אחז בן לחזקיהו

Billy asked, “What does that mean?”

Dolly Jane translated slowly, “Belonging to Hezekiah, son of Ahaz King of Judah.”

Billy smiled ear to ear. “It’s not the symbol we were hoping for, but it’s pretty clear.”

“I think we found it.”

They gave one another a fist bump, then exploded it as their hands withdrew.

Billy focused on the jar. He measured it carefully and was certain that it would fit through a tunnel drilled by Checkers.

A motley group from the United States sang from the front of the church. Their worship song beautifully illustrated Dolly Jane’s heart. She closed her eyes and silently thanked God for their discovery.

“Now that we’ve found it. Let’s take a quick break and figure out how we can retrieve the prize.”

Billy said, “We need to decide where to tunnel from, map out a route. I also need a few supplies. Is there a auto parts store nearby?”

Dolly Jane laughed, “We’re in a city of a million people. Everything we need is here somewhere.”

# Chapter 20

## Aqua Lakeshore Apartments
## Chicago

Chase awoke from his first restful slumber since the accident. Remaining still on his bed, he thought about how best to move without causing pain. Motionless, he remained for a few minutes until his bladder convinced him to make a fateful trip to the bathroom. He reached for the end table by his bed and used it to help him sit up. He managed to sit, and eventually to stand without searing pain. He opened his eyes and smiled. Improvement was reason to celebrate. After an uneventful trip to the bathroom, he made breakfast and sat down at his computer.

He longed for rest and to be free of pain. He closed his eyes and thoughts of sun drenched beaches passed through his powerful cerebrum. He imagined another vacation scuba diving in the tropics. He felt comfortable underwater, and thought the use of scuba equipment felt like cheating at first, but he soon preferred it to any other type of aquatic exploration. While in college, he continued his scuba training for years and became a certified master diver with experience in warm and cold-water climates. As a graduation celebration, he traveled to South Australia to explore the Great Barrier Reef. While he was there he teamed up with a group of locals and explored a series of sinkholes. While underwater and in a dark and foreboding atmosphere, he felt like he truly came to life. They dove in cave after cave. He stayed long enough to join the Cave Divers Association of Australia. He had gone where the guides and dive shops had told him to stay away from, and had come out with the thrill of a lifetime.

Chase opened his eyes, sitting in his apartment he knew that he had too many questions to ask and far too much to do before he could enjoy a vacation. He gazed at the computer and sorted through the files that were still open. He saw a list of dozens of miniscule adjustments to be made on the sensors on Billy's drilling robot. He distinctly remembered having made each of these. In spite of the explosion, he was convinced that the testing was a complete success. The drilling machine was a technological wonder.

Chase spent a little time researching First Constitutional Bank in Cranbury. When he found that the facility had their safety deposit boxes on the ground level, he took a keen interest in it. He researched the security systems, focused on the number of security guards present during operating hours, and the monitoring systems they had in place around the building. He sat back and thought, *Oh, the possibilities.*

Chase took a break from his thoughts and picked up his iPhone and checked in on Billy's location. *Where is the genius today?* The tracking app clearly showed that Billy had 74% of battery life left on his phone and was in ... Jerusalem!

*Why would he be in Jerusalem?*

He wondered what his connections could be on the other side of the world. What would make him travel over there? His contacts were limited. He knew that if Billy were doing something with Checkers, the drilling he would be doing wouldn't be legal. He knew better than to text or email him. He figured that Billy would log onto the Internet through his Wi-Fi. He tracked back to Billy's ISP address and through a little computer wizardry; he traced Billy's Internet search history. He focused on what he had done since the accident.

He found sites on Biblical healing, IHOP, various injuries and medical sites. Then the focus was on something called

Nehushtan. For days Billy had searched through the Biblical stories, to healing sites, to a variety of relics and their meanings. He followed the rabbit trail down sites that entertained conspiracy theories and power in relics.

After a few hours of reviewing the sites he had visited, Chase grew tired of articles that discussed *The True Cross of Christ,* the *Holy Grail, Mary's Locks, Holy Nails, The Shroud of Turin,* the *Image of Edessa,* the *Veil of Veronica,* and the *Crown of Thorns.* He wondered if Billy may have been losing his mind when he saw a web site that focused on the *Holy Foreskin.*

Then he followed Billy as he dove into the meaning of Nehushtan. Chase not only could tell what sites Billy had been up to, but the time stamps revealed how long he spent on each one. The relics, though unique in their nature, were blitzed through in an hour, but Billy spent hours on each of the Nehushtan sites, and a total of several days looking, when he compiled all the time spent on these sites. Chase read along and followed the logic: if Moses created it with the power to heal, Hezekiah had been healed by it, and even Jesus confirmed it, this was no ordinary relic.

What would you do with the power to heal?

He thought of his suffering in the hospital. He knew for a fact that if someone had told him to look at a snake to feel better, he would have done it. He would have paid anything he had, sworn an oath, pledged whatever they asked, to receive the gift of life. As the one who endured suffering, he knew and understood the power to heal. But now that he was out of the hospital and feeling better, he wondered what it might be to wield that power himself.

Doctors stabilize the body. They remove the trauma, and the things that cause injury and pain. They allow the body to heal, but they don't heal it themselves. In cases of sickness, like diabetes they add the insulin that the body is missing, they reverse the disease processes and provide the body what it needs to be healthy. But they don't heal.

*What would he do with the power to heal?*

He would start with family and friends who he knew needed healing. Some had simple ailments like high blood pressure or thyroid disease. They could all be healed, simply by looking at the bronze snake. What about his aunt with breast cancer? Or his grandma who suffered through the treatment for lymphoma, they wouldn't need the treatments. They would simply have to look at it.

Could he use it to freely heal everybody? Logistically, everybody in the world simply couldn't see the snake. The world is too big and even if he placed it on a pole and everybody knew to look, they would have to be in the right place at the right time. Even with free healing, it is limited to those who can see it.

Chase thought for a moment about what it would be like to actually have the relic. Inevitably, there would have to be protection for the relic. It would have to be under armed guard – otherwise it would certainly be stolen. The guards would have to be paid for their service. So even as he imagined being the altruistic benefactor, doling out healing for all, there was a cost to owning the relic. It couldn't be free, either some organization would have to pay to protect the relic or there would have to be a price to see it. If it were the government giving out the relic, then they would use taxes, charging everybody to heal only some. That wouldn't be fair. He wouldn't let that happen. He had to be in control. What would the price be? Would it be a minimal cost to everyone, or just a little higher because of all the stress and logistics of owning such power? He thought of what his life would be like, he would be consumed with the logistics of getting the healing out to as many people as possible. This would be his full time occupation. Since there would be a cost, and it would take all of his time, the price of owning it is high. He would have to set the cost of using it accordingly.

Chase's mind was swimming.

He found a handful of reports that hinted at secret societies that were dedicated to finding Nehushtan. With a little further digging, separate from the investigations that Billy had done, he discovered portals into a secret society web site, then another, and finally a third. As he stumbled upon a site in Italian, Chase grinned. The limited language skills he picked up during his study abroad were enough to decipher that they were after not only the snake, and the *potere guarigione* – healing power. But much more importantly, they were after the *potere dal controllo della guarigione* – the power that comes through controlling healing.

He took his time with the site liečivýbronzovýhad.eu. Though it was written in a Moravian dialect of Slovak, used in parts of Poland, Czechoslovakia, and Serbia, the official language of Slovakia. Chase was able to use Google translate to understand that their mission statement centered on finding Nehushtan. Though he couldn't tell if this was a large group, or a bearded guy in his mother's basement, it was clear that the organization planned to control all of Slovakia with the power.

*How short sighted,* he thought. *Taking control of only one country.*

Chase concluded that there were plenty of people out there who obsessed over Nehushtan. He understood the fascination with healing. But now he was beginning to understand what they truly sought – power. He imagined his life with healing power in his hands. *What would he do with it? How would he control it? Who would he give access to it? He thought of some of the benefits. What type of house would he live in? What city would he choose? Where would he vacation? He would need a complete staff to handle everything. Who would he hire to handle the press, the schedules, and the requests for people to see Nehushtan?*

He thought about the old adage, "Power corrupts, absolute power corrupts absolutely." He knew that he would have to control the means in a way that nobody else could. He wouldn't be corrupted. He would be a loving, benevolent master.

Chase reminisced about his move to Chicago and his visit to the Intel International Science and Engineering Fair (ISEF) looking for budding talent. Billy was clearly among his intellectual peers and his ingenious digging machine set him apart. He had put his own projects on hold and decided to recruit Billy by working on his project. They both saw that the potential was amazing. Of course, this all came to an explosive and abrupt ending.

He pulled out his iPhone and sent him a quick text, "I'd love to resurrect Checkers. Just a little setback, don't you think?"

He sat back in his chair and placed his hands on his head. He tried to relax back and take a deep breath, but recoiled as he was struck with a pain in his chest. Though mostly free of the searing pain, he was still reminded of his injury. How much would he pay for a chance to look at that snake and be free of this pain?

He placed his hands on his lap and wondered what could have caused the sudden shift for Billy. He thought about his time in the hospital, in spite of the suffering, the fact that his family was there with him gave him comfort. He was thankful for them, for their prayers.

He wondered, *Who had gathered around Billy?* He researched Billy's family. His unassuming father had a limited Internet footprint. While he was certainly a character in his own right – larger than life, boisterous, opinionated, with an evangelistic generosity. He helped start a church, volunteered giving healthcare in developing nations, and provided for his family. Above all else, he was dedicated to his wife and children. He was certainly not the type of person who would chase after Nehushtan.

Chase found Billy's mother online very easily. She was active on all types of social media, living out loud. Other than active travel, and volunteer work in multiple nations, she had her political views but always seemed to make peace with those with whom she disagreed. Her life could be described in one word: Steady.

Then Chase stumbled upon Dolly Jane's work in Ein Gedi. He saw pictures of the dig site. He researched the site's long history and learned about the plethora of caves.

His eyes widened and understood, *She found part of Nehushtan!*

He stood up and thought, *Billy is scanning for the pieces, and he'll dig them up!*

He paused. His intellect was operating at a dizzying pace. He had to follow them. He could track Billy, and using his scanners, he could listen and watch from a distance. After he purchased airline tickets online, he packed a bag with all the sensor equipment he could think of. Fortunately, everything was tiny and most of his gadgets had multiple functions, scans that could detect heat, motion, even metal. He knew he could track Billy's phone and computer activity so he would watch and wait, then the healing power would be his.

He looked at the departure time for his flight and then at his watch.

No problem.
He headed to the airport.

# Chapter 21

## Old City, Jerusalem

Dolly Jane and Billy arrived back at the Lion's Gate where they had entered the Old City. They hailed a cab. After they loaded the suitcase into the trunk, Dolly Jane gave instructions in English for him to take them to the nearest auto parts store.

The driver gave her a curious look, "You don't have a car. Why do you need auto parts?"

Billy knew that if he divulged he was going to buy brake fluid and chlorine, any chemically literate person would be suspicious of him building a bomb. In Israel, with the volatility of terrorism at the tipping point, even hinting at elements to make a bomb was strictly off limits. In fact, any purchase of a combination of items that could be used for explosive purposes was tracked and investigated. Purchasing such items on a credit card immediately showed up at IDF headquarters.

Billy whispered to Dolly Jane, "I've got a plan, just go with it." He turned to the driver and answered for her, "I just need a little motor oil for my prosthetic leg."

The driver, accustomed to dealing with veterans of war was quick to say, "Thank you for your service." Not wanting to further discuss his medical condition, or bring on any embarrassment, the driver put the car in gear and sped off. In the back seat, Billy smiled at Dolly Jane. He had two perfectly good legs and had never been in the military, but he had successfully fabricated a reason to get the supplies he needed.

Dolly Jane and the driver patiently waited in the car, as Billy happily walked through the aisles of the auto parts store. Though most of the labels were in Hebrew, it wasn't too hard to recognize a few international brand names and he purchased brake fluid and motor oil. He paid in cash and returned to the taxi. Back at the trunk, he secured the brake fluid in his suitcase. Then, in order to maintain his ruse, he opened the plastic quart of 10W-30 motor oil, spilled a little on the ground, and wiped it on the cuff of his khaki pants with his fingers. When he returned to the passenger seat, the driver saw the oil on his pants and said, "You don't even walk with a limp. Your prosthesis is amazing!"

Billy smiled and said, "Thanks. In Iraq, I inspected a chemical weapons plant and was exposed to high levels of chlorine. Now I'm very sensitive to it and I think our hotel had pretty high levels. I need to run a quick water test back at the hotel. Can you take us to a swimming pool supply store?"

Without a word, the driver sped off. He traveled for about ten minutes on Highway 1 then turned on HaHevera Hakalkalit Bulevard. Dolly Jane saw that they were in the Mishor Adumim industrial zone. The buildings were square and plain. Lined up like dominoes separated by loading docks and unmarked streets. They pulled into a tight street and the driver stopped at the curb. Billy saw through the window of the store that it clearly was a swimming pool supply store.

While Billy entered the tiny store Dolly Jane waited with the driver in the car. She looked across the street and was surprised to see a sign in English advertising for the Yad Kashish Souvenir Company. She was quite familiar with the bronze and wooden souvenirs that they made and sold in stores all across Israel. She wondered why a souvenir company would be out in such an industrial location. She looked above the building and saw a smokestack pouring out white smoke.

She thought, *This is no gift shop.*

A digital sign on the side of the building read, "Danger, Smelting in Progress." She could see that this was no ordinary store. It was a factory. She imagined the machinations that took place inside and wondered what smelting meant.

Meanwhile, Billy used cash to purchase a water testing kit and a small container of granular swimming pool chlorine. He carefully concealed the contents of his bag and secured it in the suitcase in the trunk and they headed back to the hotel.

Still jet lagged, they were grateful for the rest and took a nap. After he awoke, Billy opened the suitcase. He threw away the testing kit and made a make-shift mortar and pestle using a coffee cup and a spoon to turn the granular chlorine into powder then filled Checker's tanks. Taking care to keep the two chemicals separate, he filled the other tank with the brake fluid. He added a large empty duffle bag in the suitcase and did a final check of his new retrieval and drag system that he developed just for this trip, anxious to put it to use.

When Dolly Jane woke up, she knocked on his door.

She asked Billy, "What would be the best way to tunnel into Malkijah's cistern?"

He smirked, "I thought it was Jeremiah's cistern?"

She replied, "We've been through that already."

Billy said, "Checkers is prepped and ready."

Dolly Jane asked, "Do you have enough information from the scans?"

Billy smiled, "In a bit. I'll have to sort through the scan and find the best possible route."

Dolly Jane asked, "Can we go today?"

Billy shook his head, "Tomorrow. I want to know where every rock, sewer line, and gas line is before we get started. No suprises."

Dolly Jane understood, "Absolutely."

## Tel Aviv Airport , Israel

Chase placed his passport on the small shelf that separated him from the customs agent. He truthfully explained to the customs agent that he was here to see the

Holy Land for the first time, leaving out a few salient details as he smiled at the agent. She scanned his passport and gave him a close look.

As the blue slip of paper printed off, she stamped it and slid it inside his passport and handed it back to him and said, “Enjoy your visit.”

Elsewhere within the same building, Chase Johnson’s face and passport lit up the computer screen on Colonel Macks’ desk. He had requested a search of all known associates of Dolly Jane and Billy and for them to be flagged if they traveled.

The Colonel raised his eyebrows at the sight of this new arrival. His plans for the day had changed. *Who are you and why are you in Israel?* He typed into his keyboard for a moment then picked up his phone and rattled off a few orders in Hebrew.

The customs agent held Chase’s passport in his hand and listened to Colonel Macks’ orders. After he put down the phone, he looked at Chase, “Your cell phone, please.”

Chase was surprised, “My phone? Why?”

“Routine security,” the agent said.

Reluctantly, Chase slid his phone across the countertop and the agent swiftly removed the sim card and placed it in a device that copied all the data and merged it into Chase’s file in just a few seconds. He replaced the card and waited, looking at his computer screen. Colonel Macks saw that he had access to Chase’s digital life and sent a “thumbs up” emoji to the agent who returned Chase’s phone and passport and said, “Welcome to Israel.”

Colonel Macks opened an IDF program that tracks cellular information. As part of his due diligence, he needed to know everything about Chase. Using the information from his sim card and passport, a quick background check revealed his squeaky-clean criminal record and incredible academic credentials. Colonel Macks dove into his Internet search history. He smiled, knowing that connection between the iPhone and desktop allowed more advanced searches than he had ever imagined. He didn’t have any trouble gaining access to his IP address and scrolled through every site Chase had visited within the last few days.

As a security professional in the world's capital of relic hunting, Colonel Macks was well schooled in every known relic that could be hunted. While not at the top of the list, Nehushtan was certainly among the hunts that were continuous and would forever be the bane of his existence. He knew the Biblical stories and could even quote the scriptures that referenced when Moses constructed it, how Jesus referenced it, and the fateful description of Hezekiah's destruction of it. He also believed that the bronze snake would never be found.

Nehushtan hunters commonly viewed most of the sites that Chase had visited. The Colonel had arrested people from dozens of countries for illegally digging at sites all across the country. They had tampered with the archeological process and destroyed countless ancient finds in their quest for power. Some were stealthy, looking like tourists. Others tried to blend in using traditional Jewish or Arabic garb. Some even knew the languages and customs of the region. Colonel Macks made it a practice to ignore their appearance and only pay attention to two things: their Internet search history and their behavior once in Israel. Chase had no archeological connections and no good reason to be in Israel, other than his connection with Billy and Dolly Jane. He was a Nehushtan seeker. Based on what he saw in the few minutes of research, Chase was guilty until proven innocent in the Colonel's mind. He just needed proof.

Out of curiosity, the Colonel ran a similar check on the web sites Billy and Dolly Jane had visited before thir arrival and found a great deal of overlap with Chase's. He thought, *We've got a few seekers with different agendas.*

Colonel Macks checked his watch; he had fifteen minutes before his next meeting. The work that currently occupied his desk could wait. His faithful Lieutenants took over the duties at the airport while he changed into civilian clothes and began a stealthy pursuit. Within a few minutes he was in the passenger seat of a sedan while his sergeant drove. He continued his research while he followed Chase.

Meanwhile, Chase checked his phone to determine Billy's exact location. He boarded a taxi and said, "Old City Jerusalem, Lion's Gate please."

## Old City, Jerusalem

Billy and Dolly Jane returned to their favorite Hookah bar and settled into a booth. After they ordered cappuccinos, Billy scooted out of the booth, grabbed his suitcase and said, "I'll be right back." He entered the men's room and remaining fully clothed he sat down on the stool, opened the suitcase, and removed the robot. He gave it a cursory examination and noted that everything looked pristine and functional, the drilling surface eager to engage the rock below.

His mind drifted to the fateful day in Chicago outside the stadium when the explosion happened. He silently remembered Chase and Maddy. If only they could be here, they would see the practical application of their efforts. A tear formed on the lateral aspect of his left eye.

Billy took a deep breath and regained his composure. He placed Checkers on the tile floor and turned it on. After a brief scan, Billy could clearly see plumbing pipes to the right and left, but nothing directly below. He tapped away on his laptop and Checkers rumbled then sank into the floor and disappeared. The initial grinding sound dissipated as she sank into the earth. There was no pile of dirt to yield evidence of the drilling, rather a well-crafted tunnel developed behind her. He smiled at the speed and ease in which Checkers operated. With a few taps on the computer, he had Checkers pause for a moment as she constructed a circular tile to seal off the tunnel behind her. He took a tiny jar of paint and a brush and camouflaged the cover to look exactly like the tile floor around it. He paused Checker's progress and packed up his laptop, closed the suitcase and exited the stall. He washed his hands to keep up the rouse then joined Dolly Jane back to the table.

"How's progress in the bathroom?"

Billy smiled. He stared at the screen for a moment and tapped a few keys on his laptop starting the robot's progress once again. Then looked at Dolly Jane, "Checkers is heading straight down bypassing all the power lines, gas lines, and every rock or piece of slate that has been put in the ground since Abraham brought Isaac here 4000 years ago. Then she'll tunnel straight over to Malkijah's property and up to the base of the cistern. We can retrieve your choice of artifacts from there one at a time."

"Only one today," Dolly Jane said.

It took about an hour for the robot to tunnel her way under the Old City to her destination. Dolly Jane was intrigued, she watched the analysis on the screen and appreciated that the semi-independent robot was doing her duty. She asked, "Where is she right now?"

Billy scrolled over and opened another socket. The computer overlaid the underground scan with the map of the Old City and Checker's location. Billy panned out so they could see the Hookah bar, Checker's location, and the cistern. He even sketched in a blue line to make Dolly Jane feel like she was on a trip guided by Google maps.

Once they were under the cistern, they viewed the array of priceless relics. Dolly Jane pointed out the jar with Hezekiah's insignia on the handle. Billy tunneled directly underneath the jar and guided Checkers through a series of robotic calisthenics to gently capture the jar, secure it with a thin inflatable nylon pillow-like protective compartment and drag it using a short leash into the tunnel. Billy was grateful that he had the ability to measure the relic before retrieving it and it happened to be small enough to fit through the tight space. Checkers was then essentially a tugboat that brought the treasure all the way back to the Hookah bar.

"Excuse me," Billy smiled, "I feel the need to return to the restroom."

He paid another visit to the bathroom stall and found it vacant. Checker's return trip was quick, without any digging, she could swiftly drag the relic through the tunnel. He tapped gently around the edged of the circular tile to loosen it then lifted it like a manhole cover. Checkers rolled out like a well-trained dog that had just performed her work and earned her rest. Billy placed her in the suitcase then reached in and retrieved the rope that held the relic. He pulled the entire protective casing from the tunnel, and placed it into the duffel bag. He was pleased with how the protective casing had functioned, but inspection of the relic would have to wait. He tapped the manhole cover back into place.

With his work complete, he departed the bathroom. He looked like a confused tourist with his two large bags. Dolly

Jane met him outside the bathroom, slung the duffel bag over her shoulder and led him outside. They walked back through the city towards the Lion's Gate.

Behind them, Chase was leaning against a wall with a Hebrew newspaper in his hands, trying to look like he was waiting for a friend. After Dolly Jane and Billy walked away, he followed at a short distance.

Twenty yards behind Chase, Colonel Macks sat in the shade of a maple tree sipping sade kahve, his favorite Turkish coffee. When Chase moved, the large man dropped a few sheckles on the table as he rose to follow him.

Billy hailed a taxi and he took the shotgun seat while Dolly Jane climbed comfortably in the back. She texted Janet, "Great day today. Lots to tell you!" In silent anticipation, they returned to their hotel.

Chase patiently remained out of sight keeping a close eye on his iPhone. He noted that the pair had gone into the Old City with one bag, and had come out with two. He waited until Dolly Jane and Billy arrived at the Jerusalem Dan Hotel, then followed in a separate taxi.

Colonel Macks also noted the accumulation of additional baggage without doing any shopping. The Colonel was concerned about the numerous laws they had broken and had somehow acquired something they were protective of. He considered making the arrest right then and there but he didn't know what they had stolen, or what relevance it had in the grand scheme of relic hunting. Certainly, the item in the duffle bag would be kept with them. These two were easy to follow and easier to catch. He knew that he could arrest them at any time. He was intrigued and decided to allow them to study it, and reveal what it was along with why they had acquired it.

He made a quick text and within a few minutes, a Sergeant swung by in a military sedan to return him to his office.

# Chapter 22

## Jerusalem
## Jerusalem Dan Hotel

Chase entered the Jerusalem Dan Hotel, unimpressed with the foyer, he watched his phone for Billy's exact position. He sat down in one of the comfortable chairs, and pulled out a device about the size of his iPhone. He scanned the building, but realized that looking for two people with luggage would be a completely impossible task in a hotel. He thought about what Billy would have that would be unique, and set his sensors to specifically look for propylene glycol. Though the quantity was small, even a tiny hit would give away his position. He set it so that every aliquot of the chemical would show up, and nothing else.

He could see cars in the parking lot. The radiators lit up like a Christmas tree. He scanned the bank of rooms in section A and on the second floor saw a tiny vial light up. He honed in on that position, and then reset the sensors, so that he could see thermal imaging in the same space. He saw two red, orange, and yellow images. One was drinking a glass of cold blue liquid; the other enjoyed something red hot. He reset the sensor to the propylene glycol again, and zoomed in to see it closely. It was difficult to tell how much was there, or what surrounded it. He shifted the sensing to only see metal structures. The propylene glycol disappeared, but the area around it lit up. Looking closely, he could see the drill head.

*Bingo*! He had found them. He scanned the rooms nearby and on the floor above them. He found an open room one floor above them, a perfect place to monitor everything they would be doing.

Chase picked up his bag and approached the desk to check in to the hotel. He told the clerk that he had previously stayed in room 323 and would like to have the same room again, if it was available. The clerk granted his request. After a few minutes he handed him the key and welcomed him to the Jerusalem Dan Hotel. Chase walked casually to his room where he would watch and wait.

## Tel Aviv Airport , Israel

Colonel Macks changed back into his military uniform and hunched over his laptop. He watched three separate views from the cameras in the room. From the camera placed just above the door, he could see the hallway, dresser, TV, and parts of the desk. The camera mounted within the TV showed the bed and living space clearly and the view from the headboard showed the rest. Though the audio wasn't pristine, he could make out what they were saying.

He watched in real time as Billy unwrapped the urn and placed it on the bed and examined it. The urn was a historical relic, the handle clearly had the mark of King Zedekiah. Dolly Jane donned cotton gloves and delicately ran her fingers over the markings on the handle, she dusted if off and examined it closely.

## Jerusalem
## Jerusalem Dan Hotel

Billy stood next to Dolly Jane and waited.

She carefully photographed the urn. Turned it ninety degrees and photographed it again. She repeated the process until every angle was documented.

"Aren't you going to open it?"

"Don't be myopic. We are doing much more than looking for clues to a treasure hunt. This jar, by itself is an amazing find. In the Lacish dig site, they found hundreds of jars marked with Hezekiah's insignia. The collection told us countless pieces of information from which a large amount of the dealings with his Kingdom have been able to be reconstructed.

Billy looked analytically at the jar and said, "The easiest way to protect the scroll and get access to it would be to carefully section the porcelain jar."

"Never!" Dolly Jane was deeply offended. "A relic like this must be preserved."

She applied a modicum of pressure to the lid and it didn't move. Closer inspection revealed that the lid was sealed to the urn with wax. Dolly Jane smiled, certainly this made for perfect preservation of the contents. She tilted the canister forty-five degrees to the side and held her lighter underneath the wax seal. Slowly and patiently, the guardian of the urn relinquished its duty and the seal silently broke. She gave a slight twist and lifted the lid off the urn. Light and oxygen flowed into the canister for the first time in over 2500 years. They brought not only the revelation of modern technology, but also all the degradation factors that come with exposure to the elements.

One at a time, the explorers peeked inside and viewed the contents. Deep within the cavernous jar they could see the rolls of some type of scroll.

Carefully, Dolly Jane reached in with a non-toothed forceps designed for delicate operations. The ancient goatskin was coiled and content with its shape. Resistant to motion, it threatened disintegration if handled without care and respect.

Dolly Jane took her time and placed the rolled up document on the bed. After photographing it, she examined it carefully and dusted the exposed portions with a paintbrush. She taught as she worked, "The scorched scrolls from the explorations of Mt. Vesuvius have been read using computer tomography with a synchrotron in Grenoble. They used a particle accelerator to detect minute deviations in the surface of the scrolls without unrolling them."

Billy added, "Mt. Vesuvius cooked everything instantly. How did they recover any books at all?"

Dolly Jane said, "They were burnt to the point of looking like pieces of charred wood. This maintained the shape and made it possible to digitally unroll and read the document."

Billy said, "Are we going to have to bring it home and spend weeks analyzing it?"

"We'll see in a minute." She loosened the brown leather strap that tied the bundle together. As the swede fell to the bed sheet she saw that the scroll was intact, without signs of flaking or tearing. The edges were roughened, having been bent slightly from resting in its sepulcher for ages, yet it retained flexibility. Dolly Jane inserted the atzei chayim, the traditional wooden dowels designed for scrolls, and gently began the process of opening the scroll.

Dolly Jane said, "We will know soon. This is going to be a Jewish scroll, they traditionally wrote on skins, not parchment. They always used the skin of a kosher animal, usually either a goat or sheep. They were meticulous in the preparation and management of the skins, then in the diction and calligraphy of the lettering. Nothing was more important to the scribes than perfection in their scrolls. The Torah scroll contains 304,805 letters, or approximately 79,000 words. It takes 2000 hours of meticulous hand-copying to produce one copy. That's about one year of work for a dedicated individual."

"So, what's the plan?"

"Let me take a look. If I can unroll it, we'll be fine. If not, then I'll get some help." She picked up her phone and texted Janet again.

She worked the edges slowly and was pleased that the skin was supple and flexible. She began to unroll it with utmost care and a minor crack appeared in the middle. She stopped. She wrapped her travel make-up case in a sock and used it to gently hold down the edge of the skin. It wasn't a scientific method, and was far from sterile, but it protected the document well. She repeated the process with another sock protected weight. The crack didn't change. The document was pliable enough to roll out slowly. Since she didn't cause any further cracks, she proceeded.

She was able to see the lettering starting at the right side. After a few hours of carefully working the ancient document, Dolly Jane had rolled out several feet of the scroll.

She and found the title on the top right:

*גדאי קינגסאוף אתה אוף היסטורי תה אוף בוק*

Dolly Jane translated, "The Book of the History of the Kings of Judah." She thought, *This may be the original or it could be the only copy of the book of the Kings.*

There was no sense in reading the text of this book since it would have to be photographed and diligently documented. There was plenty of time for that later. Right now, they needed to simply discover what it was that lay on the hotel bed. Indeed, normally experts from all over the world would meticulously analyze a text of this importance.

Dolly Jane continued working the relic until she laid it out from one end of the bed to the other. Fortunately, a natural separation in the manuscript allowed her to break the document into two sections and she worked out the second portion in a line under the first.

While she worked, Billy commented. "Isn't it strange that the beginning is on the right side?"

Dolly Jane spoke without looking up, "Arabic, Persian, Urdu, and Hebrew languages are written right to left. Once you get used to it, it's pretty easy. The hardest part was the first few weeks of Hebrew school. In addition learning to cough up phlegm whenever I said the 'ch' sound, I felt like my world was spinning because I was reading backwards."

With the entire document laid out she photographed the book. After she downloaded the images to her tablet, she sat at the desk and stared at the screen. She magnified the image and looked closely at the lettering first looking at the whole document, then piece by piece, scanning the language and style. She told Billy, "Some of it is in Hebrew, but a fair amount is written in Aramaic."

Billy shook his head. "What do we do now?"

Dolly Jane grinned, "We read it, silly!" She dove into the text and engaged in the first few lines.

Billy asked, "Why do you know Aramaic?

Dolly Jane said, "My teachers told me I was wasting my tine, but I learned it on my own."

Billy said, "I remember the 2004 Mel Gibson film *The Passion of the Christ* used Aramaic for its dialogue. Other than that, nobody uses it."

"You'd be surprised, it isn't a dead language. There is a small population of Jews, Syriac Christians, and Mandaeans of Western Asia who still speak Neo-Aramaic as their first language. Somewhere south of a million people, but almost all of them are beyond retirement age and the remnants of the language could go extinct within a generation."

Billy said, "So it's a dying language."

Dolly Jane smiled, "Aramaic was Jesus' primary language. He spoke the Galilean dialect during his public ministry – the seven distinct colloquial Aramaic dialects have sometimes been considered separate languages."

Billy said, "I suppose someone from Boston would consider a person from Biloxi to be speaking a foreign language too."

Dolly Jane smiled as she slowly examined the text.

"Why did you learn it?"

Dolly Jane said, "I learned Hebrew and Greek, so I could read the original Biblical text. I loved it and was in the mode of learning languages. Then I found out that there are four discrete sections of the Bible written in Aramaic: Ezra, Daniel, Jeremiah, and Genesis, I figured I would learn Aramaic too."

Billy said, "And I thought I was a nerd!"

Dolly Jane gave him a knowing grin, "You are."

Billy said, "You mentioned Jeremiah. This ancient book was most likely handled by Jeremiah himself! He's the one who stored it in the cistern to protect it when Jerusalem fell and the people were taken into exile."

"Yes, that's right."

Billy inquired, “Tell me about the part that Jeremiah wrote in Aramaic.”

Dolly Jane said, “Most people just know Jeremiah as the prophet of doom. Some have even memorized Jeremiah 29:11 where God declares:

> I know the plans I have for you, plans to prosper and not to harm you.

Billy nodded, “I’ve heard that promise referenced before. It’s a very encouraging passage.”

Dolly Jane continued to work the skin as she spoke. “Jeremiah 10:11 is in Aramaic:

> Tell them this: ‘These gods, who did not make the heavens and the earth, will perish from the earth and from under the heavens.’

Dolly Jane continued, “This single sentence is written in Aramaic in the middle of an otherwise entirely Hebrew book. For some reason, Jeremiah felt it necessary to condemn idolatry in Aramaic.”

Billy affirmed, “There is no shortage of condemnation of idolatry in the Old Testament.”

Dolly Jane said, “Jeremiah was speaking not only to the Hebrew people, but to all the surrounding region. Putting it in the language most often used by the surrounding communities, he was clearly talking to them. The people of Israel only spoke Hebrew, but the businessmen and leaders who had to deal with the outsiders also were fluent in Aramaic. This is why in Hezekiah’s time the Persian General Sennacherib spoke all kinds of nasty things to the Jews on the wall using Hebrew. The Jewish leaders begged him to speak in Aramaic, so that the regular people wouldn’t be scared off by his taunting.”

Billy asked, “Hezekiah’s war story rocks!”

Dolly Jane said, “Any war story that ends with the instant death of 185,000 men is pretty amazing.”

. . . . .

One floor up, in room 323, Chase watched with his thermal imaging. The microphone picked up the sounds through the floor. It sounded as if he were in the room with them. Though he was new to the study of relics, he was certainly aware that he was in the presence of greatness as they read the Book of the Kings out loud.

He rolled his eyes as they waxed on about dialects and stories. He didn't care what language it was written in, but was eager to see if Hezekiah would make a contribution to the search for Nehushtan. He took a deep breath. The pain in his chest from his broken ribs persisted; it was manageable with a hefty dose of pain medication. He lay supine on the bed and listened.

. . . . .

Dolly Jane thought out loud, "This is clearly the Book of the Kings. I've scanned a fair amount of it and there are plenty of passages from King Abijah, Jehoshaphat, Jehoram, Ahaziah, and Asa."

Billy pondered, "Those are kings who don't have much air time in the Bible."

Dolly Jane focused, "I really would love to read this whole document but right now we are looking for Hezekiah."

"Hezekiah is after Ahaz." Billy said. "You're getting close."

Dolly Jane laughed as she read, "Some of the passages are long lists of purchases. Gold, horses, wheat. All kinds of things are recorded. They even had monkeys in the King's court for a while."

"Monkeys?"

"Unless I'm reading it wrong."

"I'm hoping you are. Skip a bit and see if you can find anything by Hezekiah."

"Patience young one."

Billy paced back and forth in the hotel room while Dolly Jane stared at the words.

Eventually she found it:

# 0yqzx

She exclaimed, "I found him!"

"Who?"

"Hezekiah!"

# Chapter 23

## Jerusalem
## Jerusalem Dan Hotel

Billy rushed over and asked, “What do you see?”

Dolly Jane said, “After a while, I can just see the words and read them without translating.”

“That’s great. What do you see?”

“So far, it’s just his name. Let me digest this a bit more.”

She dug into the text for the remainder of the day. She focused on the enlarged images on her tablet. There were plenty of actuarial lists. She scanned over a lot of kingly duties. In small font she saw a long list of awards that were given out to various builders, architects, and soldiers. Then she saw a poem that was quite different from the rest of the documented items.

Dolly Jane saw something different and looked up at Billy, “It looks like our favorite king was also a poet.”

“What do you mean?”

“Take a look at this script.” She directed his attention to a section of the text that was completely set aside, different in font, handwriting, and style.

Billy looked it over and noted it looked like poetry. He said, “It reminds me of the Psalms.”

“Absolutely.”

She took her time translating the entire poem. Billy could see that she was definitely in a zone and wouldn't be coming up for air any time soon. He slipped out and grabbed a hot chocolate from the local café.

. . . . .

Chase rolled his eyes. He slipped down to the cafeteria and enjoyed a Kosher dinner. He thoroughly enjoyed a comforting bowl of Matzoh Ball soup, then a spicy Shakshuka with potato latkes, a side of figs and fried artichokes and braided Challah bread. For desert he savored a chocolate rugelach. All the while, he made mental pictures of his diet when he had a team of minions in his own personal gourmet kitchen.

. . . . .

Colonel Macks sat in his office. He searched Chase first and found where he was located in the hotel. Then he tapped in through the cameras on their phones, laptops, and tablets and watched Dolly Jane, Billy, and Chase closely. Expectant that something would change quickly, he buzzed through his daily barrage of email, moved up his scheduled Lieutenant meeting, and blitzed through his daily tasks.

. . . . .

After an hour Billy returned to find Dolly Jane sitting in an oversized armchair sideways with her feet tucked under her. She held her iPhone with both hands and her thumbs worked furiously.

Billy asked, "How's progress?"

When she saw him she jumped in the chair and her feet landed on the floor. She said, "Oh you've got to see this! The poem is the key." Together they shared the chair and looked at her tablet as she continued, "I wrote the words down left to right, that way the translation comes easier. Take a look at this." She turned the tablet towards him.

ðiː mɛtəl biːst ɪz eɪ dɪˈsiːvəɹ
eɪ sneɪk n evrɪ sɛns əv ðiː wɝd

ət spəʊk swiːt wɝd wɪð prɒmɪs əv laɪf
bʌt brɔt deθ n ðiː ɛnd

ət wəz eɪ snâr tu ðiː priːst
eɪ hʊk n ðiː maʊð əv ðiː raɪtʃəs

ʃʊd nɛvɛɹ hæv bɪn kɛpt
brəʊkən wɪð ðiː sɪn ðæt brɔt ðiː venəm

fɪfˈtiːn jiəɹz ði lɔɹd geɪv mi θrʌf ðiː wɔrɚ sneɪk
wɪð tɛn stɛp heɪ pɹəʊv hɪz eɪθ

ðiː haʊz ʌv gɒd ɪz tʊ hæv eɪ swiːt əˈroʊmə
ðiː plɛzənt smɛl ðæt ɹiˈfɹɛʃ ðiː səʊl

nɒt ðiː smɛl əv sneɪks
nɔːɹ ðiː əˈroʊmə əv aɪdəl

aɪ stɻʌk ət ɪntʊ tltb piːs
ðiː kɪŋz hɪmˈsɛlf wɪð eɪ hæmər n hænd

aɪ brəʊk ðiː wɪkt sneɪk fəɹˈɛvɚ
ðiː bɹeɪk tʊ ˈbɹɪŋ daʊn ðiː aɪdəl

bɪˈniːθ ðiː ˈtʃænəl diːp bɪˈtwiːn ðiː sprɪŋ ænd leɪk
meɪ wɑrɚ ænd stəʊn ˈkəvɜ ət fəɹˈɛvɚ

Gɔd rɪmembər mi foʊɹ maɪ ˈstɛdfəst ɹɪˈzɒlv tʊ ˈɒnə joʊɹ neɪm
lɛt ðiː piːs ɪˈmeɪn n ðeər gɹeɪv fəɹˈɛvɚ

Billy had a blank stare

"Don't you see it?"

"See what? What you've written out is as unreadable as the original manuscript."

"It's Hezekiah's poem."

"It's gibberish."

"Just kidding. I've done the translation. It's the meaning that will take some time to decipher." Her fingers danced over the tablet and she opened a second window then handed the tablet to Billy and commanded, "Read."

Slowly, he read out loud:

*The metal beast is a deceiver*
*A snake in every sense of the word*

*It spoke sweet words with promises of life*
*But brought death in the end*

*It was a snare to the priests*
*A hook in the mouth of the righteous*

*Should never have been preserved*
*Annihilated with the sin that brought the venom*

*Fifteen years God granted me through the slippery serpent*
*With ten steps He proved His faithfulness*

*The house of God is to have a sweet aroma*
*The pleasant scent that refreshes the soul*

*Not the stench of snakes*
*Nor the smell of idolatry*

*I struck it into three pieces*
*The King himself with hammer in hand*

*I destroyed the wicked snake forever*
*The fracture to bring down the idol*

*Beneath the foundation the worm is dead*
*The armies never to conquer it*

*Beneath the channel deep between the spring and lake*

*May water and stone drown them forever*

*Lord remember me for my steadfast resolve to honor only you*
*Let the pieces remain in their graves forever*

. . . . .

Back at his office, Colonel Macks watched in rapt attention. Stunned by what he was hearing, he lost track of what Billy said. He took solace in knowing that the conversation was being recorded. He would certainly replay everything later.

He reviewed his favorite passages in Numbers 21, 2 Kings 18-20, and 2 Chronicles 29-32. Then logged into the web site BronzeGod.com. After entering his login and password as the web master and administrator for the site, the screen lit up with a dozen messages from around the world. He sorted through the casual observers and conspiracy theorists and eventually found messages from other believers. Nobody had any recent news of any archeological findings. He wondered if the Bronze Snake would ever be found.

. . . . .

Billy was pacing back and forth in the room as he read. Dolly Jane sat back and sighed, "There's a lot there to process. *The metal beast spoke sweet words but brought death*!" She pointed a little farther down on the page, "You remember Hezekiah's story, he was healed from anthrax and received fifteen years added onto his life, he certainly used the snake for the healing!"

Billy said, "And it was confirmed with the sign of the shadow going back. It's pretty clear that the line *with ten steps he proved his faithfulness* is about the confirmation by the shadow moving back ten steps." He looked up and said, "It's like a poem about his life!"

Billy read out loud, "I love the line, '*I struck it into three pieces. The King himself with hammer in hand.*' You've just gotta love that. Very masculine."

Dolly Jane chuckled, "You're becoming a Hezekiah groupie!"

Billy laughed and continued, *"I destroyed the wicked snake forever. The fracture to bring down the idol."*

"There are lots of clues in there!" Dolly Jane said. "We know that it was three pieces! That's never been reported before! Everybody assumed it was a few pieces, but we never knew how many or where to look for them!"

Billy agreed, "Three pieces."

Dolly Jane declared, "In archeological circles, that discovery alone would spawn a dozen articles in various respected Archeological journals and might even be the topic for an international conference."

Billy continued, "The King wanted everybody to know that he was intimately involved with it. He says that he broke the snake himself. The following lines confirm it twice: first he says *destroyed the wicked snake forever.* Then he repeats himself with *fracture to bring down the idol.*"

Dolly Jane confirmed, "In Hebrew poetry, the style is to generally say the most important points twice. So we know that it was important enough to repeat. She continued reading. *Beneath the foundation the worm is dead. The armies never to conquer it."*

Billy looked up and asked, "What does he mean beneath the foundation the worm is dead?"

Dolly Jane narrowed her gaze, "Calling a snake a worm would be an insult. To Hezekiah, the worm was the lowest of snakes. He was semantically diminishing it."

Dolly Jane grew impatient, "So where did he hide the pieces?"

Billy wondered, "*The foundation* could refer to a building."

Dolly Jane thought for a moment then said, "Or *the foundation* could have been the very start of something. Possibly the temple?"

Billy said, "He wouldn't dig under the foundation. He must have put it under the foundation of something major that he was building. But the only major construction project that Hezekiah built was –"

Dolly Jane declared, "The Broad Wall."

They made eye contact and said in unison, "He hid it under the wall."

Dolly Jane almost dropped her tablet. She squealed and gave Billy a hug.

She said, "That makes perfect sense. He was building a huge wall. It was one that could never be torn down. Bigger than any other structure in the country. It expanded the city from 32 acres all the way to 125 acres. The wall is older than the Ottoman Old City Wall, 2700 years ago. The discovery of Hezekiah's Broad Wall represented one of the most rare and satisfying occasions when archaeology reveals something that nobody can deny appears in the Biblical story."

Billy added, "He did everything he could to protect his city."

If he wanted to hide the pieces of Nehushtan in a place that would never be found, the city wall was a great place for it. He could even brag that he put it under the wall, and in his day, nobody would ever find it!"

Billy tapped on Checker's suitcase and said, "Until now."

Dolly Jane thought about the wall. She said, "The foundations remaining today are 10 feet tall and 20 feet wide. If you don't know what you are looking at, it seems like nothing more than a pile of rocks. But in fact, it is a part of Hezekiah's masterpiece in protecting the homeland. Tourists hurry by without bothering to glance at it."

Billy nodded.

Dolly Jane continued, "The Wall protected Jerusalem from the Assyrian army as it grew. The small contingent of men was added to over and over again until the vast army boasted 200,000 men. Hezekiah's wall separated the Israelite army from the Assyrian army when 185,000 Assyrian men were slaughtered. An angel walked through their camp with death in his hand. In a single night he obliterated the largest army to ever come against Jerusalem. You can read about it in the Bible, or in the annals of Sennacherib in Babylon. The record is clear. Jerusalem was saved."

Billy added “Hezekiah did everything he could. For years he prepared. He sacrificed in order to have food stored up. He dug the tunnel to bring water into the city. He built the wall. But most of all, when it came right down to the time of crisis, Hezekiah went into the temple and laid out his request before God. He spent time there. It was not a quick prayer. Not something he did to check the box and say, ‘Yes I prayed.’ He poured out his heart before the Lord his God!”

Dolly Jane looked at Billy and said, “Think about it for a minute. Pilgrims to the Holy Land carry a cross down the Via Dolorosa to reenact Jesus’ last hours. While this isn’t quite at that level of spiritual importance, they could do the same at the Broad Wall. They could reenact Sennacherib’s mocking and the soldier’s steadfast faith right there on the Broad Wall.

Billy concluded, “God showed up and protected his people.”

Dolly Jane said, “There should be a museum dedicated to Hezekiah right next to the excavation of the Broad Wall in the Old City of Jerusalem.”

. . . . .

Chase returned to his room and continued monitoring the treasure hunters. He traced back through the recordings and noted everything that he had missed.

. . . . .

Dolly Jane re-focused, “Let’s start by scanning the excavated portions in the middle of Jerusalem!”

Billy opened his laptop and said, “We may already have part of it with the scans we’ve already done.”

Dolly Jane said, “It was a long wall. There’s a fair amount of distance to look over. Archaeologists only uncovered 213 feet of the wall in the middle of the Old City. That’s the part that we can see from the railing in the Jewish quarter of Jerusalem, but the endeavor to protect the city was closer to 2000 feet."

Billy agreed, "That's a lot of wall. Good thing we can scan without digging."

Dolly Jane beamed, "Now that we know where to look. We can map it out. There can't be very many pieces of bronze under the Broad Wall!"

Billy said, "Excellent! We can start that tomorrow."

Dolly Jane took a deep breath. It wasn't lost on her that they had made more progress on this discovery in one day than in the previous 2700 years. She thought about packing up Checkers and heading over there right away.

Billy interrupted her thoughts, "What about the other two pieces? Certainly he hid different pieces in different locations. What does it say?"

Dolly Jane read, "*Beneath the channel deep between the spring and lake. May water and stone drown them forever.*"

Billy was puzzled. "There aren't any lakes near here. What is he talking about? The Sea of Galilee or the Dead Sea?"

Dolly Jane's eyes traveled up and to the left as she dug deep into her vast expanse of linguistic minutia. "The Aramaic word for lake is the same word that they used for pond and puddle. Really it's any freshwater body of water."

Billy pointed to a glass of water on the counter, "Pass me the lake, I'm thirsty?"

Dolly Jane ignored him, "The 'lake' he's talking about has a channel under the ground and a spring on the other end." Her eyes widened.

Billy said, "What?"

Dolly Jane declared, "The lake is the Pool of Siloam. That's certainly Hezekiah's other major construction project. He chipped and hauled limestone rocks from the Gihon Spring underground all the way into the city. He made a *Channel Deep between the spring and lake.* He created The Pool of Siloam when he brought water into the city. This was all to help them survive the impending Babylonian siege led by Sennacherib."

Billy's jaw dropped.

Dolly Jane's eyes widened, "He hid the snake somewhere near Hezekiah's tunnel!"

Dolly Jane threw her hands into the air. She gave Billy a bear hug and screamed in delight.

Billy said, “Let’s go find the rest of Nehushtan!”

Dolly Jane looked for her phone, “I’ve got to call Janet.”

. . . . .

Chase dropped his iPhone when he heard Billy say, “The rest of Nehushtan!” He thought, *They already have a piece.*

He looked around the room. Surely nobody was competing for the pieces. There were just two kids, no security, and not a worry in the world. He made plans to watch and wait until they had collected the pieces.

*Healing is power.*

*I’m going to be rich!*

He began formulating plans for his empire.

. . . . .

Janet’s phone went to voicemail.

Dolly Jane texted her, “I really need to talk with you.”

She turned to Billy, “Something’s wrong. Janet never ignores her phone. I’ve texted her countless times now, and haven’t heard anything at all.”

Billy said, “Why don’t you visit with her?”

Dolly Jane agreed, “I’ve got the address of the place she stays in the Old City. I’ve never been there, but she told me where it was, pretty easy to find.”

Billy said, “Go ahead.”

Dolly Jane checked her watch and shook her head, “It’s too late. I’ll head over there first thing in the morning.”

“No problem. I can scan the wall while you visit with her.”

“Okay. Let’s get some shut-eye. It should be another big day tomorrow.”

. . . . .

Colonel Macks' mind was racing like a motorcycle on a windy road. *Hezekiah buried the pieces!*

He burst to his feet, flinging his chair against the bookshelf behind him like a cigarette butt. He took a step to the side, then returned. He leaned over and placed his fists firmly on the desktop.

He thought, *The pieces of the bronze snake weren't destroyed, they were hidden. The treasure hunters were right. They really could be found! Dolly Jane already had found one of the three pieces. It wouldn't be long until they found the rest.*

He stood upright and thought, *This changes everything. Healing power is real. Nehushtan is real.*

He thought through the quirks of the Nehushtan seekers that he had known about for years. He had always written off their proclamations of grandeur as schizophrenic, delusional, and narcissistic. Now he realized that all this time, they were seeking a real and anointed Biblical relic that actually does exist and conveys God's healing power. They were correct all along.

He thought through the mission statements and bizarre plans they had once they found Nehushtan. While they may be crazy, and unsafe, and utterly the wrong people to wield healing power, he recognized that they were searching for the same thing he was: a connection with God. Healing.

Suddenly, he realized that the young siblings he was following were not only correct – they were in danger.

He thought, *If they find the other two pieces, they will need help, guidance, protection. This is so much larger than either of them could possibly imagine.*

He typed out a series of email messages to his lieutenants. He explained that he would be taking a few personal days and would be unavailable. He closed his laptop, stashed it in his satchel and left the building.

# Chapter 24

## Hadassah Medical Center
## Jerusalem

Janet opened her eyes and saw that she was once again in a hospital bed. She had been released on oral medications, but once again took a downward turn and was readmitted. It took her some time before she remembered where she was. She tapped on her phone and saw a litany of text messages from Dolly Jane. She checked voicemail and was grateful for the transcription feature on the phone. Her voicemail messages echoed the texts: Dolly Jane had found something.

She tapped the phone a few times until she saw Dolly Jane's smiling face. She dialed the number. The IV tubing restricted her arms, she was unable to bring the phone to her ear so she put it on speaker.

"Janet? Where have you been? I've been trying to contact you!"

"I'm fine. I'd love it if you could come visit me."

"Absolutely. I checked your apartment in the Old City, you're not there. Where are you?"

"You've been worried about me?"

"Are you kidding? You don't answer my texts or calls. After what we found, and the security issues that go with it, I'm very worried!"

"I'm fine," she repeated. It wasn't a lie, she had convinced herself that in spite of her ailments, she would conquer this and move on. "I'm at Hadassah Medical Center in Jerusalem." She looked at the label next to the open door, "Room 8517."

"Oh my word! What's wrong? Are you hurt?"

"I'm not hurt. I've just got a little medical issue. I'll tell you all about it when you come."

"I'll be right there."

Dolly Jane relayed the conversation to Billy. He said, "Go ahead. I can get started with the scanning and let you know what I find."

They walked to the lobby together and got in different cabs, Dolly Jane headed to the hospital, Billy to the Old City.

. . . . .

Billy enjoyed being in the Old City by himself. He hunkered down in a Hookah bar opened his laptop and started scanning – he was in his comfort zone. He enjoyed the cultural aspect of the different personal expressions around him. He scanned the region efficiently. He checked the map and figured out a plan for his day, hopping from one coffee shop or Hookah bar to another, all across the Old City.

Eventually, he overlaid the maps that showed the Broad Wall's position and scanned one position after the next. His scans looked like a Venn diagram, overlapping circles all across the map. The computer was once again pushed to its limits with incredible amounts of information being retrieved, stored and stitched together. The manipulation of the data became routine as Billy continued his progress, one location after the next.

. . . . .

Dolly Jane arrived in the hospital room and was shocked by Janet's appearance. She was in a hospital gown, with an intravenous in her right arm, she didn't portray the image of the strong professor that Dolly Jane had always seen. Here, she was weak and vulnerable – a patient.

Dolly Jane exclaimed, "What's going on? What happened?"

Janet gave a weak smile to her protégé. Dolly Jane wanted to give her a hug, but with all the equipment, wires, and tubing, she settled for a gentle grasp of Janet's hand.

Janet said, "I'm fine. Don't worry about me."

Dolly Jane was shocked. Before she could retort, a clean-cut gentleman approached Janet's bedside with a nurse at his side. He introduced himself to Dolly Jane, "I'm Dr. Ben Wildenstein." Dolly Jane shook his hand.

He addressed Janet, "You're looking better than when we first met."

Janet replied, "Thanks, I think."

Dolly Jane stepped back, a flurry of questions in her mind. She waited while the doctor spoke.

He continued, "It appears that you gave the community at the Holy Café a scare. You collapsed and they brought you here. We stabilized you with IV fluid and steroids. There was no evidence of any trauma to your body, but you certainly need more testing to see why you collapsed."

Janet interrupted him, "MS."

"I see," Dr. Wildenstein's eyes widened. "Multiple sclerosis is an unpredictable, often disabling disease of the central nervous system that disrupts the flow of information within the brain, and..."

Janet finished his sentence, "And between the brain and body. I don't mean any disrespect, but I've been dealing with this for a long time."

He asked, "What medications have been tried?"

Janet rolled her eyes, "I've been through so many. Injectible – Extavia, Glatopa, and Rebif. Infused – Lemtrada, Novatrone, and Ocrevus. And Oral – Aubagio, Gilenya."

Dr. Wildenstein took a deep breath and asked, "You obviously know your way around a neurology clinic and pharmacies. How many MRIs have you had?"

"Countless. Listen, I know all about inflammatory demyelization. This is just another exacerbation. Give me some prednisone and I'll be out of your hair."

"We've given you a high dose of dexamethasone, which is why you're doing better already. We've also taken blood and sputum cultures, because there could be a serious underlying infection. Give us a little time to see if there's a treatable cause for this relapse."

"I know the game, doc. Just let me go home. If there is something that needs to be treated, I'll come back and you can do your finest work."

The doctor looked at the nurse and nodded. He tapped a few times on the tablet. Without any further discussion, the nurse and doctor exited the room, anxious to see patients who would be more appreciative of their efforts.

Dolly Jane was shocked, "Multiple Sclerosis? All those medicines? Why have you never told me?"

Janet looked at her and said, "One thing at a time, my dear Dolly. I'll tell you everything. But first, we're gonna head out of here. Can you grab us a cab please?"

Dolly Jane shook her head. She had gone from being surprised that Janet was sick, to astonishment at her flippant view of her own medical treatment. It was also clear, that her mind was set and there was no changing it. Dolly Jane said, "Fine." She opened the Uber app while Janet sat up in bed.

The nurse returned a few minutes later and said, "I'll prepare the paperwork for you to sign, then we'll get your IV out and let you get going."

Janet said, "Thank you."

Dolly Jane sat in silence for a few minutes. Eventually she asked, "Can you translate for me? What's MS?"

Janet relaxed a bit, "Have you ever had pigs in a blanket?"

Dolly Jane was surprised at the question, "Hot dogs in croissant rolls, sure."

"Or sausage wrapped in pancakes," she smiled for the first time since she awoke. "Nerves are surrounded by a sheath like that. The nerve is the hot dog, the sheath is the croissant."

Dolly Jane smiled, "I'm remembering high school biology class."

Janet said, "Multiple sclerosis is a condition where the croissant dissolves and the hot dog can't do it's job. The nerves don't conduct their messages like they should."

Dolly Jane said, "I've always loved your teaching."

Janet said, "Doctors should learn how to say things so people can understand."

Dolly Jane asked, "How does that affect you?"

Janet said, “It comes and goes, but I have all kinds of trouble. I hurt all over. Sometimes I can’t talk, can’t walk, and am numb in various parts of my body.”

Dolly Jane let out a groan.

Janet said, “Yeah, it sucks.”

Dolly Jane asked, “I’ve known you for years. I’ve been in your classes, Bible studies, and study abroad trips but I’ve never heard you say anything about it.”

Janet said, “MS is not a pretty thing to talk about. Most people don’t understand it at all. It’s a condition known for exacerbations and relapses. It comes and goes. It’s not there all the time. So when I tell people that I’m struggling, then a week later I’m feeling fine, they think I was blowing it out of proportion, or faking it.”

Dolly Jane was defensive, “But it’s weird to see you this sick, and you didn’t even ask me to pray for you.”

“When I ask for prayer it gets weird.” Janet looked out the window and continued, “People pray for healing in all kinds of different ways. Later they will check in on me and most people assume I’m healed when I’m in remission, then they get very disheartened if I have another exacerbation. When this happens – and it often does – they become frustrated. Often, they accuse me of not having enough faith.”

Dolly Jane looked at the ground, “So they make it your fault!”

Janet nodded, “Adding insult to injury. Sometimes they tell me that I’m sick because of un-confessed sin in my life. Then if I deny it, or try to explain the nature of the disease, they refuse to speak to me.”

Dolly Jane lamented, “I’m sorry, I didn’t know.”

Janet said, “Christians can eat their own sometimes.”

Dolly Jane added, “All in trying to love one another.”

Janet agreed, “It’s not your fault. I hate to dump this on you like this. But I’m very happy you are here.”

Dolly Jane smiled. She recalled what she had learned from Brian while they prayed together for Billy. She had plenty more to say on the subject, but realized that this wasn’t the time or the place to lecture. She chose to listen.

Janet continued, “At this point in the conversation, most people, if they are still speaking with me, start giving me advice. They suggest a vegan diet. Or tell me about their cousin or uncle who overcame MS with acupuncture or some other treatment. I've been dealing with this disease for years, it's like a guest who refuses to leave. I tried everything that can be tried."

Dolly Jane added, "Suggestions from the masses don't help, I guess."

Janet said, "I know they mean well, but it really is insulting. Rather than make suggestions, they should ask questions. I've been studying this disease for decades. I've read dozens of books, and thousands of articles. With the exception of neurologists, I really am an authority on the topic."

Dolly Jane patiently listened.

Janet said, "So, you wonder why I became so excited when I saw Nehushtan?"

The nurse returned. They halted their discussion while she removed Janet's intravenous line and gave a few instructions for her to follow at home. Then she had Janet sign a form on the tablet agreeing that she was leaving against medical advice. Janet signed without hesitation.

When she had left, Dolly Jane focused on Janet. Her eyes revealed her understanding, "I get it."

Janet said, "If only I could look at the bronze snake on a pole. I'd be healed."

Dolly Jane waited a few minutes. She could see the solidarity in Janet's face. Her lifelong struggle with MS had been her silent daily battle. Cursed with the disease, she knew too much to sit back and be complacent. She saw Nehushtan as everything she needed.

After a few moments of silence, Janet relaxed. She looked at Dolly Jane. The wordless exchange at that moment spoke volumes.

Dolly Jane sought a little change of pace and teased, "I should tell you about my cousin. He has a great story, he overcame MS..."

Janet gave her a stern look.

Dolly Jane put her hands up defensively, "Actually, he's a neurologist in Denver, Dr. Zachary Macchi."

Janet laughed, "Maybe I'll seek out a fourteenth opinion." She went behind a curtain and grabbed her belongings. She checked her bag and was relieved to see the priceless relic still there. As she got dressed she asked Dolly Jane, “Hey! You’ve been texting and calling me. What’s going on?”

Dolly Jane’s eyes lit up. “Where do I start! My brother was in an explosion so I visited him...”

While they waited for the Uber, Dolly Jane quietly shared the details of everything she and Billy had been involved with. She told Janet all about Checkers, the scanning they had done. Janet had lots of questions about the scanning. Dolly Jane walked her through the whole process. When she told her about digging and retrieving the Book of the Kings she turned on her tablet and showed her all the images including the scroll unrolled on the hotel bed, Hezekiah’s poem, and, most importantly, the translation.

When she got to the end of the story she said, “Billy is scanning the base of the Broad Wall as we speak.”

. . . . .

Beneath the wall, Billy saw several metallic structures that needed further investigating. He zoomed in carefully on the first one and refined the image. He ran an analysis on the metal it was iron, the image showed that it was sharp on one end and blunt on the other, with a hole on the blunt end. This was clearly an ancient axe head. He was surprised that they would bury a valuable tool like this, but mistakes happen in every building project.

The second metallic structure was 175 yards to the east, still under the Broad Wall, 35 feet below the terrain. Metal analysis revealed an alloy of 82% copper and 18% tin. *Bronze.* The refined image showed a metallic structure that looked like a solid, slightly curved pole. The irregular and jagged edges were suspicious of having been fractured.

Billy thought, *The King with a hammer in hand.* He noted the location then set the computer to work out a path of retrieval.

He pulled out his phone and texted Dolly Jane, “Found piece #2.”

. . . . .

A blue Mercedes waited for them at the hospital entrance. Dolly Jane knew that if she asked the driver out loud to make a stop, Janet wouldn't allow it. Prepared to avoid the conversation, she slipped a paper to the driver with instructions:

מלאכי השלום, ירושלים
המתן 30 דקות
שער ציון

The driver was quite familiar with the city, especially tourist destinations. Though traveling from the hospital to a church, then another tourist destination was unusual, but the card was clear. He set a price for the entire trip. They haggled for a minute, settled on a slightly lower number, and the two women climbed into the Mercedes.

Dolly Jane checked her phone and happily showed Billy's message text to Janet.

Janet said, "Oh dear! This is truly amazing. A great find. And apparently with much more to come!"

Dolly Jane smiled from ear to ear.

The driver turned up the radio and the two passengers spoke in private. Janet's face changed. Suddenly she was solemn, disappointed. She said, "But you've broken so many protocols! You violated so many laws. I don't know if I can be a part of it!"

"Violated laws?" Dolly Jane was flabbergasted. "What's in your bag right now? Did you tell anyone about that? Did you record it as an archeological find? Did you submit it to the Israeli Anglo-Israel Archaeological Society as soon as you found it?"

"I apologize. I don't mean to be a pot calling a kettle black. I've just never been involved with anything of this nature before. I suppose my moral compass is a bit askew with all of this." She looked out the window at the city she loved. "Let me look at the original document again." She perused Dolly

Jane's summary of the documents on the tablet once again. She put down the device and said, "So, according to the poem, there were three pieces. They were hidden under the wall, and somewhere along Hezekiah's tunnel, and somewhere else. We don't know where ours was found."

"The tunnel is a major attraction. It's always full of tourists."

"That tunnel has been analyzed forwards and backwards for hundreds of years."

"But nobody has ever looked under it!"

"Or in the little crevices along the sides."

"It's a great place to visit for a couple of treasure hunters!"

They smiled at one another, then Dolly Jane said, "We've got one stop to make before you go home and get some rest."

# Chapter 25

## Old City, Jerusalem

Through light traffic, the four-kilometer trip took only sixteen minutes. When they stopped, Dolly Jane exited the vehicle and waited at the curb. Janet recognized the Church of St. Peter in Gallicantu. Built on a sheer hillside, the Church stands on the eastern slope of Mount Zion. On its roof rises a golden rooster atop a black cross. This recalls Christ's prophecy that Peter would deny him three times "before the cock crows." The scene of Peter's disgrace was the courtyard of the high priest Caiaphas; this church was built on the site of the high priest's house.

Dolly Jane was light-hearted, "When I first visited here I had no idea that Gallicantu means cockcrow in Latin."

Janet remained in the car. She rolled the window down and said, "Why are we here?"

Dolly Jane motioned for her to come and meet her at the curb.

Janet reluctantly opened the door, got out of the car, and stood in front of her on the sidewalk. She scoffed, "Are you going to accuse me of denying that I have MS? Sure I've denied it. But I've also lived with it."

"Actually, for some reason, I feel that we need to visit the dungeon."

"What?"

"Follow me."

They passed a courtyard statue depicting Peter's denial including the rooster, the woman who questioned Peter, and a Roman soldier. They entered the Church of St. Peter in Gallicantu at the upper level. As expected there was a busload of tourists already there. Janet rolled her eyes, "I just want to go home."

Dolly Jane said, "Thirty minutes, no more, I promise."

When the tour headed downstairs to the middle church Dolly Jane and Janet were alone in the sanctuary. They found a seat on one of the pews. Dolly Jane said, "I will stand on the promise that God gives in John 14:12-14."

Janet asked, "What promise is that?"

Dolly Jane recited, "Very truly I tell you, whoever believes in me will do the works I have been doing, and they will do even greater things than these, because I am going to the Father. And I will do whatever you ask in my name, so that the Father may be glorified in the Son. You may ask me for anything in my name, and I will do it."

Janet said, "I know the promise."

Dolly Jane continued, "He will heal because He said He would."

Janet made eye contact with Dolly Jane, "We've had this conversation before. But the roles were reversed."

Dolly Jane said, "Yes, and now, I'm the teacher."

Janet smiled.

Dolly Jane said, "I'll ask the classic question. What if you ask Him for a Bugatti?"

Janet answered, "Of course He wouldn't give me something like that. That's not how he operates."

Dolly Jane said, "He doesn't want us to get something for nothing. He doesn't want simply the life that we see as the best – our happiness. He wants much more than that."

Janet heard herself say, "Okay, that's fine. There are some times when God allows us to go through hard times."

Dolly Jane corrected, "Some times? The Psalms are full of laments like this. Jeremiah wrote an entire book called Lamentations. It's awful!"

Janet said, "There have been plenty of struggles in history. I know I'm not alone."

Dolly Jane said, "The book of I Peter is all about persecution, struggles, and pain. He mentions struggles 16 times in the tiny book."

Janet said, "I know I'm not alone. But it certainly feels that way sometimes."

Dolly Jane counseled, "You feel alone in this part of your life, because you've sequestered yourself. You don't let anyone in."

Janet looked up at the ceiling, an enormous cross-shaped window designed in a radiant variety of colors dominated it. "Like I told you, I hate the attention. I am Janet, not MS. When you let people in, they take a disease or disability as your identity. I just want to be me, not a representative of MS."

Dolly Jane said, "Not everyone will do that."

Janet put her arm around Dolly Jane and wiped her eyes before tears had a chance to escape.

Dolly Jane gave her a gentle squeeze, "Let's head downstairs."

They entered the middle church where stained glass icons depicted Peter's denial, repentance and his reconciliation with Jesus on the shore of the Sea of Galilee after the resurrection. Dolly Jane noticed for the first time that many of the inscriptions were in French, the Church was maintained by the Assumptionists, a French religious order. They bent over the guardrail and looked through the hole in the floor and saw that the tour was just leaving the lower levels.

Dolly Jane said, "Not only is this the site of Peter's denial, but it is also the home of the high-priest Caiaphas, where there was a prison cell. At the time the prisoner would have been lowered and raised by means of a rope harness." She pointed to the staircase, "Fortunately, we have an easier way down."

They stopped in the guardroom, waiting for the rest of the tourists to exit. The prison was a surprisingly unadorned space, a sandy dark cave. After a minute or so, they followed the sign engraved in a grouping of six decorative yellow tiles that stated:

ONE WAY CRYPT
BLESSED SACRAMENT CHAPEL
COURTYARD & HOLY STAIRS
SACRED PIT (DUNGEON)

Dolly Jane mused, "Sounds inviting."

The base level was a simple square room equipped not with an altar, but a lectern.

Dolly Jane said quietly, "Think back to April 7, of the year A.D. 33. Imagine this place quiet and desolate until Jesus was held for the night. He had been betrayed by one of his own disciples, tried in a kangaroo court, beaten, then sent across town, tried again, and held for at least three hours right here. What happened in this place has echoed through history."

Janet asked, "Why are you saying all of this?"

Dolly Jane ignored the interruption, "What was going through his mind? He had been asking God to take the cup from Him. But God didn't answer that prayer. Jesus was held as a prisoner right here. Can you imagine what He endured in this space?"

Dolly Jane and Janet were the only two occupying the ten by ten foot light brown cell.

Janet thought about it, "God didn't answer Jesus' prayer."

Dolly Jane took a few steps and looked at the book on the lectern. It was a Bible, open to Psalm 88. "The words of Psalm 88 sum it up well. Certainly, Jesus, the great student, had this memorized. She read softly:

Lord, you are the God who saves me;
day and night I cry out to you.
May my prayer come before you;
turn your ear to my cry.
I am overwhelmed with troubles
and my life draws near to death.
I am counted among those who go down to the pit;
I am like one without strength.
I am set apart with the dead,

like the slain who lie in the grave,
Whom you remember no more,
who are cut off from your care.
You have put me in the lowest pit,
in the darkest depths.
Your wrath lies heavily on me;
you have overwhelmed me with all your waves.
You have taken from me my closest friends,
and have made me repulsive to them.
I am confined and cannot escape;
my eyes are dim with grief.
I call to you, Lord, every day;
I spread out my hands to you.
Do you show your wonders to the dead?
Do their spirits rise up and praise you?
Is your love declared in the grave, your faithfulness in
destruction?
Are your wonders known in the place of darkness,
or your righteous deeds in the land of oblivion?
But I cry to you for help, Lord;
in the morning my prayer comes before you.
Why, Lord, do you reject me,
and hide your face from me?
From my youth I have suffered and been close to death;
I have borne your terrors and am in despair,
Your wrath has swept over me;
your terrors have destroyed me,
All day long they surround me like a flood;
they have completely engulfed me.
You have taken from me friend and neighbor—
darkness is my closest friend.

They sat in silence as the cool limestone walls echoed her final words. A reverence of Jesus' holiness came over them.

Finally, Janet broke the silence, "That's pretty intense."

Dolly Jane stood with her eyes closed.

Janet said, "I had no idea."

Dolly Jane opened her eyes and said, "What do you

mean?"

Janet said, "We will never be able to trust what God is doing in our lives until we figure out and personalize his ultimate goal. His primary purpose is not to make us happy, healthy, wealthy, and wonderful."

Dolly Jane nodded, "God puts things in our path for us to grow, to expand our horizons, and to force us to trust Him. Nobody ever got to the place of maturity with an easy life. He doesn't promise to make our lives easy and guarantee that things go smoothly. Though he is eternally committed to providing the best for his children. That 'BEST' may or may not coincide with what many of us consider 'making it' in life, or feeling good all the time."

Janet said, "Jesus didn't feel good all the time."

Dolly Jane agreed, "Especially when he spent the night here."

Janet looked around at the dungeon, "I can only imagine how he felt."

Dolly Jane said, "God is good. He is sovereign. And even in a fallen world, we can rest in the assurance that He is actively working to bring about the best possible results by the best possible means, and in the end, to make you and me like His Son, Jesus."

Janet said, "So what about our talk of the Bugatti?"

Dolly Jane replied, "To assume that He will act as a heavenly vending machine is inane and immature. Life isn't always easy, but God in His wisdom always brings about the best possible results, by the best possible means, for the longest possible time. The truth and promise from God keeps us from giving up or giving in when life seems utterly impossible."

Janet nodded in silence. She checked the staircase to see if another group was coming in. The stairs were vacant, and from the silence in the corridor, it felt like they would be alone for a little while longer.

Dolly Jane asked, "So, I'll ask a harder question. What if He doesn't heal?"

Janet said, "You know, I don't like that question."

Dolly Jane retorted, "It's a valid question."

Janet said, "I understand. But whenever anybody talks about Biblical healing, that's the first place they go. It's either

'Does God still heal?' or 'What if He doesn't heal?'"

Dolly Jane said, "That's just human nature. We've all prayed for things that didn't happen – like the Bugatti example. But we need to be prepared for the 'What if…'"

Janet motioned to the dungeon walls around them, "Look at this place. How can we expect perfect health all the time when we are standing in Jesus' own prison cell? If He suffered, we certainly will too."

Dolly Jane felt chills on the back of her neck and down her spine. She wasn't sure if the sensation was from the coolness of the cave, the realization of the sheer harshness of what Jesus went through, or if it was the Holy Spirit speaking to her. She said, "We live in a fallen world. How can we expect to have anything but trouble in this world?"

Janet said, "I'm not a fan of the prosperity Gospel."

Dolly Jane scoffed, "God wants us to be happy! That's simply not in the Bible. In fact, when he called his disciples, he called them to follow him… and die."

Janet thought for a moment. Then she said, "He has the authority to answer your prayer by saying no. He did it to his own Son! I wouldn't be so presumptuous as to think that He would never say no to me. If He chooses to not heal at this point in time, then He is working out something else in my life."

Dolly Jane reached out and grabbed Janet's hand.

Janet didn't bother to wipe the tears from her face. She said, "Let me ask you this. If He says no, does it mean we don't have enough faith?"

Dolly Jane's eyes grew wide, "Absolutely not!"

Janet nodded.

Dolly Jane said, "He said no to Jesus! He asked for the cup to be taken from him and God said no. Do you think that was because Jesus didn't have enough faith?"

Janet's shoulders slumped. "No, but when those who pray for me accuse me of not having enough faith…"

Dolly Jane looked her in the eye and said, "Nobody should ever say that. Have you heard of Todd White?"

Janet shook her head no.

"He's a healing minister who loves Jesus. He's a crazy looking guy with dred locks and a tremendous testimony. He used to be a drug addict, now he preaches about Jesus."

Janet said, "You've got my attention."

Dolly Jane looked her in the eye, "He tells the story of a six-year-old family friend who was very sick. He had prayed for him for years, and he got sicker and sicker. Finally, he prayed for him as he died. He was there when the boy died. As his mother was holding him, many hours later, he was still there. The coroner came in, Todd felt a word from the Lord and said to the coroner, 'You have a football injury in your right knee and it never healed.' The coroner freaked out a little, he wasn't a Christian. Todd prayed for the knee and he was healed. He freaked out a lot at that point, and he became a Christian.

"Another time, Todd's father had a serious ankle injury. His father wasn't a believer. He prayed for his father but he wasn't healed. Eventually, he had to undergo surgery. Afterwards, while still in the hospital, Todd prayed for a nurse who had a headache, and a doctor whose right shoulder was healed. Todd's father witnessed all this and became a Christian."

Janet laughed, "This guy is really out there."

Dolly Jane continued, "Another time, Todd tore his knee at work. He heard it pop and knew it was bad. All of his co-workers knew that he prayed for people, and people were healed, so they were tuned in when he was hurt himself. Todd prayed for his knee, but got nothing He wasn't healed. He prayed and prayed, but didn't receive healing. He needed surgery for his knee. While he was in the hospital, he was coming out of anesthesia and the nurse came and checked on him, he told the nurse, 'You get migraine headaches and you have one right now.' She said, 'That's right, but you need to rest.' He prayed for her headache and it went away."

Janet furrowed her brow, "Why are you telling me this?"

Dolly Jane said, "It was the same guy praying for everybody, some were healed, some weren't. So just using simple logic, it can't be a matter of faith. He had the same faith for one person as for the next. It can't be a matter of him wanting the healing more, since he himself wasn't healed. It's simply a matter of submitting to God."

Janet paused, "I don't know. That's weird."

Dolly Jane said, "If healing always comes, then its based on our experience, not faith. Our faith is not in our prayer, it's in Jesus, our God. This stirs up all kinds of issues."

Janet was solemn, silent.

Dolly Jane said, "I don't pretend to understand it all, but when He doesn't heal, we can rest assured that He is working out something else in us."

Janet was quiet, "I understand."

Dolly Jane said, "Let's pray for you."

Together they bowed their heads, respecting the place where they stood, Dolly Jane said, "Father God, we know that you are loving and kind and want the best for Janet. Please bring her healing. Stop the inflammation and restore the myelin throughout her nervous system." She opened her eyes, and while continuing to pray, she said, "Fix the pancake around the sausage." Janet looked at her and grinned. Dolly Jane continued, "Reverse the affects of the disease and bring complete health to her body. I speak the healing power of Jesus Christ over Janet's body."

Dolly Jane gave her an embrace.

They held onto one another for a few moments. Another tour group was gathering in the guardroom, clearly it was time for them to leave.

They made it up two levels and exited out the back door. Janet looked up at the sky and enjoyed the warm sunshine on her face. However, she could barely manage the stairs and it took all of her energy to make it to the bench to rest. Janet looked at Dolly Jane and said, "I need to get to the apartment and lie down.

Dolly Jane saw that the cab driver was checking his watch. She said, "Let's get you home."

Their driver dropped them off just a short walk from the apartment. Dolly Jane helped Janet up the stairs and into bed.

Janet said, "Lock the door behind you. Go find the other pieces of the bronze snake."

Dolly Jane smiled, "Yes ma'am."

# Chapter 26

---

## Rabinovich Square
## Old City, Jerusalem

Billy sat on a stone bench at the base of the Golden Menorah in Rabinovich Square. He enjoyed the view from his seat, overlooking the Western Wall Plaza and the Temple Mount. He was respectful of the historical significance of the structures around him and intently worked on his laptop, being the first to document, in detail, every square inch beneath the hallowed grounds.

He hardly noticed the hundreds of people passing by every few minutes as he embraced his digital toil. He took a moment and looked up at the centerpiece of the square. Encased within bulletproof glass over six feet tall and weighing over a thousand pounds, the Menorah would have been an impressive structure even if it didn't contain a precious metal. However, ninety-five of those pounds were twenty-four karat gold, covering the exterior of the structure. The Golden Menorah was made possible through the generosity of Vadim Rabinovitch, a leader of the Jewish community of Ukraine, thus the name of the square in which it currently resides.

Billy understood that this was much more than a simple seven-candle lamp stand. Its design was based on extensive research carried out by the academic and biblical researchers from the Temple Institute. The Menorah is an exact replica of the Menorah from the second temple. It is one of the seven elements in the Holy place of the temple where the priests offer their daily sacrifices.

The temple will be rebuilt. Christians know this fact via a diligent study of the final book of the Bible, Revelation. To Jews, however, the rebuilding of the temple is simply a fact of their persistence and dominance as a people. Devout Jews pray three times a day. The scheduled times are 9:00 am, noon, and 3:00 pm. Just like Daniel in the Old Testament. Part of the daily ritual prayers is the Amidah Prayer. In the Amidah prayer are nineteen statements. They start with worshiping God, asking for repentance, forgiveness, health, and prosperity. The seventeenth paragraph states:

> Be pleased, O lord our God, with your people Israel and with their prayers. Restore the service to the inner sanctuary of your Temple, and receive in love and with favor both the fire-offerings of Israel and their prayers. May the worship of your people Israel always be acceptable to you. And let our eyes behold your return in mercy to Zion. Blessed are you, O Lord, who restores his divine presence to Zion.

The Jews are keenly in tuned with the need to restore the temple. They pray for it every day and have prepared their nation for it. They are determined to rebuild the temple on the original site - currently occupied by the Golden Dome, the second most holy site in the Muslim tradition. While not a fact that is appealing to the Muslims, the Jewish community pulls no punches with regard to the temple. When the temple is rebuilt, God-fearing Jews will worship the God of Abraham, Isaac, and Jacob in the place where Solomon built the first temple. Just as Isaiah, Ezekiel, and Josiah worshiped there.

Even in a wedding ceremony, the Jewish custom is to take the most precious time in the ceremony and remember the temple. In American weddings when the Pastor or Priest says, “You may now kiss your bride,” they celebrate and the crowd cheers for them. But in Jewish weddings when the rabbi announces the new couple, they take a glass and crush it with their foot in remembrance of the destruction of the temple.

In the new temple, this Golden Menorah will take its place in the Kodesh Sanctuary. The display is not a simple pretty display, rather a religious and political statement to the world - *WE ARE READY TO REBUILD THE TEMPLE.*

Billy finished scanning the area and looked at his laptop. He traced the map of the Broad Wall and saw that he had completed his goal. The city on a hill brought numerous topographical challenges as he scanned the vast number of undiscovered underground tunnels, buildings, cisterns, and modern underground plumbing and electrical lines. He had been able to scan the most archeological rich city in the world without causing any public disruption. He closed his computer and picked up his iPhone.

. . . . .

Dolly Jane's phone vibrated in her hand. *Meet at the Menorah.* She picked up her bag and tossed her phone in her pocket and started walking. Though Menorahs were everywhere in Jerusalem, there was certainly only one of significance, it was a site where he would be scanning. She headed through the busy streets toward Rabinivich Square.

. . . . .

Billy took a break from his digital efforts and decided to pick up a little lunch. Dozens of restaurants were within a hundred yards, but he was far from an adventurous eater and enjoyed the pizza and burgers he was familiar with. He shopped at a nearby store and passed by the Shawarma, Kanafeh, and Israeli Bourekas. Instead he picked up a Jerusalem Bagel. Though not the familiar circle he was accustomed to, he knew he couldn't go wrong with bread. He declined the offer for olive oil, hummus, tahini, or za'atar. He found that the bagel was a different texture than he expected, since Jerusalem bagels are not boiled like American bagels.

With the bagel in hand, he returned to the Menorah and enjoyed the beautiful day.

. . . . .

Dolly Jane joined him with her lunch in hand.

Billy asked, "What's that?"

She said, "They called it Israeli Bourekas, but I haven't had it before. I'm not sure what I've gotten myself into."

"It looks like something I wouldn't put in my mouth."

She took a bite. After a minute she said, "It's a flaky pastry with salty cheese, spinach, mushrooms, and mashed potato." She took another bite and smiled. "There are also pickles, hard-boiled eggs and three different dipping sauces."

Billy attacked his bagel with his teeth. While he chewed he looked at her and said, "I'll keep to the safety of my bread."

She laughed at him and asked, "How goes the scanning?"

Billy opened his laptop and showed her, "I've scanned the entire Broad Wall."

Her eyes widened as she looked over the scan, overlaid with the city map. "When you put this together with the previous scans, you've scanned underneath about 80% of the Old City!" Her mind drifted to a presentation of an underground map of the whole city. Billy narrowed down the map to the section that potentially held their precious bronze relic.

She quickly re-focused and asked, "Can you use any parts of the tunnel we used last time?"

"Not really, it's a different direction. There's a public restroom between Cardos and the Holy Café, I think that will be a perfect spot."

"You can tunnel from there, and we can hunker down at the Holy Café."

Billy asked, "Janet's apartment is not far from here. Do you think we could sit in there? It would give us a little more privacy."

"I wish. I just came from there. That place is tiny, 250 square feet, tops. There's no way we could relax in there and still allow her to rest."

"Maybe we could check in with her after we do a little tunneling."

"Perfect."

Billy brought his suitcase into the stall with him in the public restroom and sent Checkers underground. When the hole was sealed off, he joined Dolly Jane for a cup of tea at the café. They guided Checkers deep underground right up to their metallic structure under the wall. Looking at the metallic structure closely, Billy said, "It doesn't look like it's encased in a jar or protected in any way. Rather it was simply a part of the earth. Who knows how much corrosion will have destroyed it."

Dolly Jane asked, "What do you mean?"

"Bronze is an alloy of copper, tin, and a variety of other metals. It is prone to corrosion, especially when in contact with anything that contains chlorine, or other oxidizing agents."

"If it was protected, somehow, like the scroll was, and the other piece was, then it will be fine."

"Would limestone protect it?"

"Possibly."

"We can only hope." He guided Checkers through the soft dirt, right up to within a few feet of the treasure, then Checkers slowed.

"Limestone," he said. "This will take a few minutes."

Dolly Jane said, "That's good right?"

Billy shrugged, "It's possible that they put a layer of limestone at the base, then the bronze snake, and then more limestone."

Dolly Jane looked closely at the scan, "It looks like a little sarcophagus."

"Indeed," Billy said as Checkers pressed through the rock and into a thin layer of air around the bronze. He tapped a few keys and the robot obediently reached out and retrieved the relic from its sanctuary. He reused the protective casing and began dragging it back to the opening.

"I think I have to visit the restroom again," he smiled.

Dolly Jane gave him an empty bag and he disappeared down the walkway. He entered the restroom and waited a few minutes for his stall to be available. He washed his hands several times, and combed his hair over and over again. Finally, a Hasidic Jew in full regalia exited the stall and he hastily entered.

He packed Checkers into the roller bag, retrieved the relic and replaced the cover over the hole. After some artistic work to camouflage the tile cover, he held the relic in his hands. The edges were ragged and irregular, but it clearly had elements that looked like scales on the sides. Other than a few areas with greenish corrosion, it was surprisingly intact. He packed it into the bag and slung it over his shoulder.

. . . . .

On the opposite side of the street, Colonel Macks enjoyed a piece of baklava. He was relishing the time away from his post and had no responsibility to check in with anybody. He simply listened to the young explorers from a dozen yards away. He was confident in his assessment, they were after the final pieces, and he could easily overpower them any time he chose.

. . . . .

Dolly Jane waited expectantly outside the men's room. Here eyes begged the question, *Did you get it?*

Billy nodded and tapped the bag. She grabbed him by the arm and together they made a quick left turn, past the exposed portion of Hezekiah's Broad Wall and went right to Janet's apartment.

. . . . .

Chase stood a dozen yards up the walkway with a newspaper under his arm. Inside the daily paper, he held a multiphase scanner. He was watching and recording every motion they made through the apartment walls. He waited for the right time to move in. He looked up and noted the cameras on the corners. Though outside and visible to the public, the outdoors security was like a vault in a bank. This was no place to make a move. He would be patient.

. . . . .

Dolly Jane opened the front door, after they crammed into the tiny hallway, she locked the door behind them and guided Billy inside. She tossed the keys on the counter and saw Janet curled up in the bed. She saw Janet's bag in the corner and couldn't contain her excitement, "We've got two of the three pieces!"

Janet woke to the sound of the opening door. She quickly wrapped herself in a robe and exited the bedroom.

Dolly Jane was slightly embarrassed, "Sorry to wake you."

Janet waved her off, "No problem, with news like that you can wake me any time."

Dolly Jane motioned to her partner. "I brought Billy with me."

Janet said, "It's a pleasure to meet you. I've heard so much!"

Billy extended his hand for a greeting, "Likewise."

Janet said, "So, this Checkers. It seems you've developed the single most useful tool in the history of archeology!"

Billy averted his gaze.

Janet smiled, "You don't have to be so modest, young man. It's quite an accomplishment."

Billy said, "The price paid in its development was too high."

Janet saw pain in his eyes. She reached out and squeezed his shoulder. After a moment, she looked at Dolly Jane and asked, "What did you find today?"

Dolly Jane placed the bag on the round wooden kitchen table. Janet stood in front of the bag, looked at Dolly Jane, and said, “May I?”

“Absolutely.”

She smoothly unzipped the duffle bag and half expected the heavens to part and angels to sing as she exposed it. She donned cotton gloves then reached in and grasped the bronze relic. She took her time examining it. Instantly she looked at the end and saw the ragged edge. She admired the piece of metal like a newborn baby. Eventually, she realized that she hadn’t taken a breath in over a minute. Drained, emotionally and physically, she sat down.

Dolly Jane reached her hand out to her shoulder and steadied her.

Nobody spoke for quite some time.

Eventually, she said, “Top shelf.”

Billy smiled and nodded, “Yes it is.”

Janet pointed to her kitchen cabinet and said, “The other piece is in the top shelf. There’s no real safe or secure place in this apartment. Can you grab that for me please?”

Billy apologized and quickly opened the cabinet. He saw the leather wrapped package and set it down next to Janet. She unwrapped it and set the two pieces next to one another. The broken ends matched up perfectly.

Janet clapped her hands together and squealed in delight, “This is easily the biggest find since the Dead Sea Scrolls. When we find the final piece, we’ll have everything!”

Dolly Jane said, “That’s only part of the excitement. Let me show you the scans Billy made.”

Janet nodded.

Billy opened his laptop, opened the program, and handed it to Dolly Jane. She began to show Janet the scans of the Old City.

Janet seemed to lose interest quickly, she brushed the scans aside, “All that matters is the third piece.”

Dolly Jane was stunned. Janet had never before neglected such an archeological discovery.

Janet was suddenly physically overwhelmed. Unable to maintain her balance, she sat down on a kitchen chair. With her hands on the kitchen table, she realized that she might go down.

She uttered, "I need to get back to bed."

Dolly Jane said, "Certainly, let me give you a hand." She helped Janet to her feet and together they walked back to the bedroom. Without Dolly Jane's help, Janet certainly would have collapsed on the floor.

Billy said, "We'll let you get some rest."

Dolly Jane said, "It's great to see you. We'll check in tomorrow."

Billy added, "I'll scan Hezekiah's tunnel tomorrow as a part of their very first tour group."

Janet took a deep breath and said, "That's a good plan. Make sure you aren't followed. We need to protect not only what we've found, but what we are looking for."

Billy scoffed, "Nobody knows what we are doing. It's been just between Dolly Jane and myself until now – just us three."

Janet warned, "I hope that's true. You have no idea of the people who will swarm to steal this when they find out about it.

Billy nodded.

Janet said, "The banks are closing now. First thing in the morning, I'll take these to my safety deposit box."

# Chapter 27

---

## Old City, Jerusalem

Billy bought a pair of tickets to Hezekiah's tunnel and waited with Dolly Jane for the first tour of the day to begin.

Dolly Jane asked, "How are you going to scan through the tunnel? The tunnel is long and narrow. There isn't a descent place to stop."

Billy smiled, "I've scanned all across Jerusalem. At first we sat quietly, and I watched every detail. Then I was able to watch InstraGram while it was going on."

"You're not instilling confidence."

"We also had trouble dealing with water at first. Water caused scatter, but I modified the sensors until I found the best resolution. The more I do it, the better I get. The water in the tunnels is not going to be a problem."

"How about tunneling through it?"

"Still a problem."

"What do you mean?"

"I can't tunnel through water. We can go above, it, around it, even below it. But never through water."

Just then they were ushered into a small theater and along with forty other visitors they watched a video of ancient Israel under Hezekiah's rule. The narrator explained:

> "In 701 BCE Jerusalem was under threat of war. Sennacherib, King of Assyria had conquered Lacish and several other cities, and

> Jerusalem was next. King Hezekiah prepared the city in every way he could. He built up the army, armed them with the best weaponry, he built food stores, but one of the biggest challenges was to bring water into the city. Hezekiah dug a tunnel from the Gihon Spring in the Kidron Valley outside the city wall, weaving 1750 feet through the bedrock of the Eastern Hill to the Pool of Siloam."

The video illustrated their digging technique including Warren's Shaft, a natural sinkhole that extended down to the tunnel from Gihon Springs. It functioned like a well, with a person at the top of the shaft lowering a bucket on a rope to the bottom of the 38-foot shaft to get fresh water from the reservoir below. The shaft was now a covered well, and part of the city's water system.

At the conclusion of the video Billy said, "I slept through the video last time I was here. It made a lot more sense this time around."

Dolly Jane rolled her eyes, "Let's go".

Billy turned on the scanner and carried it into the cavern. They walked down a set of stairs, through a series of small rooms and into the tunnel. The spring water that varied from an inch up to ankle deep cooled their feet as they walked. They were so close together they were practically stepping on each other's feet.

Billy shouted, "Dolly Jane!"

She turned around, worried that something was wrong, but found Billy laughing. The brown walls were smooth and made excellent acoustics. He enjoyed the sound of his voice coming back to him like a boomerang.

Billy scanned as he walked with Dolly Jane through the tight space.

Dolly Jane laughed, "You look ridiculous."

Billy chuckled. He noticed that bringing a suitcase through the tunnels was a little crazy. "I'll just play the role of the confused tourist."

Dolly Jane turned on her iPhone flashlight and guided them through the cool, damp walls. She turned it off for contrast and the darkness was overwhelming. Billy's broad shoulders brushed against the walls constantly as he mulled his way through, ducking every few feet to avoid cranial trauma.

The tour group in front of them was full of high-energy teenagers who sang at the top of their lungs. Their voices reverberated off the solid walls as they finished their first song. After the singing, their laughter surrounded them like a blanket. Then they burst into another song, and another, and another, all the way through the 1750-foot tunnel.

Dolly Jane looked back at Billy with her flashlight on, "Are they ever going to stop?"

Billy shook his head and continued on. Eventually they reached the knee deep water of the Pool of Siloam. Dolly Jane was curious about the five pillars within the pool, and the bizarre platform. They ascended the steps and were thankful for sunlight on their shoulders once again.

Billy found a comfortable shaded bench in the corner of the waiting area. He sat down and opened his laptop. Dolly Jane was impressed with his efficiency in the process, significantly quicker than when they first started in the Hookah bar. The scan showed not only the tunnel but also the areas a dozen yards in each direction. Because of the serpentine course the tunnel takes, there was a fair amount of overlapping of the scans in the central portion, resulting increased detail at the middle of the tunnel. Billy stared at his screen. He panned back to the City of David and looked at everything. He looked through the stairway and gift shop.

Dolly Jane interrupted his thought process. "We're looking for a piece of bronze that should be by itself somewhere along the tunnel."

"Sorry, I'm just re-living every step, without the singing teenagers."

Dolly Jane smiled, "I think you'll be able to see it pretty easily."

Billy sped up his journey through the digital scan, 1200 feet into the trek he saw something that didn't seem to fit. He focused in and saw what looked like a pile of sticks in the water. The computer enhanced the image and Billy focused closer and saw that he was looking at bones. A skeleton.

He jumped back. Surprised at the gothic appearance deep within the tunnel. He scanned further and saw another collection of bones, and another. After a while, he lost count of the number of people who had been perished in that desolate dark place.

Billy thought out loud, “What does that mean?”

The human remains didn’t frighten Dolly Jane. They were separated by distance and simply viewed on the screen, not all around her while she was by herself with them. Dolly Jane pointed at another section, “Isn’t that Warren’s shaft?”

Billy agreed, “Yes. And to the right and left are a labyrinth of caves and tunnels. Below it are more caves and tunnels. This place is like a hodgepodge of underground pools. Most of it is natural, but some of it was cut by hand.”

Billy stopped and focused on a particular pool in the middle of the miasma of subterranean mazes. He zoomed in and said, “Do you see the piece of metal right there?”

Dolly Jane asked, “You found the third piece?”

Billy pointed at the screen, “Let me check.” He ran an analysis on the material and saw that it was bronze. The size and shape were clearly appropriate for the tail section of Nehushtan.

He said, “Definitely.”

Dolly Jane clapped her hands together and grinned. “Great. Let’s go get it.”

Billy cautioned, “Not so fast. This is kind of worst-case scenario. Look at where it is positioned.”

Dolly Jane said, “It’s kind of in the middle of the cistern.”

Billy sighed, “Right, but it’s also sitting on the top of a skinny pillar.”

Dolly Jane wondered, “How did it get there? It looks like someone intentionally set it right there.”

Billy panned out and looked at the whole region. “It must have been placed there while the tunnel was being dug.”

Dolly Jane quoted Hezekiah’s poem:

*Beneath the channel deep between the spring and lake*
*May water and stone drown them forever*

Billy tossed his head back and let out a guttural exclamation of frustration.

Dolly Jane said, “It’s enshrined in a subterranean watery tomb.”

Billy sat with his eyes closed.

Dolly Jane remained hopeful, “Let’s put this on hold for now and visit with Janet. Maybe she has some ideas.”

. . . . .

Within a half hour they were back at Janet’s apartment. They opened the door, bounded up the steps and gently knocked on Janet’s bedroom door.

Dolly Jane hollered, “Janet we’ve got good news and bad news. Which do you want to hear first?”

There was no response.

A light sleeper, Janet would certainly be awake. Dolly Jane called out again, “Janet? Can you hear me?”

There was no retort from the bedroom.

Dolly Jane approached the doorway, “Janet? Are you okay?”

There was no movement whatsoever. Dolly Jane entered and looked at her mentor. She appeared to be sleeping. She tapped her on the shoulder. “Janet?”

No response.

Dolly Jane grabbed her by the shoulders and gave her a little shake.

Nothing.

Billy wondered, “Did she have a heart attack?”

Dolly Jane placed her fingers on her neck, in the crease between the trachea and the sternocleidomasteoid muscle to feel the carotid pulse. The slowly rhythmic bounding of the artery gave her hope.

“She has a pulse.”

Dolly Jane watched her chest slowly rise and fall and felt the warmth of her breath, due to the closeness of her observation. “She’s breathing.”

She looked back at Billy, “She’s in trouble.”

Billy asked, “What do we do?”

Dolly Jane said, “We need help.”

Billy pondered, “Who can we call? What is 911 in Jerusalem?”

Dolly Jane picked up her phone, “I’ll call ZAKA.”

Billy said, “Who?”

Dolly Jane said, “I’ve read about the ZAKA international rescue unit paramedics. They are like 911.”

. . . . .

Just outside the apartment, Colonel Mack’s eyes broadened, he had been watching the events unfold and was wondering what they would do.

He exclaimed, “No! Not ZAKA!” He sprang into action. As he traversed the short walkway to the apartment, he reached into his coat pocket and pulled out a lock picking kit. He quickly inserted a steel pick and a tension wrench into the tumbler lock. Within a few seconds his experienced hands worked the driver pins on the shear line and picked the lock and entered the room.

He bounded up the steps and ordered, “Put down the phone.”

Dolly Jane and Billy were shocked, “What?”

The Colonel said, “If you call ZAKA, everything in this room will be exposed.”

Dolly Jane asked, “What do you know about what is in this room?”

He continued, “You don’t need ZAKA. They are an emergency response team, but they are for disaster relief. Plus they work with the IDF and if you involve them, everything in this room will be revealed to the public.”

Dolly Jane stopped the call and put down her phone.

Billy recognized him, “Colonel Macks!”

Dolly Jane repeated, “What do you know about what is in this room?”

“Everything that I need to,” he looked over Dolly Jane, Billy and saw Janet lying in the bed. He walked over to Janet and made a quick medical assessment of her condition, non-responsive but still breathing. “You have two of the three pieces of Nehushtan and a professor with MS. The third piece is gonna be a challenge. We don’t need ZAKA, we just need to get her to a hospital.”

Dolly Jane stammered, “How do you know all that?”

Colonel Macks continued, "Listen, ZAKA stands for Zihuy Korbanot Ason. זיהוי קרבנות אסון. ZAKA is designed for Identification, Extraction, and Rescue after disasters. That is not the same as 911 in the USA. It's not the organization to call for an ambulance."

Dolly Jane said, "I'm sorry, I didn't know."

Billy looked at him and asked, "Why are you here?"

Colonel Macks realized that he had revealed himself in an awkward manner. At this point there wasn't any use in hiding anything. He said, "You two never went to Ein Gedi, so I've kept my eye on you. It's clear that you found the Book of the Kings and used that to find Nehushtan."

Dolly Jane's mouth was open, "But how..."

The Colonel interrupted her, "I've got as much interest in finding Nehushtan as you do. But we can't let it fall into the wrong hands."

Billy said, "How do we know that you aren't the one we should be worried about?"

He held up his hands defensively. "Listen, I'm keeping you from exposing Nehushtan to the world. When you retrieve the final piece from the tunnel, you'll have the ultimate power. Do you have any idea what you are dealing with?"

Billy shrugged, "Obviously more than a relic."

Dolly Jane motioned to Janet, "She needs healing, desperately."

The Colonel said, "She needs all three pieces of the bronze snake."

Dolly Jane's face revealed the flash of understanding and she was beginning to feel like they were on the same team. She said, "She was in the hospital..."

"I know," the Colonel interrupted, "for an exacerbation of MS. We don't know what brought on her exacerbation because she didn't stay in the hospital long enough. She's in real trouble now. She needs to be in the intensive care unit."

Billy said, "Modern medicine has failed her."

Dolly Jane affirmed, "When we find the third piece, all she will have to do is look at it."

The Colonel said, "I understand. But what happens after that?"

Dolly Jane said, "She'll be healed. She can go on with her life."

Colonel Macks said, "That's not what I'm talking about."

Dolly Jane was confused, "What do you mean?"

He said, "You will need help to build your organization, use it wisely, help as many people as you can, and keep the power safe. I'm after the same thing you are. But without help, the pieces of bronze will be stolen from you."

Dolly Jane looked at Billy, her eyes begged for help.

Billy said to Colonel Macks, "Give us a minute."

He walked down the stairway and stood next to the door while they spoke.

Dolly Jane asked, "Can we trust him? He's part of the IDF."

Billy said, "I don't know. But it looks like he's the only one we can trust, if we decline his help, then he'll arrest us."

Dolly Jane was skeptical, "What if he steals it, and uses it for his own purposes?"

Billy looked at the enormous man, "If he wanted to do that, he would have done it already." He approached the military man and they stood face-to-face. He pondered his options. Though a physical mountain of a man, Billy wasn't intimidated. He thought of six ways to incapacitate him in a heartbeat. But with the Colonel's Special Forces training, he would be ready and able to counter any attack Billy would levy.

The two men stared at one another.

Neither backed down.

Neither blinked.

Eventually, Billy set aside his testosterone and engaged his supreme intellect. He imagined the three of them together as a team. He looked at the mountain of a man and said, "The three of us can work together."

Dolly Jane agreed. She took a deep breath and said, "Somehow he feels like family, like a brother."

Billy reached out his hand.

The Colonel smiled as he shook it and said, "Call me Richard."

Billy said, "Thank you for not turning us in."

Dolly Jane added, "Or letting us get caught."

Richard said, "By the way, you need to do a better job of preserving the Book of the Kings than lying it flat in your hotel room. That relic is priceless."

Dolly Jane was shocked, "How much do you know?"

Richard said, "Everything, I'll explain after we get Janet to the hospital." He picked up his phone and said, "I could call 1221, the equivalent to 911 in Jerusalem, but I'd rather keep things simple and have one of my Lieutenants help us out." He spoke in Hebrew then waited a few minutes for the support to arrive. He took the time to explain how he had been monitoring them.

Billy said, "Listen, I'll take care of the technological stuff, and the Colonel can handle the security and political connections. Dolly Jane, you will dominate the Archeological world. Together we can be an unbeatable team."

Dolly Jane said, "Janet was going to take the pieces to the safety deposit box at her bank today." She looked in the bathroom and saw that everything was just as she left it the night before. "But it's pretty clear that she hasn't gotten out of bed. Billy, why don't you take the two pieces and secure them. I'll accompany Janet to the hospital."

Billy said, "Sure. Where did you put them?"

Dolly Jane said, "In the cabinet where they were before."

Billy opened the cabinet where the relics had been stowed. It was void. Empty. Nothing was there.

He looked on the counter, in the other cabinets, in the drawers, and under the sink. He searched every square inch of the apartment.

Nothing.

Billy turned to Dolly Jane and Richard and said, "They're gone!"

# Chapter 28

## Highway 1
## Between Jerusalem and Tel Aviv

The bronze relics rested like a pair of swaddled newborns inside hotel towels zippered safely within Chase's backpack. He kept a hand on the bag as he drove on Highway 1 north toward Tel Aviv. He mentally reviewed the conundrum before him. He hadn't reviewed the entirety of the most recently acquired scan, but he overheard their lament that bordered on despair regarding the difficulty in acquiring the final piece.

Never one to back away from a challenge, he was confident that he'd find a way to acquire the final piece before Billy or Dolly Jane could come up with a plan.

. . . . .

Inside the apartment, Richard was on his phone, in Hebrew he ordered his Lieutenant to track his cell phone and bring up the street footage for the last twelve hours for the front door of the apartment where he was located. He waited thirty seconds then said in English, "Review it, find anyone who went in or out and send the video to my cell." He hung up and waited. In a few minutes, a text announced that another Lieutenant was waiting with a sedan just a hundred yards away.

Billy and Dolly Jane looked at one another. He commented, "Very resourceful."

Dolly Jane was at Janet's side. She asked Richard, "Can you help us get Janet to the hospital?"

Billy said, "Let's get a wheelchair."

Richard said, "Nonsense, I've got this." He picked her up like a child in his arms and cradled her. She looked tiny as his pectoralis became her pillow. Richard looked at Dolly Jane and Billy and said, "Let's go."

. . . . .

Chase parked his rental car at HaTahana HaMerkazit, the main bus station of Tel Aviv, and marched inside. He dropped a few sheckels into locker number 17, opened the door and stowed his backpack safely within it. He removed the key and tucked it into his front pocket then returned to his vehicle and took a few minutes looking up his next destination. With the address entered into the dashboard computer, he was satisfied that he could navigate the roads. He smirked as he pressed the accelerator.

. . . . .

By the time they had reached the hospital, Janet's breathing was shallow and her pulse was weak and thready. Her facial pallor was dusky and her lips were deep blue.

Richard burst through the ambulance door with the sick woman in his arms. One look from the emergency room triage nurse and she called for help. Instantly, they were ushered into a treatment room. Nurses attached a slew of monitors, and started an intravenous line. Her initial pulse oximeter reading was 88%. The respiratory therapist provided supplemental oxygen by ventilating with a facemask. A radiology tech rolled a portable chest X-ray machine over the bed and began snapping images.

Dolly Jane stood at the doorway watching and praying. She didn't know what to do. Tears welled up and escaped her eyes. The emergency room doctor did a cursory examination and ordered some tests. Dolly Jane waited in the hallway. She was beginning to hate hospitals. The pain and suffering that goes on there is just too much for her to deal with. She looked down the hallway and saw more patients, each sicker than the last, all being tended to by a variety of nurses and doctors. Eventually, she saw Dr. Ben Wildenstein down the hall typing on a laptop. She ran to him, "Doctor!"

He looked up and recognized her immediately. Within a second he knew why Dolly Jane would have been there. He walked over and said, "Where's Janet?"

Dolly Jane motioned to the room where the team was working fervently. The emergency room doctor was looking at the chest X-ray images on the computer when Dr. Wildenstein approached. The image showed bilateral asymmetrical consolidation with a bilateral whiteout appearance and pleural effusions. Dr. Wildenstein asked the ER doctor to look up the results of her recent blood cultures. He did so with a few clicks of the mouse. When they had reviewed the results, the ER doctor gave a slew of orders in Hebrew.

Dr. Wildenstein approached Dolly Jane and said, "I'm sorry to see you back here so soon."

Dolly Jane asked, "Is she going to be okay?"

The doctor took Dolly Jane, Billy, and Richard to another room and sat them down. "She's very sick. When she left the hospital, we didn't have all the answers. But now it appears that it was an infection that caused her relapse. She felt better because of the steroids we gave her, but now, her lungs are in dire straights. She has Acute Respiratory Distress Syndrome. We can treat her with oxygen positive end-expiratory pressure steroids and antibiotics. We will do everything we can, we will bring in a pulmonologist and they will consider partial liquid ventilation treatment with Perflubron, but she's in critical condition. I honestly don't know if she'll make it."

Dolly Jane looked at Billy. They were stunned.

Richard excused himself. He was as familiar with hospitals as he was with firearms. He made another phone call. "I saw the thief. Trace his passport number, and track his position with his credit card purchases, and phone GPS position."

The Lieutenant said, "We did that, his phone is either turned off or disabled. He hasn't made any purchases except a plane ticket. He's scheduled to leave tonight at 18:28 on flight 3634 from Tel Aviv to New York."

Richard said, "Keep looking. Use the facial recognition to locate him. Check Tel Aviv and the area around the City of David." He hung up and approached the others.

Dolly Jane said, "What are we going to do?"

Richard said, "Chase Johnson stole the bronze pieces."

Billy shook his head, "Chase. Why wouldn't he join us?"

Richard said, "He stole it to make his mark on history with Nehushtan's healing power! He wants to find the final piece and leave on a plane tonight."

Billy said, "Not if we can stop him."

Just then Richard's phone vibrated. He saw the text and said, "Three minutes ago our friend visited a scuba shop in Tel Aviv."

Dolly Jane was shocked, "Tel Aviv? Why would he go there?"

Richard stroked his chin, "If he's going to dive, he would have to go to Tel Aviv. There are no scuba shops in Jerusalem."

Billy asked, "I suppose you're an expert in scuba, too?"

Richard shrugged, "You pick up a lot in the navy. You know, Tel Aviv is next to the Mediterranean. It's cold and the visibility is low. There are only a few scuba shops there, but the vast majority of diving is done further south, in the beautiful Red Sea."

Billy shook his head, "We know what he's going to do. Let's get over to the City of David. I researched Warren's Shaft. It's got a connection to the city's fresh water system that can be accessed through a three foot fresh water conduit under the Silwan Mosque, just a dozen yards from the Pool of Siloam."

Dolly Jane asked, "Do you think he's even healthy enough to scuba dive down?"

Billy shrugged, "I know his chest was pretty beat up, but he was healed enough to fly all the way here. With his level of determination, I'm sure he'd do anything to get the last piece."

Richard said, "That would be incredibly foolish. Irregardless of his level of physical fitness, the water system is a labyrinth of caves and tight passageways. When people have tried to explore the area, men have died."

Billy added, "It's 'regardless', drop the 'ir'. Besides, he's a master diver with cave diving certification. Cave diving is his passion."

Richard shook his head, "That doesn't mean anything down there. The Israeli Special Forces unit, Shayelet 13 are the best warriors in the world. They are right up there with Anerica's Navy SEALs. These guys are the best divers in the world. Even they don't go down there. It's just plain too dangerous."

Billy said, "That would explain the dead bodies we saw down there."

Dolly Jane wondered, "But Chase doesn't know that."

Billy confirmed, "Nor does he care about the danger. He already purchased the gear. He sees caves and treasure and loves the challenge of cave diving. There's no doubt he's going in."

Richard said, "We can only pray that he makes it out." He pulled up a map on his phone while they spoke.

Dolly Jane looked at the ground, "I'm gonna stay here with Janet."

Richard added, "I agree with Billy. Chase is set on his mission. He is going to go down there. He has to come out somewhere. When he comes out, we can overtake him. We'll get the final piece." He pointed at the map and said, "We need to station lookouts at the Mosque, the Pool of Siloam, and Hezekiah's tunnel."

Dolly Jane looked at him, "You want me to come?"

Richard said, "Absolutely."

They all looked at Janet. The ventilator made a rhythmic sound as it forced life-giving oxygen into her ailing lungs. Richard said, "You can pray from anywhere. She'll be out for a while. I understand that you want to be there for her when she wakes up. Right now we need all three of us."

"Fine," she acquiesced. "Give me a minute, I've gotta go to the restroom."

Richard said, "Take your time. We've got a few minutes, we would beat him there if we go right now. We want him to dive and be successful. We'll leave the hospital in fifteen minutes."

The men waited in the ER waiting room. With the crowd of people around them, they didn't speak to one another and were looking for a diversion from the topic. They found open seats by the television in the waiting room. The BBC was in the middle of a report of a mass school shooting in the USA. They watched in silence as the reporter spoke:

> *Shots rang out just before 7:30 am. Police say that the majority of those dead and wounded at Santa Maria High School in Oklahoma are students. The shooter, a seventeen-year-old classmate, Jacob McManeus. He gave himself up. Two weapons were used, a 45 revolver and a .223 semiautomatic rifle. He didn't have the courage …*

Richard turned away and faced Billy, "Let's get out of here. We don't need more bad news today." They moved into a hallway and waited for Dolly Jane.

Billy said, "I can't believe that happened again."

Richard added, "How long will it be before the news pivots to talking about banning guns?"

Billy said, "I hate these political battles."

Richard said, "In Israel, the teachers carry guns. I've trained some of them myself. They know what they are doing. We've never had a school shooting."

Billy retorted, "So that's the solution? The problem is gun violence, so the solution is to bring in more guns?"

Richard said, "The problem is much more complex. If you come from a family with two parents where the parents are directly involved in the children's education and activities, the chances of violence are low. But mental health is much more complex than that. Family structure, discipline, a healthy self-worth – these all get mixed together like a viscous soup of the mind. We want everybody to be healthy, but many aren't. The fact is that unhealthy people get their hands on weapons and then use them."

Just then Dolly Jane joined their group, she saw the television report in the distance and realized that they were discussing it.

Billy said, "I'll bet we get a law introduced within the next few weeks. It will ban certain types of magazines, or barrels, without any affect on gun violence." He rolled his eyes, wanting nothing to do with a discussion of guns or politics.

Richard said, "When I hear politicians and news reporters talking about guns, I can't help but laugh because they don't know what they are talking about. Listen, I've worked with a gun in my hand for the last 30 years. I can take apart and put back together just about any gun in the arsenal – blindfolded. I've taught gun safety, marksmanship, even military sniper school. I could wax eloquently about caliber, accuracy, rounds per minute of just about any military or civilian weapon. I know guns. But politicians who barely know the parts of a gun make the laws that regulate them."

Dolly Jane said, "Hang on a second." The other two looked at him. "Your logic is fantastic. It's the same with healing."

Richard and Billy together said, "What?"

Dolly Jane repeated, "Healing is talked about by two different camps. There are those who either believe God doesn't heal anymore, or don't believe in God. And there are healing ministers who live it, study it, know the Bible's teaching on healing like the back of their hands"

Billy nodded, "Your friend Brian Pendleton."

"Right," Dolly Jane agreed. "That guy knows healing. He's worked in a healing room at IHOP for thirteen years, every day he prays for healing for people. He sees people healed on a regular basis. He's taught healing to church leaders and prayer warriors all over the world."

Richard pondered, "He knows healing like I know weapons."

Dolly Jane said, "That's exactly my point. If I want to know about guns, I shouldn't ask a politician, or a reporter. I should go to the person who knows guns professionally. I'll ask you."

Billy picked up her logic, "If I want to know about healing, I shouldn't ask a minister who doesn't believe in healing. I'll ask the expert who knows."

Richard said, "Let's go."

The three of them sauntered out of the hospital as a unit. As they approached Richard's car, Dolly Jane picked up her iPhone and dialed Brian Pendleton. He answered with a sleepy voice, "Dolly Jane? What's wrong?"

"Brian, oh I'm sorry, I forgot about the time change. I'm in Israel again."

"No problem. How can I help?"

"When we were in Chicago, praying for Billy, Chase, and Maddy, you told me a few things about how to get healing."

Brian walked into his living room and sat down on the couch. "Go on."

Dolly Jane got into the car and buckled her seat belt. "I'm just so confused," Dolly Jane said. "God didn't heal Maddy, I'm afraid he's not going to heal my friend Janet."

"Tell me more," he requested.

As Richard pulled out of the parking lot and drove toward the City of David, she told him a brief version of her relationship with Janet, her Multiple Sclerosis, and her current condition.

Brian digested the information and said, "Wow! It sounds like you've been through a lot."

"We asked for healing before. Billy was healed, but Maddy died. Now how do we get healing for Janet?"

Brian counseled, "You're on the right track. We should go to God on all occasions with all kinds of prayers and requests."

Dolly Jane replied, "You are quoting Ephesians 6:18. I understand that we need to go to God. I'm trying."

"Healing isn't something you get. It's something God does, at His discretion. It's all about Him."

Dolly Jane sighed, "I know. I just don't like that part."

Brian said, "You don't have to. When God tells us to ask for anything, He reserves the right to say no. But that shouldn't keep us from asking."

Dolly Jane asked, "Is there some technique that always works? If you lay hands on them in a certain way? If you anoint them with a certain kind of oil? What about one of those prayer napkins you can get in the mail?"

Brian said, "You can even make your shadow pass over them."

Dolly Jane said, “Yes! That’s it!”

Brian shook his head. “No. Not really. It’s all about Jesus healing. It’s not how we ask. It has nothing to do with the technique. It’s really us making the request and getting out of the way for God to work.”

“But when the Israelites looked at the bronze snake, they were healed. Why can’t it be like that?”

Brian was shocked. “I haven’t heard anyone ask it that way before. I was just reading that story in Numbers 21. It was after they repented, and asked for forgiveness that God provided the means for healing. In spite of the short nature, it’s actually a very complex story.”

Dolly Jane said, “We should have something to look at and get healing.”

Brian said, “We already do. His name is Jesus.”

Dolly Jane was quiet. Tears welled up in the corners of her eyes. His words resonated in her soul. She thought, *All I need is Jesus.*

Brian continued, “Do you remember what Jesus said about that bronze snake?”

Dolly Jane cleared her throat and replied, “He was talking to Nicodemus at night.”

Brian said, “That’s it, what did he say?”

Dolly Jane thought for a moment, “Something about lifting up the snake.”

Brian said, “He explained, ‘Just as Moses lifted up the snake in the wilderness, so the Son of Man must be lifted up, that everyone who believes may have eternal life in Him.’ The whole purpose of the bronze snake that Moses made was to point to Jesus.”

Dolly Jane paused, “I never thought of it like that before.”

“Jesus was lifted up on the cross – just like the bronze snake was lifted up in the wilderness. He was killed on a real cross by real Roman soldiers on April 6, 33 AD as a substitutive sacrifice for my sins.”

Dolly Jane said, “And mine.”

Brian continued, “He atoned for our sins on the cross.”

Dolly Jane finished his sentence, “And healing comes through the atonement.”

Brian smiled at her acute memory, “Yes.”

Dolly Jane said, “So we keep praying.”

Brian agreed, “Pray without ceasing.”

She laughed, “Now you’re quoting another scripture.”

He said, “I Thessalonians, 5:17”

She said, “I get it, Brian. Thanks.”

Brian said, “Before you go, let me pray for Janet with you.”

Dolly Jane agreed, “Sure.”

Brian closed his eyes and said, “Father God. You know Janet, every cell in her body. You know her nervous system and her lungs. In the name of Jesus we speak healing over her body. Complete healing from the top of her head to the soles of her feet. We ask this in Jesus’ name, amen.”

Tears rolled down Dolly Jane’s face, “Thank you.”

She pushed the red button on her iPhone screen and looked up. Billy and Richard looked at her.

Silently, each of them continued to pray for Janet. After a few minutes, they were within sight of the Hezekiah tunnel parking lot. Richard said, “We’re here.”

Billy said, “Let’s find Chase.”

# Chapter 29

## Old City, Jerusalem

Richard drove past the Hezekiah tunnel lot and pulled in to the Silwan Mosque parking lot. His phone buzzed in his pocket, he received a text from a Lieutenant informing him of the license plate on Chase's rental car. Being Thursday, it wasn't busy. The following day would find the lot packed with worshipers. Within a few seconds of entering the lot Richard recognized the license plate, "There's his car." They parked and got out of the car.

Richard instructed, "Dolly Jane, take the car over to the Hezekiah tunnel parking lot and wait there. He might exit that way. Billy, do you think you can find a way to the water conduit without entering the Mosque?"

Billy pulled out his laptop and examined the scans. He answered, "This place is so confusing. There are probably five possible entrances to the cave system. Three of them are outside the mosque, but none of them are very direct to the bronze piece. It's like a maze down there."

"You go down to observe the entrances by the Mosque. I'll wait here by his car." Richard looked at Dolly Jane, "He might exit the tourist entrance then take a cab to the bus station.

Dolly Jane retorted, "But his car is here. He'll come back."

"Once he has what he wants, he won't care about anything."

They staked out their assigned positions and waited.

Fifteen minutes went by.

Then another fifteen.

Billy texted Dolly Jane and Richard, "How long can an air tank last?"

Richard replied, "Let's give him another thirty minutes, then change plans."

The time passed painfully slowly.

After the allotted time had gone by, Dolly Jane texted, "Nothing happening on my end."

Billy was quick to reply, "Mine too."

Richard said, "It's time to re-scan the tunnel."

Billy was already opening his scanning program on his laptop. He asked, "Can you bring my suitcase to me?"

Dolly Jane pulled the car back around and brought the suitcase to the backside of the Mosque. Together they watched the screen as Billy scanned again. The second time through added detail to the nooks and crannies of the cave system, he added labels to the pools and connection tunnels, to help prevent repeating his scans. Billy was enjoying it until he realized that the extra detail wasn't helpful for the task at hand. They went over the whole region the scan reached from that location, then he looked at Richard and shrugged.

Richard instructed, "Let's go to where the bronze piece was."

Richard packed his laptop and rolled the suitcase to the Pool of Siloam. He set up at the base of the stairs, though there was no good place for him, he hunkered down with a suitcase in the awkward location.

The three of them watched as he scanned over to the underground pool with the pillar that held the treasure. He quickly labeled the pool the *Treasure Room* and focused on the pillar and found that it was empty!

"He took it!" Dolly Jane said.

"Oh no!" Billy gasped.

Richard said calmly, "We'll find him. Keep scanning."

Billy's fingers swept over the keyboard as he scanned the region from one end to the other.

Dolly Jane looked at Richard, "What if we can't find him?"

"We can put him on the terrorist watch list and pick him up at customs when he goes to the airport."

Dolly Jane thought for a moment, "But then the IDF would confiscate the relics."

Billy added, “They’d arrest him.”

Richard closed his eyes, “And us.”

Dolly Jane said, “What?”

Richard answered, “There’s no way to get a hold of relics like that by yourself. They would investigate.” He looked at Billy, “His computer is full of images from your computer and they would be able to connect them.” He looked at Dolly Jane, “Connecting you and me would be just a few clicks after that.”

Dolly Jane said to Billy, “Find him.”

Billy remained silent in his contemplative diligence as he worked the machine. He saw something on the floor of a pool. “Look! That wasn’t there on the previous scan.”

They looked closely. It was another pool outside the treasure room with an irregular floor and three feet of water. On the bottom was an air tank and vest.

“His BCD!” Richard said.

“His what?” Dolly Jane asked.

“Buoyancy control device. It’s the scuba equipment that holds the tank.” Richard began thinking out loud, “When you dive in caves, the tank on your back gets held up on the walls. If you are desperate, you grab your backup air tank and drop your BCD. He must have been in trouble.”

“Keep looking.”

Billy never looked up. While Richard had been talking, he switched to the thermal image, and found that the tank and BCD was 55 degrees Fahrenheit – the same as the ambient temperature of the cave. He switched views to the overall image once again and swept over the series of caves.

Richard said, “He would be swimming with nothing but the relic and his reserve tank. It’s about the size of a can of tennis balls.”

Dolly Jane inquired, “How long would that last?”

Richard said, “The reserve tank provides 57 breaths. Then he’s out of air.”

Dolly Jane sighed, “Oh Chase…”

Billy was about 150 feet away from the BCD before he found anything else. Richard put a hand on his shoulder, “Look below.”

Billy scanned deeper into the labyrinth of waterways until something appeared on the screen.

Richard commanded, “Stop!”

He zoomed in and could see a body face down deep inside a natural underground cistern. The cistern was connected to the water system, but at least ten yards deeper than any of the other cisterns or tunnels.

He got closer and could see one hand on the spare air canister and his other arm outstretched in a lifeless reach for air.

Billy wondered out loud, “How did he get down there?”

Richard whispered, “Anoxia causes confusion. He made a wrong turn, then couldn’t tell which way was up or down. He is completely trapped.”

The three of them were speechless.

Billy switched to thermal mode and read out the body’s temperature. The blue water and walls surrounded the yellow body. He focused on Chase’s chest and neck to read out his core temperature – 72 degrees Fahrenheit. He had been dead for one to two hours.

They looked on in awe. Billy sat as motionless as the corpse he observed. He switched back to the mode in which he saw the bronze relic and saw the metallic piece tucked into a bag strapped to his chest.

Richard sat back. He wondered if there was any way to dive in to retrieve the body and the relic, but quickly concluded that it was a fool’s errand.

Dolly Jane said, “We can use Checkers to tunnel down and get to him.”

Billy worked furiously on his laptop. He continued scanning the pool, looking for a way for Checkers to access the relic or the body. Chase was in the middle of the pool. Completely isolated. There was no way to tunnel close to him.

Dolly Jane asked, “Could we go in from above and reach down to him?”

Billy said, “There’s an eight foot gap between the ceiling and the water level. Even if we dropped in from above, we couldn’t reach him.”

For the first time, Richard looked around them. Happy tourists frolicked in the Pool of Siloam. Their joy was a striking contrast to the painful realization the trio of treasure hunters felt. He tapped Billy on the back, “Let’s head up the stairs.”

The three of them climbed the staircase and got away from the crowd. Richard led the way to a nearby concrete bench where Dolly Jane sat with her elbows on her knees, her head rested in her hands as she sobbed. Her thoughts shifted from Chase to the relic, then to Janet. “Oh God, what are we going to do for Janet, now?”

Billy set the roller bag on the ground, tossed his backpack next to it and sat down on the ground.

Richard stood motionless with his hands on his hips facing away from them. He said, “We can’t dive.”

Billy said, “We can’t tunnel.”

Dolly Jane looked up to the sky and said, “What are we going to do?”

# Chapter 30

## Old City, Jerusalem

The three overachievers sat docile at the bench near the pool of Siloam for an extended period of time. They had no dig to accomplish, gadget to invent, or criminal to arrest. They were without a schedule to maintain. Internally, they searched for answers.

Billy had a spark of creative thinking and said, "If we rerouted the water to another channel and drained the cistern..."

Richard sighed, "Years ago in Adana Turkey, I helped a group reroute the water table to a natural well to unearth a stash of second century coins. It was a multi-million dollar gamble and a geological engineer's nightmare. But it worked."

Dolly Jane shook her head, "There is no way to obtain a permit to do any of that near Hezekiah's tunnel. It's a holy site. And you would be rerouting the water table of the entire city of Jerusalem. Plus, there is no historical reason for a piece of Nehushtan to be located there unless we divulge how it got there – our illegal activities."

They sat in silence for some time.

Richard turned towards Dolly Jane and Billy and summarized, “We have illegally obtained a relic that very few people knew existed.”

Billy thought about Chase, “Now, even fewer.”

Dolly Jane said, “But Janet needs healing! We have to retrieve the piece.”

Richard and Billy looked at her blankly and shook their heads. Billy said, “It’s gone.”

Eventually, they left the bench and without words they drove to the bus station. In the car, Richard reviewed the surveillance video of the locker areas and discovered that locker 17 had their treasure. They quickly found the storage locker and Richard pulled out his lock picking kit and worked the lock. They retrieved Chase’s bag, verified that the two pieces were inside and returned to Richard’s car. He tapped the bag, “The pieces of bronze in this bag can’t stay with us.”

Dolly Jane agreed, “We can’t take what we have to a museum.”

Richard found a silver lining, “At least we don’t have to worry about investigations, or interrogations. Nobody in my office knows about this. The pieces of Nehushtan are not missing, because technically, they’ve never been found.”

Billy looked at Richard, “So, law dog, how many crimes is that? The illegal digs. Trespassing on holy sites. Theft of priceless multiple Israeli national treasures.”

Richard shook his head. “Even the use of ground penetrating radar on holy sites without specific permission from the Anglo-Israel Archaeological Society is a crime.”

Dolly Jane laughed, “By their definition, any piece of dirt from Egypt to Turkey can be considered a holy site.”

Richard looked at both of them, “I’ve lost track of how many crimes have been committed. Believe me, you do NOT want to see the inside of an Israeli prison.”

Dolly Jane said, “We need to pray.”

The others looked at her.

Billy said, “We can write our prayers on paper, and tuck them into the Western Wall.”

Dolly Jane agreed, “Sure. There’s nothing wrong with that. But I’ve got something else in mind.”

Richard said, "We need to do what David did, what Hezekiah did, what all the good leaders did in their times of crisis."

Dolly Jane said, "Hezekiah approached God at the temple. He took the letter from his enemy and laid it out before God, then he prayed."

Billy thought for a moment, "David didn't care for himself at all, he basically lived in the temple during the time his child was sick."

Richard added, "The child from his illegitimate union with Bed Bath and Beyond!"

Dolly Jane laughed at the unusual reference, "The temple is gone, but the steps are still there."

Richard said, "Something special happens when we sing the Psalms of Ascent on those steps."

Billy said, "Let's petition God the way it was designed thousands of years ago, on the temple steps."

Dolly Jane agreed, "There is no better place in all the world to ask God what to do with what we have found."

They got into Richard's sedan. He drove the short distance to the Zion Gate and pulled into the parking garage. As if they were tourists on their first visit to Jerusalem, they entered the Davidson Center and purchased tickets to the temple site. They quickly passed through the museum. Dolly Jane was astonished at the simplicity with which the presentations were made to the public. There was so much history, so much deep theology that was there to dissect, to chew on, and ponder. Yet, the bland vanilla presentations covered only the most basic historical facts. They passed by the famed trumpeter's stone that previously stood proudly on the corner of the temple. They walked over the steel platform and through the archway to the excavated temple steps.

Dolly Jane said, "As the temple steps were uncovered it was noted that they alternated long and short steps." She didn't even realize that she had dropped into a professorial tone as she spoke, "The western flight of stairs leading to the main entrances of the Temple Mount was 200 feet wide. Excavations begun by Benjamin Mazar in 1968 were the largest and most important earth-moving archaeological projects in Israel."

The three of them stopped at the base of the stairs. She added, "Each twelve-inch step was followed by a thirty six-inch step reaching up toward the temple for thirty steps. It was intentionally built for worship. Fifteen normal steps separated fifteen platforms. Each one provided a platform for pilgrims to stop and recite the Psalms of Ascent."

Richard interjected, "Actually, they would sing each of the fifteen Psalms of Ascent in worship in the original Hebrew, irregardless of their native tongue." He winked at Dolly Jane then continued, "The process of preparing one's heart for worship began well before they stepped foot inside their destination."

Dolly Jane thought for a moment she remembered her very first archeology assignment in Janet's class and how easy it had been for her to put herself in the coffee shop in Nicaea. She applied the same discipline to this holy location, "Imagine that you're a first century Jew hoping all year long to travel to Jerusalem. Your heart longs for a pilgrimage to the holy place. You've scrimped and saved your Shekels to bring your family to the holy temple in Jerusalem. You desperately need to hear from God about something."

Billy said, "Possibly looking for direction, or forgiveness for something you may have done."

Richard added, "Or what to do after you've found something precious or committed a series of crimes."

Together they looked out over the brown terrain and were just about to take the first step when a rag tag collection of twenty-three Americans poured onto the holy scene. They wore sun hats, backpacks, and athletic shoes. Anyone could recognize them as American tourists from a single glance. They were loud, though they wore radio communication devices so that they could hear the whispers of their guide, and they argued with one another as they found a place to sit together in the shade.

Dolly Jane, Richard, and Billy did their best to ignore the tourists and huddled closer to one another. Richard reached into his satchel. His hands found the towels that covered the ancient bronze. He handed one of them to Billy and the other to Dolly Jane and zipped up his bag.

Dolly Jane looked up the temple steps and said, "What are we to do with these pieces of the relic?"

She placed her foot onto the first thirty six-inch platform and recited from memory the first of the Psalms written for this occasion. She sang slowly with an angelic voice:

| | |
|---|---|
| לאדון שלי הצרות את לקחתי | I took my troubles to the Lord |
| ש על ענה והוא ,לו צעקתי | I cried out to him |
| משקרנים ,אדוני ,אותי הצילו | And he answered my prayer |
| הרמייה האנשים ומכל | Rescue me, Oh Lord from liars |
| לך יעשה אלוהים מה ,מטעה לשון | And from all deceitful people |
| שלך העונש את יגדיל הוא איך | How will he increase your punishment |
| חדים חצים עם פירסינג תהיה אתה | You will be pierced with sharp arrows |
| זוהרות בגחלים ונשרף | And burned with glowing coals |
| הרחוק במישך סובלת אני איך | How I suffer in far-off Meshech |
| הרחוקה בקידר לחיות לי כואב | It pains me to live in distant Kedar |
| לחיות לי נמאס | I am tired of living |
| שלום ששונאים אנשים בקרב | Among people who hate peace |
| שלום מחפש אני | I search for peace |
| ,שלום על מדבר כשאני אבל | But when I speak of peace, |
| מלחמה רוצים הם | they want war |

Richard and Billy joined her as they took in the magnitude of the site. Together, all three paused and breathed deep. Inspiration of the holy air at the holy site made holy by their holy God.

They paused.

There was no hurry. No agenda. No meeting to attend. They only wanted to seek God.

Richard reached his foot toward the next step. He stepped through the narrow step and ascended to the platform. He imagined watching the shadow go down the steps as the sun traversed the sky. He wondered how Hezekiah felt when he saw the shadow go back ten steps. The glory of God was visible and real in that place.

Reverently, he looked up at the temple site. Then, as he considered the text of the Psalm that he was about to recite, he turned facing away from where the temple was and looked all around. The mountainous terrain was bustling with life. Motorcycles and busses, businesses covered the closely compacted city. He sang:

| | |
|---|---|
| אני מביט אל ההרים | I look up to the mountains |
| העזרה שלי באה משם | Does my help come from there? |
| העזרה שלי באה מן האדון | My help comes from the Lord |
| שעשה שמים וארץ | Who made heaven and earth |
| הוא לא ייתן לך למעוד | He will not let you stumble |
| מי ששומר עלייך לא יירדם | The one who watches over you will not stumble |
| ואכן, מי ששומר על ישראל | Indeed he who watches over Israel |
| אף פעם לא נרדם או ישן | Never slumbers or sleeps |
| אלוהים עצמו צופה בך | The Lord himself watches over you |
| ה' עומד לצידך כגונך המגונן | The Lord stands beside you as your protective shade |
| השמש לא תפגע בך ביום | The sun will not harm you by day |
| ולא את הירח בלילה | Nor the moon by night |
| אלוהים שומר אותך מכל נזק | The Lord keeps you from all harm |
| ואת צופה על החיים שלך | And watches over your life |
| האדון שומר עליך כמו שאתה בא | The Lord keeps watch over you as you come and go |
| גם עכשיו וגם לנצח | Both now and forever |

The three of them waited. Dolly Jane thought about the Psalm. She knew that each of them could preach a sermon series on that Psalm alone. The words could be cut and dissected a thousand different ways yet they do not lose their importance or reverence. She whispered, "In the movie *The Sound of Music*, Julie Andrews, playing Maria, misquoted the scripture. 'I look to the hills, where my help comes from.' No! She didn't finish the line. She should have said, 'My help comes from the Lord, the maker of heaven and earth! I'm only looking to the hills, because I'm standing here, on the second of fifteen platforms designed to sing this song in this place, to seek the Lord and His glory!'"

Billy and Richard were quiet. A myriad of thoughts went through their minds, yet they remained still.

As the trio stood on the second temple step, they were certainly aware of the unique elements of the hand hewn stones upon which they stood. With this song, they became acutely cognizant of the presence of God in that place.

Richard intellectually knew that because of His quality of omnipresence, God was always there. But with the focus on Him, everything shifted in the spiritual realm. Even his propensity for jocularity went by the wayside as he contemplated the magnitude of God! He could quote from scripture many verses that lent to the omnipresence of God, yet as his acute eyesight picked out trees and brush on the distant mountains, he sensed a deeper presence of God. As he silently and reverently spoke with God, he expressed his love deeply. To Richard, God's love was becoming palpable. He could feel it so strongly that His presence seemed to be all that mattered.

A few minutes went by and Richard thanked God for His love. In awe of His presence and complete humility, he knew that it was time to present the question that they had come to ask. He verbally asked God, "What should we do with the two pieces of Nehushtan?"

Billy and Dolly Jane stood with him and the trio waited in beautiful silence.

After a few minutes, Billy took the lead on the next step. He danced over the short step doing a short routine that he had seen on the video game Fortnite. A moment later, he respectfully planted the soles of his shoes on the third platform. Knowing the content of the Psalm he was about to recite, he looked over the city of Jerusalem and began to feel for the city the way God does. He loved this city. Every street and café was his beloved. Each house held people that he was crazy about.

His eyes moistened as he sang:

| | |
|---|---|
| לי אמרו כאשר שמחתי | I was glad when they said to me |
| "' ה לבית נלך הבה" | "Let us go to the house of the Lord" |
| כאן אנחנו ועכשיו | And now here we are |
| ירושלים ,שעריך בתוך עומד | Standing inside your gates, O Jerusalem |
| היטב בנויה עיר היא ירושלים | Jerusalem is a well-built city |
| לפריצה ניתנים אינם תפר ללא קירותיה | Its seamless walls cannot be breached |
| – אלוהים של העם - ישראל שבטי כל | All the tribes of Israel –the Lord's people |
| כאן שלהם לרגל לעלות | Make their pilgrimage here |
| אלוהים של לשמו להודות באים הם | They come to give thanks to the Lord |
| מישראל החוק שמחייב כפי | As the law requires of Israel |
| דין פסק ניתן שבהם הכסאות עומדים כאן | Here are thrones where judgment is given |
| דוד שושלת של כסאות | The thrones of the dynasty of David |
| בירושלים לשלום התפלל | Pray for the peace of Jerusalem |
| לשגשג הזאת העיר את שאוהב מי כל מאי | May all who love this city prosper |
| שלך הקירות בתוך שלום יהיה אולי ,ירושלים | O Jerusalem let peace be within your walls |
| שלך בארמונות שגשוג ואת | And prosperity in your palaces |
| אומר אני ,וחברי משפחתי למען | For my family and friends, I will say, |
| "שלום לך יש" | "May you have peace" |
| אלוהינו' ה בית למען | Because of the house of the Lord our God |
| ירושלים ,עבורך ביותר הטוב את אבקש אני | I want what is best for you, O Jerusalem |

By the time he had finished, his lacrimal glands had poured cleansing fluid over the gates of his eyelids and streams of reverence and adoration flowed down his cheeks. He blinked, and though the tears obstructed his vision, he could see the city.

He saw God's city, Jerusalem!

But now, with fresh eyes, he saw it as a collection of individuals who were deeply loved and cared for by the Creator. While He knew their faults, He also knew their potential. He knew their wandering hearts, yet was patient and waited for them to turn to Him. As the father of a wayward teenager longs and waits for the rebellious heart to turn, God looks on everyone in this city with a longing many times greater.

Billy had confidence that in spite of their reckless manner in which they had obtained the pieces of the relic, God was bigger than his problem. God knew and understood how they had come to this place. He was ready to listen.

Once again, they waited. The revelation of the character of God was becoming more and more real as they spoke the words designed for the steps. Their hearts were crying out. They took their time.

They rose through the steps one by one.

Without looking on a page, they quoted the entirety of the Psalms of Ascent as they ascended the temple steps. Singing the Psalms in the original Hebrew seemed to not only take them back in time, but also honor God's chosen people, the city as a whole, and, of course, the temple.

By the time they reached the final step, it was no longer three of them on the steps. Jesus had joined their group. Each of them felt the presence of the second member of the trinity standing right there next to them.

With her eyes closed Dolly Jane pictured Him as He is drawn in children's picture Bibles with a beard, white robe, and a blue sash. Just for fun she even imagined a lamb on His shoulders. She listened to hear what the loving shepherd would say.

Richard saw Jesus wearing a plaid flannel shirt and jeans, as a modern day carpenter. He held out his hands in a receptive gesture, waiting for the master carpenter to give him direction.

Billy's image of Jesus started with His eyes. A Pakistani artist who had experienced a near death experience saw Jesus of Nazareth. She painted the image of her savior afterwards. His blue eyes were captivating. Billy had been introduced to this image after his parents read to him a book that was later turned into a movie about heaven. He had the picture displayed in his bedroom for his entire life.

Standing on the top step, the trio waited in patient silence, enjoying the presence of God. They felt the refreshing breath of the Holy Spirit, and the loving touch of Jesus as they worshiped the Father in the public space.

After some time, Dolly Jane sat on the top step with her hands on her knees.

Billy knelt in reverence, with his forehead on the ground.

And Richard stood with his hands raised to the heavens.

Each of them felt God give them a warm loving embrace. In their own ways, they melted into His presence and wept.

# Chapter 31

---

## Temple Steps
## Old City, Jerusalem

The busload of Americans had long since departed, Having checked the box on their list of sites to visit and taken their many photographs, they meandered off, quite possibly completely missing the spiritual reality of the temple site altogether. The sun shone brightly in the cloudless sky and the warmth from the infrared radiation poured over Dolly Jane's face as she looked up. She bowed her head and opened her eyes. She looked at the bronze relic in her hands.

Billy unwrapped his relic, stowed the towel and dropped the ancient bronze piece on the ground. It hit with a thud and all three of them looked at it. The action would have brought a collective gasp a few hours previously. But now, the relic was inconsequential, insignificant, and irrelevant. It had gone from being the spawn of a world regime to being trivial, inane, and powerless.

Richard said, "What was it that Jesus said to Nicodemus?"

Billy quoted, "As Moses lifted up the bronze snake on a pole in the wilderness, so the Son of Man must be lifted up, so that everyone who believes in Him will have eternal life."

Richard smiled, "Jesus wasn't saying that we need to find the parts of the bronze snake and re-create Moses' means of healing. He was saying that Nehushtan was simply a type of Christ. A metaphor. This bronze snake is symbolic of Jesus."

Billy said, "There was no way that Nicodemus could have understood that Jesus would be lifted up on a cross by the Roman army just a thousand yards from this location".

Dolly Jane no longer cradled the bronze relic. She held it lazily, like a walking stick, as if she didn't care if it fell from her hand and struck the ground. "Jesus was clear in saying that the snake was no longer important."

Richard said, "For God so loved the world that he gave his one and only Son–"

Billy continued, "That whoever believes in him would not perish but have eternal life."

Dolly Jane smiled through tears and finished for them, "God sent his Son into the world not to judge the world but to save the world through Him."

Richard looked around him and said, "Jesus is the reason for this temple."

Dolly Jane removed the towel and dropped the relic. It fell to the stone platform and landed with a clunk like a discarded piece of refuse. She turned toward Richard and placed her left index finger on his chest saying, "And this temple." Then she turned to Billy and placed her right index finger on his chest and gently repeated, "And this temple." While she stood there touching them she quoted, "Don't you realize that your body is the temple of the Holy Spirit, who lives in you and was given to you by God? You do not belong to yourself, for God bought you with a high price."

Billy smiled, "I'm also a fan of I Corinthians 6. But my favorite is I Peter 2, where he says that you are living stones that God is building into His spiritual temple. What's more, you are His holy priests. Through the mediation of Jesus Christ you offer spiritual sacrifices that please God."

Dolly Jane said, "The temple is a metaphor for us."

Billy added, "And we are a metaphor for it."

Dolly Jane looked at Billy. She dropped her hands to her sides and took a breath. "That's a little deep. Let's just stick with 'It's all about Jesus.'"

Richard nodded, "When Jesus was talking to Nicodemus, he mentioned Nehushtan simply to point to Himself."

Billy said, "But what of the rumors of healing power?"

Richard shook his head, “I looked into this one a bit more over the past few days. Hezekiah destroyed the snake and he also received healing from God that added fifteen years to his life. Were the two events linked? Who knows?”

The intellectual trio was silent for a few minutes. They looked around and enjoyed the view from the top of the temple steps. Dolly Jane looked at the various buildings, the city wall, the gates. She pointed to the gate and said. “Right there is another important historic site.”

Billy and Richard were puzzled.

Dolly Jane said, “In the third chapter of Acts we see the story unfold. It was after the Pentecost, and the new church was growing. At three o’clock in the afternoon, Peter and John were coming here to pray. Right there, at the gate called Beautiful was a man who spent all his time there. It was his place of employment, so to speak. He was a lame man, unable to work, so he was brought to this place to beg. Notably, it was the best place in the world for his profession.”

“Who wouldn’t give alms to a beggar as they prepare to worship almighty God?” Billy gave a knowing smile. “In this place.”

Richard nodded, “Who did he receive more from, those preparing their hearts to seek God, or from those who had just had an encounter with the God of the universe? Generosity springs from a heart that loves God.”

Dolly Jane continued, “Peter and John stopped right there, and looked at him intently. Peter said, ‘Look at us!’” I imagine that he was pulling out his pockets showing that they were empty. Then Peter said, “I don’t have any silver or gold for you, but I’ll give you what I have.”

Dolly Jane tapped the relic with her foot, “He had something worth more than gold. More than a priceless bronze relic.”

Billy tapped his piece with his foot and shoved it towards the other piece. The bronze pieces clinked together as they lay on the limestone. He said, “They had seen their savior lifted up like Moses lifted up that thing so many years earlier.”

Dolly Jane said, “He said to the beggar, ‘In the name of Jesus Christ of Nazareth get up and walk!’ Then Peter took the lame man by the right hand and helped him up. As he did, the man’s feet and ankles were instantly healed and strengthened.

He jumped up, stood on his feet, and began to walk. Then, walking and leaping, and praising God, he went into the Temple with them."

Richard said, "Healing comes at the atonement."

Billy's eye's widened. "The atonement. Jesus has provided for healing through his resurrection! Peter, John and the formerly lame man climbed these steps together! The lame man leapt up each one of them!"

Richard wondered, "Do you think they recited the Psalms of Ascent that day?"

Billy said, "I bet they completely forgot and ran up the steps!"

Dolly Jane picked up the pieces of bronze and waved them around, "Do you think this thing had anything to do with that healing?"

Billy blurted out, "No way!"

Richard said, "In a way, yes!"

Dolly Jane's forehead wrinkled in confusion, "Wait, what?"

Richard explained, "They were not living in a vacuum. Jesus said that just as that thing in your hand was lifted up, so the Son of Man would be lifted up. That thing no longer had the anointing of God. That piece of metal is a memory. It points to Jesus on the cross."

Dolly Jane frowned, "How many people burned incense to this piece of metal hoping it would bring healing?"

Billy added, "They only burned incense to it because they knew it had conveyed healing in the past. It had power."

Dolly Jane said, "For a moment in time."

Billy agreed, "For a moment."

Richard said, "Then it became a teaching point."

"A distraction."

"A footnote in history."

"A footnote that was quoted by Jesus Himself."

Billy was silent for a moment. Then he said, "Only in reference to salvation did He mention the snake. He used the piece of metal as a teaching point to introduce Nicodemus to the doctrine of substitutive sacrificial salvation. That was the first time that Jesus spoke about being lifted up for our salvation. It was the earliest mention in the Gospels. Jesus must have thought very highly of Nicodemus to entrust him with the message so early in his ministry!"

Dolly Jane and Richard nodded in contemplation.

Billy continued, "From then on, the message was about God's love. Jesus taught through parables. He also healed and performed miracles all in a message of love and redemption."

"It's all about Jesus."

Billy smiled, "The solitary reference to Nehushtan was not to the masses who might misconstrue his message, but to the teacher who understood what it was. Nicodemus knew his history. He knew Jesus was referring to an incident of sin, repentance, forgiveness, and restoration."

Richard was puzzled. "Why would he know all of that?"

Billy said, "It's clearly in Moses' account of the bronze snake. Nicodemus certainly had that memorized and had taught from the passage many times. God only gave the order for Moses to build the snake after the people had repented. The snake came into play for the Israelites when sin had engulfed their hearts. They were bitter and angry at God for bringing them into the desert where they had no food or water. Just as the Israelites humbled themselves, acknowledged their sin, God provided healing through the snake. This occurred after their hearts were right before Him."

Billy said, "What happened in me as I ascended these steps was profound. I felt the presence of God so strongly. Not because of a piece of metal that was lifted up, but because of Jesus Himself!"

Richard said, "The story of the bronze snake has nothing to do with power coming from a piece of metal. The story of Nehushtan is a window into Jesus' salvation. The snake was a microcosm of restoration that brought healing. Jesus is the new covenant."

Billy agreed, "It is clear. Jesus is the replacement of the snake. Our job is to do what the Israelites did. Repent first. They had to tell Moses that they were deeply apologetic for their bitterness. Repentance is nothing if they plan to go back to it again. With snakes killing people right and left, it was clear that their only other alternative was death."

Dolly Jane grabbed both pieces and waved them in the air, "Then they had to look at a piece of metal."

Richard nodded, "And God healed."

Dolly Jane said, "Because He loves the world. The same reason that He sent his Son. So that whoever believes..."

Billy interrupted, "Just like looking at a piece of metal brings healing."

Dolly Jane continued, "Whosoever believes in Jesus will have eternal life."

Silence permeated the temple steps.

Nobody spoke for some time.

Richard whispered. "Hezekiah had it right."

Billy asked, "What?"

Richard said, "Nehushtan is a distraction. That piece of metal was perfect for it's moment in history, but ever since then it has taken the attention away from the Savior it represented. Hezekiah broke it to pieces for the right reason."

Richard held out his hand and Dolly Jane gave the pieces to him. He continued, "The whole reason God did this is because He loved His people. He didn't want them to die because of their sin. He provided a way out at that time, for those people. But when we have this in our possession, our attention is diverted to the relic, rather than to the wonderful God who ordered it to be made and anointed it with healing power."

Charles Spurgeon had some thoughts on it. He had an entire sermon on Nehushtan. He said, "How can they understand it? It is a thing too sacred for the common people to see! No, wrap up the brazen serpent; wrap it up in a cloth, do not let it be exhibited."

Dolly Jane wondered, "What should we do with it?"

Richard shook his head. "Hezekiah broke it to pieces and hid it in a place that, until our technology was created, could never be found."

Billy said, "A museum is out of the question."

The trio was quiet for a few moments.

Richard said, "Through the search for the bronze snake, all I've seen is strife, tension, and a complete misunderstanding of both healing and salvation."

Dolly Jane agreed, "It is nothing but a distraction away from Jesus."

They looked at one another in silence.

Eventually, Dolly Jane said, "I've got an idea."

# Chapter 32

---

## Jerusalem

As the shadow extended down the temple steps, Dolly Jane gave Richard directions to drive back down Highway 1 towards the Mishor Adumim industrial zone. Across the street from a pool supply store on HaHevera Hakalkalit Bulevard was a building labeled, “Yad Kashish Souvenir Company.”

Billy knocked on the door but there was no answer.

Richard pulled out his lock picking kit and made quick work of the dead bolt on the front door. He turned to the others and nodded, “Follow me.”

They walked casually at the pace of an inspector with a job to do. Against the far wall, a furnace burned under a large vat of glowing orange metal.

Billy looked around the building, “There’s nobody here.”

Dolly Jane said, “But the furnace is still hot.”

Richard estimated the width and depth of the cauldron and calculated, “There’s anywhere from 800 to 1000 gallons of molten bronze in there.”

Dolly Jane smiled, “Let’s make it a little more.” She reached into her bag and retrieved Nehushtan’s head. She looked at it under the light of the glowing metal and could easily see the hastily carved details of the eyes and mouth – thousands of years old.

Richard retrieved Nehushtan's middle section and held it next to the head. He said, "No longer a distraction."

Billy looked at them and said, "Go on, now."

The two of them looked at one another. In unison they tossed the relics into the vat of molten bronze. A splash of liquid metal sprang up and safely landed within the confines of the boiling vessel. The midsection sunk quickly, but the head wavered within the metal bath and remained at the surface for a few moments. It was the only piece of darkness within the sea of glowing heated alloy. As it took on heat, the head glowed like the sun, then dissipated into its surroundings.

Billy looked to the side of the furnace. Drop by drop, the bronze would be poured into molds of various shapes. Though the mechanical devices were off they could see the workings of the machinery. A large belt carried the molds to a separate device where they were cooled, finished, and polished. One by one dropped into a box labeled "Yad Kashish Souvenirs".

Dolly Jane said, "Hezekiah had it right."

Without any further fanfare, they left the building and locked the door on the way out. They drove off from the industrial complex.

Richard looked at the two of them and asked, "Are you okay?"

Dolly Jane looked at her phone, and said, "I need to speak to Janet. But I can't imagine that she would be awake. I've been praying for her."

Richard interrupted, "We all have."

Dolly Jane said, "When we left her she was on a ventilator. She probably won't be able to speak for days."

Billy chimed in, "God can heal her."

Dolly Jane sighed, "Thanks. I'll just send her a text, and we can talk when we go back to the hospital."

Just then the iPhone vibrated. Janet's face appeared on the screen. Dolly Jane looked up. Billy and Richard beamed.

She pressed the green button to receive the call and said, "Janet?"

A soft voice came through, "Dolly Jane?"

Dolly Jane quickly put the call on speakerphone, “How are you feeling?”

Janet said, “Better.”

Billy said, “We have so much to tell you.”

Janet said firmly, “Me first. I know how much this means to you, but I want you to stop the search.”

Dolly Jane said, “What?”

Janet confirmed, “Don’t search out the other piece.”

Dolly Jane asked, “What are you talking about?”

Janet paused a moment then spoke clearly, “I’ve been sick before, but this time I was close to death. It’s a long story, but the short version is this. I was dead for a few minutes. I saw everything around me, outside my body. I had an experience. I saw Him.”

Dolly Jane asked, “Who?”

Janet said, “I saw Jesus.”

Dolly Jane said, “What do you mean, you saw Him?”

Janet said, “He has the most beautiful eyes. Piercing blue eyes.”

Dolly Jane said, “What are you saying?”

Janet’s voice was smooth, like a DJ on a late night radio show, “The bronze relic doesn’t heal. Jesus does.”

Dolly Jane smiled, “I know. We’ll be right there.”

# Chapter 33

**London**
**Supreme House**
**300 Regents Park Road**

**Six weeks later**

Billy and Dolly Jane traveled with Janet to London. They had been summoned by the ASIS where they met Nahman Mavigad PhD in the lobby of the beautiful conference center. Dolly Jane was thrilled to meet Dr. Mavigad.

While they waited for their meeting to begin, Dr. Mavigad tucked his tablet under his arm and pulled Janet aside and said, “I’m pleased that you were able to use the apartment.”

Janet smiled, “It worked out very well while I was in town. Thank you very much.”

He added, “I never told you about the other nearby properties my family owns.”

She smiled, “I have no interest in that. I’m grateful for what you’ve given.”

Dr. Mavigad said, "We own an entire city block in the area and for many years my brothers and I have been looking for something meaningful to do with it."

Janet's eyebrows elevated. She was speechless. An entire block of property within the Old City of Jerusalem would be priceless.

The grandiose double doors to the conference room opened. They entered the elegant conference room and Colonel Richard Macks appeared in his formal IDF uniform. He greeted each of them warmly and introduced Dolly Jane, Billy and Janet to General Mordechai Zimbelman of the IDF.

Dr. Mavigad made the formal introductions to the men and women on the AIAS board. They took their seats around the table along with two members of the IDF. Richard pulled out a chair for Janet and sat next to her. Billy nervously fidgeted with the cuffs on his shirt as he sat between Dolly Jane and Richard. The four of them were lined up directly across the table from General Zimbelman. The IDF and AIAS members filled in the seats at the ends of the table.

General Zimbelman sat with several stacks of folders in front of him. He brought the meeting to order. He looked across the table and said, "The account of what you three have unearthed has been processed by a limited number of individuals. Only the members of the IDF and AIAS who are in this room know the intimate details. No one else knows about the relics you found, the advanced techniques used to retrieve them, or how the bronze relics were destroyed."

Billy looked to Dolly Jane for hints of what was coming. She shrugged and looked at Janet, who was respectfully looking at the General. Richard sat with a ramrod spine and stared straight ahead as if looking for a boat in the distance.

The General pulled out a piece of paper and read from the prepared document. "The crimes committed by the individuals of concern are numerous: Theft of historic relics from an active dig site, unauthorized digging in an historic site, trespassing in an historic protected area, theft of historic relics from an undocumented site, unauthorized underground scanning, vandalism of a public toilet, and illegal cave diving."

Billy almost came out of his chair. He said, "We didn't scuba dive, that was Chase."

The general looked up at him. It was clear from his stern facial expression that this was not a negotiation, nor a deliberation.

Dolly Jane placed her hand on Billy's elbow and whispered, "Relax."

The general paused for a moment before he continued reading, "We have a history of firm adjudication of all criminal activity against the state of Israel. The crimes listed here are extensive, deserving many years of imprisonment." He paused and looked around the room.

Dolly Jane's eyes grew wide.

Janet was sweating.

Billy's face was parallel to the table.

Richard was expressionless, looking forward.

The general continued, "However, this case has special considerations."

Billy took a breath and looked up at Richard hopefully. Richard remained still, looking forward.

The General motioned to Dr. Mavigad. The archeologist rested his hands on his tablet and said, "Proper protocol was not followed. Artifacts were handled according to neither the prescribed archeological processes, nor the legal requirements. But the reasons for this are connected to the security for the relics of concern. Their activity is understood to be not only for the safety of the individuals involved but ultimately for the protection of the State of Israel."

The General said, "In cooperation with the AIAS, the IDF acknowledges that there were extenuating circumstances to the crimes involved. The IDF and AIAS would like to extend an element of grace to each of you and is prepared to come to an agreement."

Dolly Jane, Billy, and Richard waited anxiously.

The General continued, "We will agree to exonerate those involved with said activities in exchange for something from each of you."

The room was silent. Billy and Dolly Jane looked at one another with wide eyes.

The General said, "I'll let Dr. Mavigad explain."

Dr. Mavigad said, "The Book of the Kings and the other relics found within Malkijah's cistern will be recorded as if they had been retrieved from an approved experimental dig site. The dig site has been pre-dated and retroactively approved by AIAS."

Dolly Jane smiled at Janet.

Dr. Mavigad continued, "All the documents and relics found there would be combined with a trove of other artifacts from Hezekiah's reign and displayed at a new 12,000 square foot museum dedicated to Hezekiah. This structure will be built next to the remnants of Hezekiah's Broad Wall. An anonymous family has donated the property and construction of the new facility will start immediately."

Janet looked at Dr. Mavigad with her mouth open.

He looked back at her and raised his index finger to his mouth saying, "Shhhh." He turned his tablet to face her and pressed the button. Janet saw that the images were digital renderings of the new facility. She swiped the screen and it showed a large arched entryway with the words "Hezekiah, King of Israel" emblazoned across the top. There were hallways full of displays, a small theater, and a gift shop. The entire facility was centered around the Broad Wall, giving proper honor and respect to the battle in which 185,000 Persian soldiers died.

Dr. Mavigad said, "Janet, in exchange for exoneration of your crimes, the IDF and AIAS requests that you take the position as the curator of the Hezekiah museum."

Janet said, "I would be honored. This is the most wonderful tribute to the great king."

Dr. Mavigad looked at Richard, "The new museum will need someone to be in charge of the unique international security issues that we have in Jerusalem. In exchange for exoneration of your crimes, the IDS and AIAS would like to offer you the position of security attaché. Of course, you will have freedom to hire your own team and develop the security with all the technology in coordination with the IDF."

He extended a hand to Richard who stood and smothered the professor's manicured hand with his own in a grip of a gentle giant. He smiled, "I'll get right on it." Richard faced the General and gave him a salute. The General stood and returned the salute then gave him a warm handshake.

Dr. Mavigad approached Billy. "The AIAS will be putting together a task force on the best practices for use of tunneling technology in Archaeology. Would you be able to help with that?"

Billy was shocked, "Of course I would."

Dr. Mavigad said, "I took the liberty of doing the paperwork to create a research and development company dedicated to tunneling technology." He handed Billy a small stack of papers. "You are the sole proprietor, founder and CEO. The AIAS will contract with you for all the scanning and minimally invasive tunneling services that you can offer."

Billy held the papers in his hands, "I don't know what to say."

Dr. Mavigad said, "Take your time to review the legal issues involved, we are not in a hurry. I would suggest that your first official interaction with the AIAS would be to bill them for services previously rendered. The scans you have done in the Old City are top quality. Nothing like this has ever been possible with any technology. You should be well compensated for your work."

Billy's jaw dropped open. He looked at the heading on the page. The new company was called, "Shekar Byron, Incorporated."

Billy said, "It's perfect." He sprung to his feet and broke out into a celebratory dance. Dolly Jane and Richard applauded him.

Dr. Mavigad looked at Dolly Jane and said, "I'm impressed with your tenaciousness, my dear. I've always considered Professor Zimmerman to be like a daughter to me. Of course, this makes you like a granddaughter."

He took the tablet and pressed the screen a few times. The underground scans of the Old City popped up in vivid detail. He said, "This is an amazing advancement, a discovery of historic proportions, the information has tremendous value. In 1946, the discovery of the Dead Sea scrolls brought in thousands of experts to study the documents for decades. In the world of geographic archeology, this is the equivalent. The ASIS and IDF would like to charge you with the task of leading a team to document the geographical, biblical and cultural history to every square inch under the Holy City."

Dolly Jane's mouth dropped open.

Janet beamed with pride.

Dr. Mavigad explained, "I think you'll find plenty of people who will be interested in helping you with the project.

Dolly Jane was speechless.

Dr. Mavigad continued, "Please understand, this will be a paid position and you can perform the duties while you use the work to complete your Master's and PhD thesis."

Dolly Jane said, "I don't know what to say!"

General Zimbelman closed the file in front of him and concluded, "This meeting is adjourned. You are dismissed."

A wave of emotions flooded over the room. Billy stood up, raised his hands to the sky, and cheered. Even Richard broke out of his rigid military exterior into a wide smile. Billy gave Richard a bear hug and was joined by Dolly Jane.

Dr. Mavigad looked on like a proud father. He was pleased with the progress. "This has been wonderful, but at this time I'll take my leave."

Dolly Jane caught his attention and said, "Excuse me. I don't mean to be intrusive, but what about Nehushtan?"

Dr. Mavigad looked at them and said, "The Bronze Snake of Moses? Yes, this Biblical object has never been officially recognized as a modern day relic. There might be various societies out there looking for it, but it is clear that Hezekiah destroyed it. He probably threw the pieces into a furnace."

He made eye contact with Dolly Jane, Billy, and Richard and winked.

# Acknowledgements

This piece of fiction would not have been possible without a tremendous amount of patience and tolerance from my beautiful wife, Anna. She not only tolerates my unusual hobby but is also my primary source of wisdom. She has input with the content of the story, cultural relevance, language, geography, and even my attempts at humor. She not only puts up with me, but proofreads every page. Her fingerprints are on every page of this book.

As I tell a story that involves healing, I would be remiss if I didn't get expert guidance on the theology of healing when dealing with it. Brian Pendleton is my friend who prays for a living! He's been a wonderful servant working in ministry for many years. He has been with IHOP—KC for over a decade and serves as the director of healing rooms. For this project, Brian worked tirelessly to give me coaching in the nuisances of healing ministry. He not only supplied me with articles on the theology of healing, was my sounding board for theological issues, but he also proofread every word of the manuscript giving countless helpful editorial comments. I can't thank him enough.

On our 2018 visit to the Holy Land, I credit all of our co-travelers with creating the perfect trip. Dan Allison was our fearless leader and itinerant preacher. Along with his wife, Sara, and kids Calvin, Mitchell, Russell, Bob and Suzie they were a big happy family. The other team members including Brian and Lynette Schatz, Annette and Kate Lance, Rex and Debbie Hanson, Karen Hudek, Diane Gotto, Sally Shearer made the tour group a tremendous experience. Our bus driver Munir, and our phenomenal tour guide, Olga provided an atmosphere of peaceful, studious reverence to the land and the history of what happened there. This gave a proper framework for the backdrop to this story.

I was inspired to write by my mother. She has gracefully proofread hundreds of chapters over the years. She's encouraged, guided, and coached me every step of the way.

I've used a lot of languages in the process of telling this story. I'm not a scholar of Greek, Hebrew, Aramaic, or other historically important languages and I can guarantee there are errors in my rendition of the text. I take the blame for any errors herein.

I give any and all credit to the ideas and creative nature of this work to the Holy Spirit. I simply inquired of the Lord how he wanted this book to look, and ideas flowed.

# *Notes*

**Chapter 15**

1. Charles Haddon Spurgeon, "The Mysteries of the Brazen Serpent," September 2, 1857, https://www.spurgeon.org/resource-library/sermons/the-mysteries-of-the-brazen-serpent#flipbook/.
2. ibid.
3. ibid.

www.ingramcontent.com/pod-product-compliance
Lightning Source LLC
Chambersburg PA
CBHW030818310726
48980CB00006B/537/J
*9781732649439*